FLIGHT OF THE CUCKOO

By

K. L. Smith

For my late-husband Shaun who made this book possible by making me laugh so much.

For my late-husband Shaun who made this book possible by making me laugh so much.

I must say, it's quite liberating knowing that I'm going to die. Thinking of all the things I could say and do without fear of repercussions. I do have a wicked sense of humour and it's been rearing its ugly head since I made the decision to end my life around a week ago. (More on that in a bit, I promise.)

Draft four,

"To my daughter Louise,

I send you my love and admiration,
respect and affection,
but I hope you get clap and a urine infection!"

Shit this is gonna take a while!

Forgive me; I haven't formally introduced myself have I? If I'm going to tell you the truth, I better start off properly. My name is Sarah Pemberton; I am Forty-five and a quarter, five-foot-four, and a little underweight according to fat women. I'm now a bottle blonde, or should I say 'Natural ultra-blonde'. My eyes are my own colour though, boring grey. (Like my roots.) I've been told I'm attractive when I'm not scowling; but unfortunately, scowling's my natural expression, my forehead wrinkles cause me to scowl, it's a vicious circle.

Contrary to what people think, I am not mad, or cuckoo, a little eccentric perhaps, but I think it's part of my charm. I think the problem is that I don't really care what people think anymore. For years I've tried to rationalise my hobbies and interests to small minded boring women who have no interests beyond their designer handbags and designer children, who come complete with their own arsey little attitudes, carbon copies of their boring parents. They look at me with a patronising little smirk as though they have a piece of rotten egg under their nose. I have nothing in common with these people, I'm not deliberately rude to them, I just can't relate to them. My conversation repertoire is thus: - "That's a lovely handbag", and "I like your shoes." After that I find myself stumped for something to say, particularly if they look down at my feet, about to return the compliment until they see my green wellies.

I no longer have time or patience for these people, for years I've bottled up my thoughts for fear of offending these people. Well not anymore! I'm not going to be around long enough to worry about hurting their feelings anyway.

One of my neighbours is one of these offensively boring women. Melanie. She's in her mid-twenties, around the same age as my daughter Louise, all designer handbags, manicures, and has that annoying habit that so many people her age have, were they make every sentence that comes out of their head sound like a question, and every other sentence is "ya know?"

She was pleasant enough to my face so I was willing to look past her blandness and give her a chance. I regularly took her fresh eggs from my hens, and vegetables from my garden, as she'd told me she liked 'organic' you see. Well, she said orgasmic but I knew what she meant. *Then* when I was weeding in my garden last week I overheard her talking to her gardener about me. My ears pricked up as I heard my name mentioned.

"Yeah, she lives next door." I heard Melanie reply.

"Is she as bad as what I've heard?" The gardener laughed.

"Worse! You know she's certified insane don't you?"

Ouch! I bit my lip and bided my time.

The next day she was trying to reverse her brand-new Range Rover into her driveway (badly) when she took off the wing mirror of my poor little Mini. I locked eyes with her as she did it. She was devastated, and was desperate to pay me directly for the damage without involving her insurance company. I did what all good neighbours would do, and agreed wholeheartedly....on one condition. She must come around to my house and cut the half an acre of lawn at the back. Not her gardener, she must do it *herself.* Ha, should have seen her face!

"You want ME to cut YOUR lawn? You can't be serious!"

"I am." I stared her down innocently. "You need a favour, so do I."

She was horrified, but I had her backed into a corner.

The woman pays ridiculous fees to the gym in the city, spending three days a week 'working out', yet was completely unable to use a lawnmower. She lasted ten minutes before she decided to go through her insurance company after all. It was so worth it though, the ten minutes she spent parading up and down was priceless. I never told her the lawnmower was self-propelled, and set to 'fast'. Imagine her face when she started it up and it took off with her!

I was especially amused when she skidded on a wet patch and went down face first in dog shit.

God, revenge is sweet, and incredibly addictive. After that, I started writing a list of people who have offended me over the years, and I've spent all week working my way through it. Top of the list is my daughter Louise. I have a strained relationship with her, who as you may have deduced is an insufferable snob. I have tried desperately with her all her life, yet she treats me like dirt. Nothing I can do is good enough for her. She is desperately ashamed of me and goes to huge lengths to keep me at a distance. She's also terrified I am going to corrupt her son, my grandson Malcolm. She's right though, I would corrupt him given half the chance. Better than to have him grow up like Louise. He's a six-year-old with a wicked sense of humour like my own. She does everything she can to deter him from becoming like me, but to my delight, the more she tries, the more he tells her to get lost. It amused me no end when she refused to let him visit me and he retaliated by shaving her cat. She also didn't see the funny side when her boyfriend at the time wrote on Facebook that she'd shaved her pussy.

Also, I used to have a husband until I killed him. Only joking.

As I'm writing this I'm in my study overlooking the back lawn and orchards. I've spent years restoring and caring for the gardens here. It was a jungle when I first inherited the house from my great-aunt May. She was very old when she passed away bless her, and she'd let the place fall to rack and ruin. The house used to be an old Hotel up until the second world war, when it was unceremoniously bombed. This was in 1944, fortunately there had been no guests staying here at the time. It was a devastating blow for its owners, George and Edith Staines; quite literally, as the bomb dropped right over their bed. I'm pretty sure they died as they lived, as stains!

The damage wasn't too bad after the bomb. The hotel had been built in the 1871, by George Staines's grandfather, Herbert. It's a large red brick imposing building with stone window frames, large fluted chimneys and stained glass. You know the type, mini stately home. Built to impress its wealthy guests. Business had gone well, and so by the 1880's Herbert had decided to add on another wing to the hotel. This would be for his own family so that his annoying children didn't keep upsetting the guests. According to my great-aunt May the children used to terrorize the guests at every opportunity. This was the wing that the late George and Edith were living in up until the bomb of '44. Luckily the bomb only tore through this wing and not the whole hotel. The remains of the old East wing are still there in the garden if you know what to look for. Most of it's hidden behind rhododendrons and ivy, but the East wall beneath its ivy façade shows its battle scars well.

I've been in love with this house since I was a child. My great-aunt May used to invite me over often to tell me tales from her youth. She used to work in the Hotel before she inherited the place from her employers. I used to love hearing all her stories and scandals about the place. Her eyes used to light up as she told me the tales of love, life, death and of course ghosts. I think it was because of my love of the place that she left it to me when she died. She knew I would treasure the place and care for it, which I have for the last twenty years.

If only my Louise could love the place as I do, things would have been a lot easier. The only thing she loves is money. She'd boot me out and raze the place to the ground if she could and sell the land off to the highest bidder. She has no time for family, history or tradition. It's all about MONEY. I would love to see the look on her face at the reading of my will, when she realizes she's not getting her hands on this place. She's screwed me over too many times too expect anything from me.

Living in an old place like this is a joy and a burden. Keeping the place going is a complete nightmare. If it's not the roof blowing off, it's the gutters falling off. If it isn't that, it's the ongoing battle of the woodworm. Sarah vs. woodworm has been an ongoing saga for nigh on ten years. Every time I think I have won the war, the little bastards regroup and plan an alternate battle ground. We've fought for territories such as the gorgeous oak staircase that snakes up the grand hall to the third floor; the walnut parquet floors throughout the ground floor, and lately I have had to admit defeat over the wooden windows in the library. It wasn't given up without a fight though. I have been through gallons and gallons of woodworm treatments trying to kill the little blighters.

As well as fighting the woodworm, I have battled with the damp, wet rot, dry rot, green mould, black mould, spores, mildew you name it I've had it.

It has been a labour of love though, I would never want to live (or die) anywhere else. The biggest problem of all has been the distinct lack of money that it takes to keep a place of this magnitude going. It would have been an enormous help if Louise had been more willing to help me instead of hindering me, which is pretty much what got me in trouble in the first place. She is a manipulative traitor that is trying to ruin me. But again, I'm jumping ahead. If I'm going to tell my tale properly, I had better start at the beginning. I'll let you be the judge on whether you think I'm a criminal, insane, or just someone forced into a corner having to choose to fight or flight. All I can do at this stage is be honest and let you make up your own mind.

I was born in the former Davenport Manor Hotel, (my current home) which belonged to great-aunt May. The local doctor lived on one side, and the midwife on the other, and so it made perfect sense for my mother to stay there until she gave birth. Also, my aunt May was the closest thing she had to a mother as her own was as good as useless. aunt May cut my cord, and was the first person to hold me. She was the nearest thing to a grandmother that I ever had. I have three older siblings, but she never made any bones about the fact that she couldn't stand them. I was her girl from the start.

Aunt May was a character, she was beautiful and funny, she could out-drink, out-joke, out-fight any man that she came across and they all loved her for it. There were many men that fell for May, but May only had eyes for one man, so she said, although who he was she would never reveal. Even into her seventies she was still quite a catch, and could still turn many a head.

I spent much of my childhood at Davenport, playing in the grounds, climbing trees trying to find the best conkers in order to beat the kids at school. I loved playing hide and seek in the house on rainy days when my brothers were allowed to visit too. It was the perfect house for hide and seek with cupboards and hidey holes everywhere.

I adored the house, I always knew I'd live there one day. That day came when I was almost twenty-six, though the circumstances through which I came to be there were a little unusual.

Oo I've got a good one: -

Draft Five

"My Dear Louise,

I just want to make sure that you are aware that my death is your fault.
I also want to make you aware that I fully intend to haunt you,
and yes, I will see you when you are having a poo."

Part One
1994

It's important to have a starting point, and really my tale started on its path of destruction with the events from twenty years ago. Let me take you back to the starting point of my troubles if I may. Back to 1994.

In 1994 I'd been going to stay with my aunt May regularly, in order to have a breather from my husband Neil, who was driving me crazy, and making my life a misery. I had to have a break or I would've killed him.

We'd had a whirl wind romance falling deeply in love within days, drawn to each other, not despite our differences but because of them. I think we saw something refreshing and challenging in each other, delighting in our contrary ways, arguing and making up constantly.

We were married within a few months, and it wasn't long before Louise came along. Unfortunately, it also wasn't long before the rot set in. The differences that seemed so interesting at first became '*issues*'. Apparently I had a lot of these '*issues*'. Nothing I could do was good enough anymore. If I cooked his favourite dinner, it was too spicy, too bland, too hot, too cold, he was a regular bloody goldilocks, or rather in my head I called him "goldibollocks". I really tried my hardest to please him, but I came to realise some people don't want to be pleased; they want someone to use as a whipping boy. He was a bit of a snob and a control freak really looking back, he thought he was better and more intelligent than everyone else, including me. Personally I came to think of him as a complete nob. I tolerated his patronising bigoted ways for a few years, but I came to hate him. He was a pompous stuck-up arse with a napoleon complex.

The change in him happened so subtly I didn't realise what was happening, at first he was correcting my speech, mocking my accent just because I didn't sound stuck up like he was. Then it was telling me what I could and couldn't wear, and then from there - who I could and couldn't speak to. He got rid of my friends, trying to ingratiate me with the wives of the posh twits who he knew through his job as an assistant manager in a factory; the aforementioned designer handbag brigade. I'm sorry but NO, NO, NO! Who the hell did he think he was!

The next stage of his plan to control me was to get me sacked from my job. The only independence I had was working at a garden centre surrounded by my beloved friends, a lot of like-minded people who shared my sense of humour. I say he got me sacked, it's not quite true. I was ill in bed with a fever and asked him to call in sick for me; I'd probably need a week or so off. But this isn't what he told them. He told them that I had quit, but was too scared to tell them myself and so had asked him to tell them instead. He also went on to say that I found their humour distasteful and that I was thinking of suing them for sexual harassment! This was because he was too much of a snob to have a wife who did manual work, but unfortunately for him, this was the straw that broke the camel's back, this was WAR! I wasn't used to having so much time on my hands, and you know what they say about idle hands! I started to plot.

I told him after that, that I was going to leave and take Louise with me. We didn't need him; we'd be fine on our own. We'd be better than fine, we'd be free. His response was to remind me that when we married, his father had insisted that I sign a pre-nuptial agreement, with us not being together very long before we announced we were getting married, his parents had panicked and dragged in their solicitor. The house that we lived in was included in the pre-nup, as was any savings we had.

The clincher was when he told me if I left he would seek full custody of Louise. There was no doubt in my mind that there was a very real possibility that he would get custody, after all, thanks to him I had no job, no means to provide for her, and no home. His parents would discredit my abilities as a parent; my own parents now lived abroad and so couldn't help. He even threatened to have me psychologically evaluated!

So there you have it, I was cornered. The selfish bastard thought I was his to do with as he wished. I think he expected me to break after that. WRONG! He didn't know me as well as he thought he did. I thought to myself, if I'm going to be saddled with this bastard for the rest of my life, then I'm going to have a little fun and amuse myself - at his expense of course.

I started plotting my revenge. I started small at first so he barely noticed how I'd started to torture him. Little things that kept me amused, like the time he had an early meeting that he could not and would not be late for. He set two digital alarm clocks just in case one wouldn't go off. For some strange reason his alarm clock was no longer trustworthy, as every night he swore he set it, yet the next day it looked as though it had been turned off.

Wasn't me scouts honour!

Course it was.

Two alarm clocks not going off though would be suspicious, and I didn't want him to cotton on to my game yet. But, the thought of the stress and embarrassment of him missing his meeting was too much an opportunity to miss.

So, at four o'clock in the morning after listening to the son of a bitch snoring for a few hours, I got up and crept downstairs. I fumbled around for a while until I found my torch and headed for the cupboard under the stairs - where I swiftly pulled out the main house fuse. I left it a few seconds and then smugly replaced it. Instantly every clock in the house re set to 00:00. Result! There could be no suspicion on me, everything in the house was re-set, TV and video, microwave, it looked just like a brief power cut.

All night I lay awake quietly sniggering, waiting for morning. He was supposed to be up at six, however, it was nine o clock when he woke up.

"GOD!" He bellowed, as he opened one eye and saw the time on the clock. "Shit, shit, shit, shit, shit! I'm late!" He hopped around the bedroom trying to get dressed, teeth brushed and shaved all at once. He left the house in a flap with little squares of toilet tissue stuck to his face where he'd cut himself shaving.

I don't know how I kept a straight face till he'd gone. He was barely out the door before I erupted with laughter; it kept me laughing all day.

These strange power cuts became quite a nuisance for him that year, he was late for work all the time. He was threatened with the sack for poor punctuality and missed out on a promotion. He was furious and wrote repeated snotty letters to the electricity board about it. Eventually he admitted defeat and bought a battery powered alarm clock. Much to my disappointment!

During 1993-1994 amongst other things, I cooked him a meat pie with pedigree chum; stole his car more times than I can count; put chilli powder in his underpants, sent a stripagram to his work (a fat one), and subscribed him to a gay porn mag! (Our paperboy avoided him like the plague after that.)

The one that stands out for me though, was one day when I came home to find him ransacking my wardrobe.

"What the hell are you doing?" I cried as I walked in to the hurricane of clothes flying out of my wardrobe at warp speed.

"Getting rid of all these tarty clothes. Don't you know how old you are?"

"I'm twenty-five!"

"Yep five years too old for mini-skirts."

"Put them back!" I scooped a pile of clothes off the floor and tried to push past him to return them to my wardrobe. He knocked them out of my hands.

"Hey. Stop that." I slapped at his hands that were trying to grab my wrists. He caught me tight by both wrists and marched me out of the bedroom door backwards, slamming the door in my face and locking it without a word. I banged on the door for ages to no avail, he wouldn't let me in.

Later that day when I was allowed back into the bedroom I found to my horror almost all my clothes had gone. All that he had left in there was the sensible clothes his mother had bought me over the years, hideous things that I had buried at the back of the wardrobe. Clothes fit for someone in their fifties, not twenties. I looked out of the bedroom window to see the pile of smouldering clothes on the bonfire that Neil had lit at the bottom of the garden. He had lit it despite the next-door neighbours having washing hung out on the line. That should make him popular, I thought as I sat on the bed and thought about what he'd done. This could not go unpunished, He would pay majorly for this.

Unfortunately for Neil, a while later, his little white Scotty dog was 'kidnapped'. He was distraught. It's the only time he seemed half human for years. He was out in the streets for hours looking for it, I started to feel quite bad for him actually. He even called the police. But he was more distraught when it came back...dyed bright pink!

The memory of watching him walk that pink Scotty dog still makes me cry with laughing. The neighbours took the piss out of him for months. It took four months for the dye to wash out. (It took me hours to get all the pink dye out of the bath before he got home.)

He started thinking one of our neighbours must have a vendetta against him. Especially after all his washing was 'stolen' off the clothesline. He was especially affronted when he spotted the scarecrow on his way to work was wearing his best suit. (Have you ever tried dressing a scarecrow? Way harder than you'd think.)

He called the police about ten times for various things, wanting them to track down this 'criminal with a vendetta against him'. They just laughed at him for being stupid. After he'd been pestering them for a while they started calling him Victor Meldrew, and unfortunately for him, the name stuck. You could often hear calls of "morning Mr Meldrew" down our street on a morning!

It gave me fresh purpose planning and plotting my next move, thinking each time, surly he has to know it's me doing these things. After all, as he repeatedly told me, he was much more intelligent than me. Every week I told him I hated him and wanted a divorce, to which he'd laugh and tell me I could have one, as long as I left penniless and without Louise.

Another one that stands out was when he went to a restaurant without me. Apparently I was too scruffy to be seen with.

"You aren't coming out looking like that."

"Like what?" I looked down at the hideous ankle length dress I was wearing with a pair of lime green trainers. I had worn it on purpose to try and shame him for destroying most of my clothes.

"You look like a simpleton."

"It's not my fault I don't have any decent clothes."

"Don't start that again." He stood up and grabbed his car keys. "I'll think of you while I'm tucking into a nice juicy steak. I think there's a tin of beans in the cupboard if you get hungry." He left with a self-satisfied smirk on his face. I fumed....and then got creative. I decided to follow him.

He left his car in the restaurant car park, his brand-new car, that is. A white BMW 3 series, which was his pride and joy. I smiled as I looked at it, it was very pretty.

I spotted the local rugby team who were training next door to the car park and persuaded them to help me. They gathered around his car and managed to move it by lifting and bumping it in such a way that it became completely wedged, nose to tail between two bollards.

I wish I could have seen his face when he came out and saw it, but there was no way on earth I would've been able to keep a straight face, so I daren't watch.

I realised I had done the right thing later on, just listening to him ranting down the phone to the RAC was enough to make me wee, no way could I have kept a straight face.

The trouble was, this was a bit of a vicious circle. The worse he treated me, the more I tortured him, the more I tortured him, the worse his mood was and the worse he treated me. Yet he wouldn't let me leave. Worse still, was that my little girl had become a daddy's girl. She was picking up his derogatory phrases to me. She told me I was a stupid thick mummy, a mental case, ugly, a peasant. She'd mock my accent too and correct my grammar. If I asked who said something, she'd shout WHOM Mummy not who! The two of them made a game of it. Who could make me cry first won.

I had to get away for a while, and take my girl with me. Away from such a negative influence. This was what brought me back to aunt May's for a few days.

Weekend at May's

I felt better already just driving away from home. I felt the tension slipping out of my shoulders and more importantly the creases falling from my forehead. I looked across at Louise who was asleep in her car seat beside me. She'd fallen asleep after thirty minutes of driving (me driving, not her, I wasn't that bad a parent.) She looked like a little dark haired cherub fast asleep with her thumb in her mouth, the other hand curled around her hair. She'd actually been quite nice to me that day; her usual distaste for me seemed to be on holiday.

The scenery up here in East Yorkshire is beautiful, and it felt like I was driving through an oil painting. Rolling green hills and valleys, sheep and lambs as far as the eye could see. We crawled up and over the little stone bridge that marks the entrance to the village, I noticed that the water below us was much higher than it normally was, there must have been a lot of rain fall. A flock of mallards swam under the bridge, a mother and a dozen ducklings, I woke Louise up to point them out to her, but she just shrugged and went back to sleep. She's never been interested in animals at all. She once asked me what was the point in them, I was too taken aback to give her a proper answer. Animals have always been a huge part of my life, how she could not appreciate them has always baffled me.

At last the driveway came into view for Davenport. The hotel sign was still propped up against one of the oak trees at the start of the drive. It used to hang between the trees right across the driveway proudly announcing its guests had arrived at "Davenport Manor Hotel". May had it taken down after she inherited the place from her former employers. Her employers, Mr & Mrs Staines, had been childless, and after many squabbles within the Staines' family, they had decided to leave it to their employee and friend, who was very much a daughter to them in all the ways that counted.

There was nobody more surprised than May when it was announced by the Staines family solicitor that the estate in its entirety had been left to her, an outsider. The remaining Staines family were furious; they had taken it for granted that the beautiful Hotel built by the late Herbert Staines would stay within the family. They fought long and hard through the courts trying to usurp May from the Hotel. It cost her most of her inheritance in the legal battle that lasted for almost five years -which was a great shame, as May had been hoping to use her newfound wealth to repair the bomb damage to the hotel and get it back up and running. Sadly, in the end she could only afford to have the east wing pulled down, and the east side wall rebuilt and made safe again. She took in many lodgers over the years for an income, and many, many waifs and strays, but sadly it was never open as a hotel again. May, being sentimental would never let anyone remove the sign from the driveway. In the end, she compromised and had it taken down and propped against the first oak tree where it has sat for the last sixty years. Unfortunately, it's caused poor lost travellers to knock on the door for years until eventually moss made the sign almost illegible.

I turned the car down the driveway, having to weave around the many potholes that peppered the drive. Every time I'd been there lately the place seemed more and more like a wilderness. It's always been beautiful to me, even in the state it was in, but I had to admit it was starting to look like something off a haunted house movie.

I pulled up and parked in the gravel turning circle, its former pond and fountain - complete with water nymph looking decidedly sorry for itself.

Waking a grumpy Louise, I was unfastening her from her child seat as May came out to greet us.

"Hello lovies!" She beamed at us.

She'd obviously dressed up for the occasion, wearing a lovely green silk dress, and she had a new hairdo. Beautiful pearls were gathered at her throat, and a jewelled clip complimented her newly bobbed silver hair. The Barbara Cartland makeup made me jump though. Plus, I don't know what she was thinking, finishing off an outfit like that with the acid pink fluffy slippers!

"Good to see you aunt May."

We had a big hug once I'd finally got Louise untethered, although when May tried to hug Louise she wrestled away from her and stuck her tongue out at her. I could have died from embarrassment.

"Louise, don't be rude. Give aunt May a hug."

Lou shook her head and glared at May. May didn't seem that bothered and stuck two fingers up at Louise by way of reply. Lou looked at me gobsmacked but I just laughed, and followed May inside. Louise would learn, May didn't suffer fools.

Later that night once Louise was safely tucked up in bed, asleep after listening to me read her favourite story, Snow white, (she preferred the wicked witch to Snow white, should have been a warning sign really) I poured my heart out to May. My parents had moved abroad a few years before to live with my eldest brother in Spain, and I didn't realise just how much I missed the closeness of family.

I told May everything. All the cruel ways Neil had belittled me, and bullied me, robbing me of my independence, confidence, and very nearly my sanity. She sat in silence while I poured my heart out to her, crying all the tears that I'd bottled up for so long. I told her all about him taking away my job, friends, money, the pre-nup, and how he'd assured me I'd never get custody of Louise.

She was disgusted with him. "I told you he was a bastard! I never could stand that man, Mr bloody posh pants, who the hell does he think he is?"

I finally pulled myself together and blew my nose and sighed. "Yeah I know. But don't worry I've been getting my own back. He's not been getting away with it all." I smiled and filled her in on some of the things I had done to torture him. Oh my god she howled with laughter till we were both rolling around the floor laughing. What really tickled her though was the tale of the fat stripagram that I had sent to his office.

"When I say fat aunt May, I don't really mean fat, I mean half a ton HUGE!!!" I laughed and started my tale.

"I'd seen her picture on a flyer in a telephone box and thought she was perfect. I told her on the phone when I booked her that I was Neil's boss, and said he'd had a lot of stress at work lately, and so I wanted to cheer him up. I went on to say how he'd always had a thing for 'curvy girls' especially, ones dressed as *Wonder Woman!*"

"My goodness!" May interrupted.

I continued. "And so, come Monday morning, Fat Wonder Woman burst into his office, mid meeting; tried to lasso him with a bit of washing line that she'd obviously picked up along the way, unfortunately missed her target, tripped over the lasso, and landed on Neil's boss breaking his nose!"

Aunt May laughed so hard she trumped.

"So, to add insult to injury, his co-workers now think he's a pervert. Well, an unpunctual pervert, his alarm clocks hadn't woken him up again that morning."

(Actually, he got off lightly, I'd paid her to hog tie him and take pictures!)

May and I stayed up talking all night, both laughing and worrying about my situation. May's solution to the problem was a little excessive. "We'll have to bump him off love, it's the only way you'll be free of him."

I was stunned. "Don't be ridiculous aunt May, we can't just go around killing people willy nilly!"

"I'm not talking about hurting him, just...dispatching him. How long do you think it'll be before he starts getting physical? Men like him are all the same love. Sweetness and light, roses and champagne, till they've got you where they want you."

"Oh don't May, I wish I hadn't told you now." I hung my head in my hands and sighed.

"So, he won't give you a divorce then?"

I shook my head.

She stood over me, hands on hips. "Well as I see it he's given you no choice then. Desperate times call for desperate measures."

"I didn't tell you this to wind you up, I just needed someone to talk to, just to vent a bit." I paused, "I just need to come up with some sort of plan of action, stop feeling sorry for myself and take my life back."

She sat at the side of me and put her hand on mine. "You know my house is your house love, never think you haven't got a home. This has always been your home. You just concentrate on a strategy for custody, while I have a think about things." She patted my arm, her eyes shining with mischief. "Anyway, while we're thinking of a plan it won't do any harm to continue torturing him will it? After all, now you've got an accomplice!"

Life got a lot more interesting after that.

Double Trouble

I went home feeling like a huge burden had been lifted. I was no longer alone, I had an ally. We'd decided that I would go back on the Sunday morning as planned, and resume life as normal, for now. May was going to call Neil sometime during the week to demand my assistance the following weekend with something, we didn't know what yet but she'd come up with something. Neil wouldn't be able to say no to May without looking rude, which was something he never was to anybody but me. I knew he wouldn't want to come with me as he had planned a game of golf for the weekend with his boss. (This was a desperate attempt to get back in his boss's good books after the Wonder Woman incident.)

This would give May and I time to think and plan what the next move would be. Meanwhile I'd resume normal duties of mental cruelty.

I returned home to find that while I'd been gone, he'd put the house up for sale! The first I knew of it, was the for-sale sign in the front garden. I was dumb-struck, how could he do this without telling me?

Louise looked at the sign puzzled too. "What does that sign mean Mum?"

"Apparently we're moving!" I put my hands on my head, and exhaled slowly.

"Good, I hate it here; the people around here are so common!" She confirmed this by wiping her muddy shoe on the curb of the house next door, as though all they were good for was wiping her feet on. I shook my head at her. "Well lady, you were born here so that makes you common too!"

She stuck her tongue out at me. She really was her father's daughter.

We spent hours arguing after Louise had gone to bed.

"I can't believe you're making us move on a stupid whim!"

"It's not a whim." He spat. "I hate it here, it's beneath us living in an area like this."

"Beneath us? Who the hell do you think we are? We aren't bloody royalty!"

He pointed at me. "YOU might like these…commoners, but I find them …vulgar!"

"Why? What have they ever done to you?"

He paused and looked away. "I find their comments about my sexual conduct offensive." He looked down at his feet, obviously embarrassed.

I smiled inwardly. He'd obviously heard the gossip that was going around.

We argued the rest of the night away, but I went to bed happy. I'd finally got to the truth of why he wanted to leave our lovely house. He wouldn't admit it but he was frightened of the neighbours! Their constant piss taking since he was seen after dark, wearing a ridiculous mac and dark glasses, walking a pink dog had got to him. (He looked like a camp Inspector Gadget.)

Plus, our old paperboy had moved in along with his family two doors down, and proceeded to regale all the other neighbours about Neil's former subscription to the hard-core gay porno - 'Bums, butts, nobs, n nuts' - which had exacerbated the situation somewhat. I think he was getting a reputation as a pervert! (Shame they didn't know about Wonder Woman.)

I thought it a shame that we would be moving, I really liked our neighbours, I got on great with them, but I was told in no uncertain terms that I had no say in the matter. To punctuate this point, before he went to bed, he smashed up my new video camera that he had bought me for my birthday.

Later that night, from my bed in the spare room, I started to wonder if May had a point about him possibly becoming violent. He'd never physically hurt me, but what's to say he wouldn't get worse? He was a hell of a lot bigger than me, over six foot, and had at least six stone on me.

As planned, May called Neil and demanded my presence for the following weekend. She told him she needed help with interviewing a new handyman, and needed a second opinion. So it was all set. I would drive up to May's Saturday morning, while Neil was playing golf.

Saturday morning arrived, with Neil being the first one to leave. I just had time to drop Louise off at Neil's parents, before I'd have to depart. Did I mention I'd have to pass the golf course on my way to May's?

I'd made sure to have a copy made of Neil's car key ages ago in order to steal it and park in different places to where he left it. (Just to mess with him.) So, I pulled into the golf course and parked next to his prised BMW. I had to wait awhile for a quiet spell to make sure there were no witnesses to worry about. I looked about, watching for anyone pulling in near me. When the coast was clear, I quietly unlocked the driver door, and slid in. Looking over my shoulder to make sure no one was watching. I stuck the key into the ignition and switched it on. I've never been a fan of Automatic cars, but Neil only has a license to drive automatics, he says he could drive a manual if he wanted to, he just didn't want to. Bullshit! He's just a terrible driver. It took him seven attempts to pass his test. I grabbed the gear selector and pulled it out of park and into neutral. I turned off the ignition and climbed back out. After another long look around me checking for witnesses, I leaned back in and disengaged the hand-brake. I then locked it back up carefully, and scarpered bloody quickly!

I watched at a distance as it very slowly at first, started to creep forward, picking up speed as it gained momentum. He'd parked it facing on to the back of the golf course, with no obstacles at all between the car and the pond. It was perfect!

I would have filmed it if he hadn't smashed up my camera. Hope his boss was willing to give him a lift home! With a beam on my face, I set off for aunt May's.

I'd barely slept all week, plotting and planning. Plus, the bed in the spare room wouldn't be out of place in a torture chamber. It's very difficult to sleep with one spring in your back and another stuck up your arse. Not that I'd have slept anyway. My new idea was keeping my brain whirling with endless possibilities.

I arrived at May's around midday, after a very pleasant easy journey, with very little traffic for a Saturday. Pulling up outside of the House, I saw that May must have company. A very old and dirty camper van was parked in the turning circle. I got out of my car and had a nosey at the van as I made my way over to the front door. It was more of a muddy, sort of rusty colour than brown. It must have been older than I was. As I walked around it I noticed the bumper sticker: -

"I still miss my ex, but my aims getting better!" Wonder where they got that from? I like it. Who the hell was visiting her?

I got my shoulder up against the front door and shoved as hard as I could, eventually the door unstuck and creaked open. It had been a pain for sticking for years, I never knew how May managed to open it, but then again, she was as strong as an ox.

I walked into the foyer feeling instantly like I was home. The place had seen better days, but it was still very grand. The oak panelling had a stunning patina after more than a hundred years of beeswax, it positively gleamed. The floor was black and white marble tiles in a diamond pattern. A gorgeous crystal swag chandelier hung thirty feet above my head, sadly more cobweb now then crystal. But the main feature that drew the eye was the staircase. It was gorgeous, Jacobean oak, full of intricate carvings and filigree. It must have been at least eight feet wide, I suppose to accommodate the many guests that it was built to serve. It snaked up the left-hand side of the hall all the way up to the third-floor gallery

"Hello, aunt May? It's me, are you in?" I started walking towards the kitchen at the back of the hall when she appeared behind me from the parlour, making me jump.

"Hello love, how are you?" She asked as she gave me a hug.

I shrugged. "I'm fine, got another instalment to tell you about." I gave her a mischievous grin. "Who have you got visiting? I saw the van outside."

"Ah, that would be my new handyman Darren!" She pulled her glasses halfway down her nose and peering over them she winked at me. "Another lost soul come to stay. I think you'll like him."

I followed her through to the kitchen. "So you weren't completely lying to Neil then?" I laughed.

"No but it seemed like a good excuse to get you here. You'll meet him tomorrow, he's working at to the pub till late tonight." She paused while she filled the teapot. "He came looking for a hotel room to rent for a few weeks and I didn't have the heart to turn him away, so I offered him the gardener's old rooms in exchange for a few jobs about the place." She put a cup of tea down in front of me, and carried on. "He's a nice enough lad; bit of a hippy though, looks a bit girly with long hair. I caught him smoking some wacky-backy in the shed yesterday. You should have seen him start stuttering when I walked in. He tried to claim it was 'herbal tobacco'." She chuckled. "He must think I was born yesterday. It smelt terrible too. If I'd known he liked pot I'd have given him some of mine, mines better!"

I spat my tea out in shock. She never failed to surprise me.

"What?" She puzzled at my surprised face. "Half the women in the WI grow it to help with their arthritis."

After we'd gossiped awhile about the new lodger, we finally got down to business. May laughed till she cried about the golf course incident, as I described to her, the car hurtling across the putting green and into the pond.

"Oh my goodness." She cried as she wiped the tears from her eyes. "I'd love to have seen his face when he got to the last hole and his car was in it!" We both exploded with laughter again.

"I wish I could have hung around to see his face but I couldn't risk him seeing me. I don't suppose it would have improved his boss's opinion of him either; it would look like he wasn't even capable of putting his hand-brake on."

We both laughed again. When we'd finished chuckling I wiped my eyes with the back of my hand. May dried her eyes on her handkerchief.

"So have you decided to let me bump him off yet then?"

I took a long sip of my tea before replying. "Don't be daft, I can't do that aunty May, I can't even kill a spider, let alone the father of my child."

She looked quite disappointed; I think she was already planning on how to do it. I looked down at my hands, fidgeting with my cup. "There is one way to get rid of him though." lifting my eyes to meet hers. "We could set him up to go to jail."

May sat back in her chair looking thoughtful. "Mm, now that's not something that had occurred to me." She pursed her lips. "Let me give it some thought."

The Ghost

While May was planning on how best to have my husband incarcerated, I decided to bring my overnight bag in from the car and take it up to my room.

I loved my room at Davenport. It's the room I was born in. In fact, it's the same room that I use today. (Well until my dance with death later anyway.) It's the grandest bedroom in the place; what was once -according to the brass plaque on the door, 'The Honeymoon Suite'. At thirty feet by forty feet, it is the largest of the twenty bedrooms, boasting a magnificent four poster bed, with gorgeous, sumptuous, gold damask curtains, though falling to bits due to the many moths that made them their home. It has a huge Walnut wardrobe that takes up nearly a whole wall, ornately carved with roses and tulips. But I suppose the real centrepiece of the room is the fireplace. Eight-foot-tall, ornately carved oak. It must have been built by the same craftsmen who were responsible for the staircase. It is simply a marvel. It must have taken months to carve all the intricate detail into it.

The room's seven large windows are all stained glass, again with the roses and tulip theme. It's simply stunning watching the sun rise through these magnificently coloured windows. I'm sure that all the brides that had stayed in this room had to have fallen in love with the room almost as much as with their grooms.

I asked May many times why she had stayed on in her old room in the servants' quarters after she inherited the place, when she could have taken over the stunning honeymoon suite. She just used to shrug and say there were too many bad memories in there, and she didn't like sharing with ghosts. I have to tell you that scared the crap out of me. I slept with the lights on for years after that. I never saw the ghost that's supposed to haunt my room. But my mother did. She told me her tale the night that Louise was born, I believe in an effort to give me a distraction and to take my mind off the pain.

The night that I was born, she was staying in the honeymoon suite, in pampered luxury, thanks to her darling aunt May. She was very agitated and in a lot of pain, due to me being particularly active that night, or so she believed.

Unable to sleep, convinced that this would be the night her baby would be born, and annoyed that she was alone in her bedroom, as my father had stayed at home to look after the three boys, along with his sister, my aunty Peggy who was helping out. My mother had thought it ridiculous that she should stay with her aunt May for the last week of her pregnancy. All well and good, that there was a doctor living on one side, and a midwife on the other. But she wasn't a first-time mother, she'd been through this three times before, so this wouldn't be too bad. She's rather be at home with her husband and her boys. She huffed and puffed trying to turn this way and that, in order to try and get comfortable, to no avail. She knew her baby was coming.

Eventually she gave up on sleep and pulled herself up against the pillows into a sitting position and waited for her baby to be born. She had decided she would do this on her own, she didn't need help, she was an old hand at this now. She'd show them. She cursed aunt May for making her stay in this unfamiliar, uncomfortable bed.

As she cast her eyes around the room she saw the shadow move. At first she thought her eyes were playing tricks on her. As she watched, a dark shadow appeared by the fireside, like black smoke, growing in stature until it was around five feet tall, pulsing and contracting, it moulded into the shape of a woman. My mother was terrified; all thoughts of her uncomfortable bed were gone, all thought of her baby gone. All that was left was pure paralysing terror.

The dark shadow woman crossed the room towards my mother, gliding above the floor, passing through the bedside table, and slowly bent down until it was level with my mother,
eyeball to eyeball with her. It stared at her with its dead eyes, and said "Ring the bell!"

My mother's paralysis was momentarily broken, and she did as her instincts were screaming at her to do, and reached for the bell pull next to her bed. As soon as she rang the bell the spectre disappeared. A minute later appeared aunty May; And ten hours after that, so did I.

My mother's convinced to this day, that had that ghost not scared the crap out of her, forcing her to ring for help, then she would have probably died in childbirth. Mine was not the easy birth she had been expecting, and without the skill and quick thinking of both the Doctor and the midwife, Davenport Manor Hotel would've had two more ghosts.

Plan A

After I'd finished putting my things away, I went back in search of aunt May. I found her still in the kitchen where I'd left her, drinking her tea. Her cigarette dangled from the end of her ebony cigarette holder, as she twirled it through her fingers thoughtfully.

"Any ideas?" I asked, making her jump.

She looked up startled. "Well the more I think about it the more I like it". She stubbed her cigarette out and continued. "The biggest issue is him going for sole custody of Louise,
like the bastard said, as things stand, he'd win custody hands down. Big house, big income, rich semi-retired parents living five minutes away. Plus, I dare say if she was asked, Louise would choose to live with him. After all, she can see no fault in him."

I interrupted. "Plus, he said he'd have me declared mentally incompetent. Any time I try and voice an opinion on anything he threatens me with a psych evaluation!" I paused and took a deep breath. "This new threat is a nightmare. I went to the doctors last year because I was so low in condition and struggling to eat. I had no appetite at all, and the doctor said perhaps I was depressed. Well I laughed and thought 'well d'oh'. Any way the doctor gave me anti-depressants and sent me on my way. I never took them; happy pills won't give me a divorce will they? Anyway, unbeknown to me, Neil's parents knew my doctor, who blabbed about me having *mental health issues*. They in turn blabbed to Neil, so now he's got even more ammo." I sat back and sighed.

Aunt May leaned over and squeezed my hand. "Well love, all the more reason to set the bastard up. If we can somehow discredit him, it'll make his chances of getting custody impossible. What's a bit of depression compared to being a convict?"

That made me smile. "But what could we do? He's never even had a parking ticket?"

May took her glasses off to clean them, "Well we'll have to do some serious thinking pet."

We sat all afternoon in the kitchen drinking tea and pondering. We were in the middle of a fit of giggles thinking of Neil being shacked up with a big butch cell mate, when the phone started ringing. May was just doing an impression of a gruff man's voice. "Come on Neil, time to kneel!"

I spluttered and started coughing, choking on my tea and snorting with laughter.

When May managed to stop laughing she answered the phone. It was Neil, and he wasn't happy. May passed the phone over to me. Taking a few seconds to try and compose myself, I picked up the receiver.

"You need to come home now." He barked. "There's been an accident with my car!"

Oh dear he wasn't a happy bunny. I faked concern and surprise. "What sort of accident? Are you alright?" I smiled into the receiver.

"No I'm bloody not! There's been some sort of mechanical malfunction with my car. I parked up at the golf course earlier, put the car in park, put the hand-brake on as normal; and somehow it's slipped out of gear, the hand-brake failed and the car went hurtling into the bloody pond near the ninth hole!" I actually heard a little catch in his voice then, like a stifled sob.

"I was playing a brilliant round of golf, absolutely playing out of my skin, I think I was actually starting to impress old Mr Hemsworth, 'cause let's face it, that bloody mad woman dressed as Wonder Woman bursting into my office and busting his nose didn't exactly make me look good."

I put my hanky in my mouth to stifle the laugh that was trying to bust out.

"Everything was going like a dream, my aim was the best it's ever been, I couldn't miss. I also couldn't miss my car sticking up from the duck pond as we rounded the ninth hole! I thought, that can't be my car. It can't be, oh god, please don't let that be my car. But it was!" He paused, and said softly, "Mr Hemsworth's started calling me Basil Fawlty."

After a good belly hurting, side splitting laugh at his expense, I set off for home.

On my return, I discovered poor Neil had been dealt another blow. His insurance company had deemed his insurance policy void, as their vehicle recovery team had reported to them that the car had been left in neutral with no hand-brake engaged. Their conclusion, 'driver error'. He was also billed for the cost of the recovery truck. This gave me an idea, and got me thinking.

Sadly, Neil had to bicycle to work after that. As he didn't have a manual transmission driving license he couldn't even borrow my car.

Watching him wobbling all over the road the following Monday morning, trousers held down by bicycle clips, tit-head helmet on his head, amidst a chorus of "Morning Mr Meldrew" from the neighbours, was enough of a happy pill to banish depression for ever!

Neil's Rebellion

Poor Neil, life just wasn't being fair for him at that time. All he wanted from life was to be respected. His parents were both very successful and well respected professionals. His father was a stockbroker, and his mother a barrister. Both had made a huge success of their careers climbing their respective corporate ladders. Circulating with the upper classes, they had more money than they knew what to do with, and more importantly, influence. Sadly though, for all their heirs and graces, they lacked the simple tools needed in life. Kindness, forgiveness, empathy; and a bloody sense of humour!

Perhaps if they had possessed any of these skills they could have taught them to their son. Instead they taught him greed, selfishness, cruelty, intolerance, and ignorance.

Despite his many tries, he could never quite live up to his parents' expectations of him. When he passed his A levels with two A's and two A pluses, their response was: - "Why didn't you study hard enough to get four A pluses?"

When he developed chicken pox and missed so many lectures that he failed his degree in psychology, they didn't speak to him for a year. They cut all ties with him completely. Although this was probably the best thing they could have done for him, the injustice of it made him angry. For the first time in his life, it made him......REBEL!

He started his rebellion slowly at first, dipping his toe into the shallow end. Not used to thinking and fending for himself, it was a shock to his system at first.

He got his first job working in the Student Union Bar, having never done bar work before, (or any other work either.) He needed to be trained up. He was a nervous as hell trying to pull his first few pints, while all the drunken students took the piss out of him. "Oi mate, you give shit head!" Or the classic, "I wish my girlfriend gave as much head as you!"

It was a steep learning curve but one worth studying. He became a little more down to earth with each passing day, even joining in with the banter after a while, surprised to find that he quite liked his workmates and rowdy customers. He in turn began to grow on them a little too. They started to treat him like a little brother, he was a bit posh and little wet behind the ears, but he was alright.

He started to not quite mind being poor. It had its benefits, there was nobody to try and impress anymore. It was a weight off his shoulders not having to feel judged and found lacking all the time. As time passed he started learning how to smile. True it looked more like a constipated grimace at first, but with practice it got better.

Stage two of his rebellion was his appearance. He grew his hair! No more sensible short back and sides for Neil! He knew if his parents could see it they would be horrified. He'd briefly wondered if he should send them a photo? No, he'd wait until it was a bit longer, and permed!

His skin also began to lose the insipid clammy paleness he had obtained from being indoors studying for so many years. From the many afternoons he spent in the beer garden with his new friends, he started to get a tan.

Next was his wardrobe. He threw away all the pompous jumpers his Mother had bought him, replacing them with T shirts of bands that he'd discovered he liked. No more stuffy suits and shirts, and from now on, ties would only be worn on his head!

With his new-found sense of humour, new wardrobe, and newly tousled dark locks,
he began to attract the ladies for the first time. At first he was bewildered by them, assuming their compliments were mockery. His annoyed retorts to their compliments would leave the girls speechless. It wasn't until a friend pulled him aside and hit him on the side of the head for being dumb that he realised he was finally, after all these years, desirable!

It was with this new found smug confidence that he approached the pretty petite blonde, who had come into the bar and made a beeline for the table in the corner. He thought she was a stunner, and according to what his friends had told him about how women behave when they like you, she must really like him. After all, she had been steadily ignoring him for over an hour! In fact, the way she rolled her eyes at the bar, when he told her the book she was reading was crap, looked very promising. He sat down beside her. "May I join you?"

She looked up from her book with annoyance. "To what?" She turned back to the page she was reading.

He was baffled. "Eh pardon?"

"What do you want to join me to?"

This wasn't going well. "I'm sorry I meant may I sit with you?"

"Depends on if you're going to insult my taste in books again."

"I'm sorry I didn't mean to be rude, actually I've no idea if your book's any good or not." He sighed. "My friends told me that if I see a beautiful girl that I'd like to compliment, I should insult her instead. The old treat 'em mean, keep 'em keen, I suppose. I'm sorry I'm not very good at all this. I'll go away and stop bothering you now." He got up to leave, blushing furiously.

"Wait."

He looked up hopefully.

"That's the nicest, stupidest half arsed compliment I think I've ever heard." She laughed. "Come and sit down. My name's Sarah."

And so began a whirlwind romance. It was the happiest few months of our marriage. Upon the positive result of a pregnancy test, we decided to get married; And that's when the shit hit the fan.

Upon hearing about their son's impending wedding, and pregnant future wife, Neil's parents decided that Neil had been punished enough now. It was time for him to return to the fold. In private they did not approve of Neil's choice in bride, I was far too common. But, with a baby on the way, they didn't feel like there was much that could be done about it without causing a scandal.

Neil was delighted at returning to the bosom of his family, although he was determined to hang onto his new-found independence. In an effort to make amends, his parents organised and paid for the wedding, which was a very grand affair. (In order to impress their friends of course.) The only stipulation they had given Neil and I was, "do not let anyone know you are expecting!" God forbid they should be embarrassed in front of their posh friends!

After the wedding, we were given a nice four-bedroomed semi to live in, in a cul-de-sac, near his parents, in a 'nice area'. Neil was offered a job as assistant manager in a factory belonging to a friend of his father, and the rest is history.

Neil's rebellion was over. He began to wear suits again, as he was 'management now'. Next, his hair was annoying him; it was too long, much easier to look after if it was short. As his hours at work increased, his once tanned skin began to return to its former pale clamminess. Then it was his sense of humour. "No time for jokes, time is money!"

By the time his smile soured back into a constipated grimace, his parents where finally proud of him. Except now, his life had turned to shit. Everything he'd worked so hard for was slipping through his fingers. He was a laughing stock at work, his parents were disappointed in him again, his boss thought he was a twit, his neighbours were terrorising him, the paperboy thought he was a pervert, the electricity company seemed to have a personal vendetta against him, his wife hated him, he'd lost his car; and, to top it off, he had a pink dog!

Yep life was not very fair at all.

D Day

All weekend Neil had been a nightmare to live with. He'd begged and pleaded, ranted and raved down the phone at his insurance company, threatening to report them to the insurance ombudsmen if they didn't uphold his claim.

"I know my rights!" he told them. But he couldn't persuade them with either charm or threats, and by god he tried both. He couldn't get around the fact that he had the only key to the car, (mm) and that the car was found in neutral, with no hand-brake engaged. He was screwed.

Next, he started on the BMW dealership where he bought the car from. He tried to convince them that the car must have had a mechanical fault. It just wasn't good enough! He would sue them!

They put the phone down on him after calling him a 'tosser'.

Next was my turn for an ear bashing. I barely got through the front door before the assault started. It was something along the lines of:

"Where the hell do you think you've been?"

(Shops d'oh.)

And:

"Who the hell do you think you are?"

(Did he think I had Alzheimer's?)

"How dare you go gallivanting off at the drop of a hat, leaving me home all alone?"

I thought that was extremely uncalled for, he was the one that sent me out for a bottle of wine. I explained this, to which he replied:

"Yeah? Well, it's living with you that makes me drink!" He glared at me. "Staring at your ugly miserable mug all day is hard work."

Ouch.

"It's about time I traded you in for a younger, better model. A nice curvy feminine woman who knows her place and doesn't talk back. Someone that knows how to please a man!"

He was vile. I was quick to tell him he could happily trade me in for another model. Good bloody riddance to him!

"Oh, you'd just love that wouldn't you, so you can get to play the victim, crying to all your friends about what a horrid man you married. No. You are *my* wife, and you're gonna play by *my* rules!" He pointed at my face, glaring at me. "To remind you of who's boss around here, I've decided to punish you." He sneered. "I'm taking your bank cards off you. You can have them back when you learn some respect!" He then ransacked my handbag, pulling my cards out of my purse, shoved them in his pocket, and stormed out of the house slamming the front door behind him.

I just heard a faint "Morning Mr Meldrew," and a subsequent reply of "Fuck Off!" before the door slammed back into its frame.

I was quite shaken I have to tell you. I had started to feel guilty about my idea for plan A. Well not anymore!

After checking that the coast was clear, I found the car insurance policy with the phone number on it. After copying the number onto the back of my hand, I headed out of the front door and across the road to the payphone, where I anonymously reported to his insurance company that an acquaintance of mine had heard a man called Neil bragging down the pub about how he was going to dump his white BMW in the golf course pond and collect the insurance. Hearing that a white BMW had recently been pulled from the pond on the golf course, I thought it my duty as a concerned citizen to report the matter at once! And so began Plan A. Operation Insurance Fraud!

That did make me feel much better. But, I was still stinging from his comments earlier. What was it he said? He wanted a new more feminine woman about the place? Oh, I'd give him one alright. Though not quite what he had in mind perhaps.

As our sex life had been none existent for a long time now, I had drifted out of the habit of taking the pill. In fact, I probably had about a six-month supply left. Well, it would be a shame to waste them wouldn't it?

For the next three weeks Neil's tea had a new ingredient. Neil would become the new feminine curvy woman that he had wanted!

I informed May on my latest shenanigans while Neil was out. She's was horrified at the way he'd spoken to me, taking away my money as though I was a naughty child being deprived of its pocket money for bad behaviour.

Soon turned that frown upside down though.

I thought she disappeared off the phone for a while when the line went quiet. Nope. She was laid on the floor, gasping for air, holding her belly, and snorting with laughter. This was all told to me by Darren the new handyman who just happened to be passing, believing her at first to be having a heart attack. He said she would have to call me back when she stopped laughing and changed her underwear. He seemed a little bemused but fortunately didn't ask.

Every day I waited for the insurance company to send out a claims investigator, or some sort of detective, surely they took insurance fraud seriously? When would my plan pay off?

At least I had something to keep me occupied for a while though. I started watching Neil like a hawk, waiting to see what affect oestrogen would have on him. I didn't have to wait long.

The first sign for me was when I arrived home after dropping Louise off at chess club, to find him furiously vacuuming. This was new! In all the years I'd known him I'd *never* witnessed him doing house work. He looked quite absorbed in it too.

The next sign was the sudden cravings for chocolate. He normally only ate a little of it now and then, having more of a savoury palette than sweet. Now he was going through about four bars a day; which was in turn leading to weight gain! Those curves were coming along nicely! The sitting down for weeing was a shock though. I think if he hadn't taken away my bank cards I'd probably have bought him some tampons.

I absorbed all these new little changes with an evil relish - although I started to think I'd created a monster when he started crying at soap operas.

Finally, after three weeks of waiting, I got the news I had been waiting for. I was visiting at May's when the telephone call came through. Neil had been arrested for insurance fraud. He called me from the police station to ask me to arrange for a solicitor to meet him there. I made a lot of sympathetic noises while he sniffed and whined down the phone. Inwardly smiling. I asked him why not ask his mother? Surly being in the legal profession she would be better equipped to find him legal counsel? But no, she was not to be told, *under any circumstances*. He couldn't stand the shame.

He didn't seem very pleased when I arrived at the police station with his mother. Well, as I explained to him afterwards, I had no money with which to pay for a solicitor. After all, he'd taken away my cards.

Unfortunately for me, this little mischief back fired on me. She got him off with no charge. Shit, back to the drawing board.

Time for a re-think

Things were not going well. Not only had Neil's mother scuppered my plans, she'd taken pity on him on the car front too. No more cycling to work on his 'Raleigh Racer'. (Which was a shame incidentally as I had loosened his back wheel in anticipation for the following day.)

She couldn't have anybody seeing her son on a bicycle! What would the neighbours think! Well, I already knew what they thought but hey ho.

She didn't just buy him any old car either; she bought him an Audi Quattro V8. I was quite envious to be honest, it was very sexy, all wrapped up in metallic black paint. Shame I'd never be allowed to drive it, it was a car to be *really* driven and put through its paces, not to trundle along at twenty-five miles an hour as Neil would do, or bumping into bollards trying to park. At least I could steal it without his knowledge though. Shit, time to get another key cut!

At least it cheered the miserable git up a bit though. To be honest, the hormone cocktail he was on was starting to annoy me. He had PMT. Up one minute, down the next. He put two stone on, then went on a diet, cried a bit, and then binged until he was fatter than when he started! I even caught him trying to see his arse in the bathroom mirror. Yet despite this new feminine side, he was still treating me like shit!

He suddenly seemed very fixated on my hair. I assumed it was something to do with the hormones at first, as I had noticed he had taken an interest in his own hair too. His short back and sides were looking less severe these days, a little longer and softer, quite nice really, more like when we first met. But no, his interest in my hair was not a good thing.

My hair is natural blonde, quite long and thick, it was always my pride and joy in those days. I liked to wear it long and loose, and a bit wild, a bit like me I suppose.

Suddenly it was comments like: "You'd better get a haircut, you look like a hippy." Or "When are you going to do something about that hair? No wife of mine should have scruffy hair like that!"

He basically wanted me to have it cut into a sensible little Princess Diana hairdo. Like his mother and all her cronies, I might add. But I was having none of it. I loved my hair as it was. My hair had attitude. I didn't want to look like some posh inbred twit. NO!

I awoke the next day, and sat up in bed yawning and was in mid-stretch when I looked down and saw my hair still on the pillow. My hands shot to my head in horror. "Please no!"

Yes, he had. He'd crept in during the night while I was asleep and cut half of it off! He just never knew when to quit did he?

I composed myself before I went downstairs. I would not let the son of a bitch see me cry. I dried my tears, got dressed, pulled a hat on and got on with my normal chores which entailed getting Louise up, dressed, fed, and off to school.

She'd looked at my hat in disgust. "You look ridiculous."

I'd had just about enough and so pulled my hat off. "Would you prefer me to look like this?"

She was open mouthed and for once lost for words.

I took her speechlessness as a sign of acceptance to my hat, and so jammed it back on my head. I could see her looking at me out of the corner of her eye all the way to school. I know what she was thinking, 'Daddy's right, Mummy's crazy.' She obviously thought I'd done this to myself. I couldn't tell her who really did it. After all, she was Six, she didn't need the stress.

When I returned home, Neil was just getting ready to go to work. He must've been going in late that day. (Not my fault this time, I never woke up in time to pull out the fuse. Shame, I might have bumped into Neil, armed with his scissors.)

I could see him grinning at me out the corner of my eye. Just as he got up to go, I had a brain wave. I took the balled-up tear-stained snotty toilet tissue from my pocket, straightened it out,
and carefully tucked it into the waist band of his trousers as he passed by me. It dangled three foot down over his arse like an Andrex puppy. Good. At least at work people would think he hadn't wiped properly!

I watched him smugly sauntering down the path towards his new sexy little Audi, feeling eight-foot-tall, no doubt. A man in control, a man who would have respect! A man who had three foot of toilet roll billowing behind him in the wind.

By a stroke of luck the toilet paper got stuck in his car door as he slammed it. Good. The toilet roll would now have brown patches off the muddy road too.

I called May and told her what he had done. Suffice to say, she was livid. I was too exhausted to cry anymore and just felt miserable. May wanted me to come home to her straight away. But I couldn't, I had Louise to think of. I rang off promising to call her the next day after I'd had time to think about things and come up with another plan to be rid of him.

I reluctantly made my way to the hairdressers to get my hair fixed. I looked like a punk walking in, and bloody Princess Di walking out. The son of a bitch had beat me. Well, he might have won the battle, but the war was far from over. Let the battle commence!

Upping My Game

While I had been in the hairdressers my brain had been whirling. I was really going to get even this time. I couldn't think of a proper plan B yet, but while I was coming up with a scheme I would resume torturing him. In fact, sitting in the hairdresser's chair I came up with another idea.

On my way home I stopped in at the newsagents and spent the last of the money that I had managed to swipe from Neil the week before and bought industrial strength nicotine patches. If the oestrogen was making him hormonal, I wondered what discretely sticking nicotine patches to his back would do? Especially if after a week, I stopped doing it? I couldn't wait to find out.

He seemed to approve of my new hair, complimenting me on a wise decision in style choice. (Smug bastard). At least he was cheerful I suppose.

I was awake all night waiting for the sound of him snoring, to ensure I could get the nicotine patch on his back without him waking up. How the hell would I explain *that* if he woke up? I crept in, avoiding the squeaky floorboard, almost tripping over the clothes he had left all over the floor. Shit, he was asleep on his back. Bollocks, now what? Ah ha! I stuck gold! He had a plaster under the sole of this left foot.

I carefully started removing the plaster, cringing as I did it, please, *don't let him wake up!* He snorted and fidgeted. My heart was racing. I waited a few minutes until his snoring resumed, and then gingerly tried again. I finally got it off, phew! I swiftly replaced it with the nicotine patch and scarpered quickly.

We played footsie the following night too, but he had no idea.

I thought he was onto me on the second day when I saw him peal the patch off to replace it with another plaster. Fortunately, he didn't pay too much attention to the 'plaster' he threw away. He was complaining that the cut under his foot instead of healing seemed to be getting more and more sore; in fact, it felt like it was burning. I offered to put him on a new plaster. I'm nice like that.

After he'd gone to bed I emptied all the plasters out of the box and threw them away, replacing them with the nicotine patches. As long as he didn't look too close he'd never know the difference. After all, he was very short sighted, but too vain for glasses. Plus, it would save me a job replacing it every night. Labour saving!

The next morning, I watched him limping off to his Quattro. (Completely unaware of the fact that I put super glue on his wind screen wipers three days earlier). I looked up and prayed for rain. Nope, not a cloud in sight.

I set off with a heavy heart, and half the contents of my jewellery box, to the pawn brokers. After all, a war needed funds. I relinquished all the jewellery that I thought Neil wouldn't notice missing; and I came away with about eight hundred quid. Should be enough to help me get started. I was still stumped for a plan to be rid of him permanently, but not for ways to hit him where it hurts; his lovely new Audi Quattro. But first I needed to get a key cut. I had been quoted a hundred quid from the *key and heel bar* down the road. An unbelievable price for one little key! But, needs must.

I had to wait until Saturday morning while Neil was having a lay in to steal his keys and get down to the shop pronto. Fortunately, Louise was at her friends for the weekend, I'm sure if I had taken her with me she would have blabbed.

And so there I was, Monday morning, armed with a nice shiny new key, just begging to be used! I set off for his factory with a smile on my face.

I parked around the corner, so as not to make my presence there obvious. Cautiously I walked through the side gate into the car park, avoiding the main entrance. Good, the coast was clear. There was no one around at all, phew, that would make life easier. I approached his beloved car, checking around to make sure there was no one around. Yep, all clear. I got my lovely new key out and slid it into the lock. What a sweet sound that 'click' was. Hundred quid well spent.

I got in, and had a little nosey around the interior, pretty nice actually. His mother did have good taste. I inserted the key into the ignition, clicked it on, turned his lights on, and his radio too for good measure. (Volume turned off though, didn't want anyone alerted to the sound.) I then promptly locked it up and left. This was nine thirty in the morning; I figured by the time he came out at six o clock his battery should be good and dead. Ha, another visit from the RAC I think!

I giggled to myself all the way to May's house. I know it was silly and petty, but it was these little victories that were keeping me going. I knew that sooner or later I'd probably get found out, so it was best to enjoy it while it lasted. I kept imagining his conversation with the man from the RAC. "So, Mr Pemberton, last time we met, you couldn't engage your instruments properly, and now you can't remember to disengage them!"

Oh dear he wouldn't be happy.

On arriving at May's I spotted another car parked next to Darren's van. This one was in much better shape than the poor old campervan. A newish silver ford escort. Who the hell was visiting now?

I finally got through the sticky front door, hurting my shoulder from shoving it so hard against the bloody door. After shouting and announcing my presence, I heard May calling for me to come through to the drawing room across the hall.

On entering, I came face to face, or should I say face to nipple, with a very tall, very handsome, extremely naked man!

I don't honestly know who was more startled, him or me. He must've been around the same age as me, very tall, short dark hair, very annoyed looking eyes, and I must state again, very, very naked! Oh, and he was also holding up a violin for some reason.

"Erm, hello." I stammered looking away, feeling very awkward. "I'm looking for my aunty May."

His response was very bad tempered and quite baffling. "If you want to look, its fifty quid an hour."

I was completely bewildered. I can't tell you how relieved I was when I saw aunt May across the room. I went running over as fast as my legs would carry me.

"Aunt May what the hell is going on and who the hell is that?" I gestured behind me.

"Sarah, meet Darren's brother, Matthew. He's a life model at the college." Her eyebrows shot up meaningfully. "You know how much I love painting portraits, and Matthew was kind enough to do a home visit for a poor old lady who can't get out anymore."

The crafty old perve! She'd never painted a thing in her life; she couldn't even draw a stick figure!

I hadn't noticed the easel she had propped up in front of her at first. I now also noticed that her canvas was blank and her brushes were clean. She had been paying this poor man to stand naked with a violin while she pretended to paint. What the hell would she have done if he had asked to see his portrait?

My god, if she was this badly behaved in her twilight years what the hell was she like in her twenties?

"That'll be all for now love." She said to Matthew, quickly covered up her canvas with a sheet, (so he wouldn't see she was a liar and a pervert presumably) and then pulled out his 'wages'. No wonder he'd seemed in a mood!

"Come on then Sarah love; let's go have a cup of tea."

"Good idea, I think I need one now."

After aunt May had laughed at me and called me a frigid prude, we got down to talking about Neil, and my new hair! She didn't like it any more than I did. I know she was angry with me for staying after he'd practically scalped me, but I had no choice. There's no way on earth I would have stayed if not for Louise.

I filled her in on my new 'experiment' with the pill, and then the nicotine patches, finally ending with the many things that I had done to his new car.

That cheered her up no end. "My god you get your sense of humour from me!" She laughed.

After quizzing me a bit more about his behaviour since the hormones, she looked quite thoughtful, rubbing her chin. "You know, you might be on to something there, if these, what did you call 'em, 'experiments' are making him a bit up and down, other people are bound to have noticed." She stopped for a gulp of tea before continuing. "What if," she paused for dramatic effect, "instead of trying to discredit him by making him a criminal, we get him discredited as being a basket case?"

She had a point. He'd threatened me with the exact same thing hadn't he?

I said with a slow smile, "I think we have a plan B!"

To be honest I was just relieved that she wasn't still after killing him.

Plan B

Well, really plan B was already underway. He'd been on the pill for a while now, plus he was going through some serious withdrawal. When the cut on his foot became inflamed he had booked himself a doctor's appointment. Yikes! A doctor would notice that his 'plaster' was actually a nicotine patch. I made the caring suggestion that maybe he should stop putting plasters on it and let the air get to it a bit before going to the doctors? Thankfully he agreed.

The doctor suggested that it was possible that he'd had an allergic reaction to the brand of plasters he'd been using. Luckily this seemed to be plausible to Neil, after all, once he stopped wearing plasters it got much better! Although his moods didn't.

The nicotine patches that I bought were aimed at people who were on sixty a day. For him to suddenly be cut off from such a high dose seemed to affect him dramatically. He was having some major mood swings. He was like a menopausal woman. (Well he nearly was one I suppose.) Everybody copped for his wrath.

I cooked him a Sunday dinner with all the trimmings, which he promptly threw at me when I hadn't mashed the potatoes properly. Picking the peas from out of my cleavage would probably have made me cry before, but not now, everything was going according to plan.

He fell out with all the neighbours again, after demanding to know who had super glued his windscreen wipers to the screen. He tried to accuse the paperboy's dad of letting his tyres down,
who responded by punching him. And so, the following Monday morning he arrived at work, late, (power cut again.) and with a black eye!

He barked at his employees, and was rude to his boss, until finally he was sent home to 'cool off'. He had to get the bus home though as I'd arrived earlier and let his tyres down.

This 'cooling off' from work lasted about a week, during which, I made some interesting discoveries. Apparently staring at my 'ugly mug all day' was 'doing his head in'. He had to get out for a while for some 'fresh air'.

Mm, I decided to follow him. The more I could learn about his life, the easier his downfall would be.

I watched him pull out of the street before I got into my own car and began following him at a distance. I made sure to keep well back; at least three cars were between us at all times. From the direction he was going he seemed to be heading into the city centre. Strange, he hated any busy roads. He used to get confused and flustered and end up doing stupid things like turning down one way streets. I saw his indicator come on, and noted him turning into a large car park.I didn't dare follow him in there as he would have seen me straight away. I headed up to the next round about and then came into the car park from the opposite side. It was probably five minutes or so after Neil had entered. I parked right at the end near the bushes, and cautiously got out of the car to look for him. No sign yet, so I quickly shoved a pound in the machine for my ticket, looking about me as I popped it into the window. After walking up and down for a while, probably looking to any passers-by as though I was a car thief, I found his car, but no Neil. I had missed him. What the hell was he doing coming into the town centre? Normally he wouldn't go there under any circumstances. Something fishy was going on. Never mind I was here now. I might as well make myself useful.

I unlocked his car and removed his parking ticket. He'd bought one for four hours. Whoops there it went into the bin. Oh dear and what did that sign over there say?

'WARNING! CLAMPERS OPERATE HERE!'

With a smile, I headed home.

It was very late before he finally returned home, and I think it was fair to say he hadn't had a very good day by the look of him. He walked straight past me, and up the stairs, face like thunder. By the sound of it he was having a shower. Sometime later I heard him on the phone to his father complaining that due to the incompetence of the car park attendants he had in fact been clamped. The fine had been five-hundred quid. Ouch!

The next day I followed him again, different car park this time. Same result, five-hundred pound fine.

Although I'd followed him again, he'd still given me the slip. Where was he going? It was driving me crazy. I was sure he was up to something, but perhaps he thought that about me too?

The next day I was ready for him. As I've said before, he wasn't a very confident driver. I knew if he went into town again, there's no way on earth he would attempt to Parallel Park into a parking spot on the street. He would only park where he could pull in forwards, and leave forwards. The last two car parks he wouldn't return to after they had 'robbed him'. That left just one car park left. So, the next time, I made sure I was there before him, waiting.

As predicted there he was. I waited until he parked up, bought a ticket and spent five minutes making sure it was adequately stuck to the windscreen, (bless him he was paranoid), and then followed him. To my absolute shock and amazement it wasn't another woman he was off to meet. No. He was going to……………..WEIGHT WATCHERS!!

There he was, plain as day, outside weight watchers, queuing up with a load of woman, to be publically humiliated about his weight. If he wanted to be humiliated about his weight, he should have said.

I stopped by his car on the way back to mine. Bye, bye parking ticket, hello Five hundred quid fine!

I had a new goal, make Neil fat!

Fat

I observed his eating habits for a few days. The meals that he threw at me, telling me they were disgusting and not fit for a dog were the ones that were fattening and loaded with calories. The meals that he actually ate and said were 'ok' were the fairly low calorie ones. So it wasn't my cooking that was the problem, it was that he was on a diet and wouldn't admit it. He'd rather let me have a face full of food and broken crockery, then to ask me for a salad!

I started looking for ways to make him fat. It was obviously the pill that was doing it, plus the withdrawal wouldn't be helping. He was craving something but didn't know what.

I started buying fatty foods and diet foods, swapping the labels around before putting them in the fridge. For the hell of it I messed with the calibration on the bathroom scales. He looked devastated when he thought he'd put on a stone.

I spent many nights awake and plotting how best to humiliate him next. This was a tricky one, he wasn't stupid, he wasn't going to keep falling for the "Oo would you believe there's only Ten calories in this trifle I bought?" Plus, I wasn't supposed to be aware that he was on a diet was I? I was supposed to just catch the flying plates full of high calorie food with my face. Yep, this new little project wasn't easy.

It didn't take me long to get inspired though, were there's a will there's a way.

I was doing his washing the following day when the idea came to me. He was paranoid about being fat right? But, I couldn't actually make him fat. However, there was nothing to stop me making him think he was fat was there?

I had a close look at all of the clothes that he wore regularly; most of them were fairly new. Since he'd been on the pill he'd been more aware of his appearance, buying a lot of new stuff lately. I wrote down what everything was on my pad, noting his sizes too. After checking the labels I realised they were all from the same shop.

So, off I went with my list, and blew the bulk of my 'war fund' on replacing all of his clothes with ones a size smaller. It took me ages washing them all with my own detergent so that they didn't smell new, or have that stiff starchiness about them. Well worth the effort though.

Next, I crawled under his bed and loosened the legs that held the mattress supports. With a bit of luck, the bed should now collapse when he gets in it!

Later that night, I was fast asleep, when the house shook with a BANG! I shot out of bed in surprise before my sleepy brain caught up with what the noise was. Both me and a yawning Louise crept into Neil's bedroom to assess the damage. Neil was sprawled on his back on the bed, (which was almost on the floor), with his legs hooked over the side of the bed frame - which was still standing. He looked like a tortoise on its back with its legs in the air. His bewildered eyes caught mine, and I had to bite my lip from smirking.

Louise was the first to break the silence. "Daddy are you so fat now that you broke the bed?"

She'd noticed how tight his (new) pyjamas had looked before she went to bed. Unfortunately, this one backfired on me. After putting Louise back to bed, I tried to return to my own bedroom finding instead a locked door. He'd evicted me from my bedroom. Never mind, a night on the couch was worth it.

One thing had been troubling me for the last few days. If Neil had been going to weight watchers all along, why was he going every day? I thought it was generally a once a week thing, get weighed, get humiliated in public and then go home and cry into a cake. Or, was I wrong? Had he only been to weight watchers once that week which just happened to be the day I followed him? Which begs the question, where did he go on the other days?

Sadly his 'cooling off' period from work was over and he returned to work the following Monday. So, this would now make following him almost impossible. But, it meant the coast was clear for searching through his things for clues! With him safely back at work, and Louise at school, I had plenty of opportunity.

First I went through his pockets. Nope nothing but lint. For a man he was quite good at emptying his pockets. I'd only ever washed his wallet once. (And that was because I took his wallet off the dressing table and put it into the pocket of the pair of trousers I was washing.)

I went into his bedroom, ah, he'd fixed his bed, bless him. I couldn't see anything on his dressing table or bed side cabinet. Mm, ah ha! Peering under the bed I saw a shoe box. I had to really stretch my arm and shoulder under to reach it, squashing my nose into the carpet in the process. Finally, I got a grip on it and pulled it out.

Sitting down on the bed with the box on my knee, I removed the lid. The first thing I noticed at the top of the pile was the three receipts he had for having his car unclamped, he obviously didn't want me to know about them then.

As I worked my way down through the pile of receipts and bills I found my bank cards. Yes!!! Thank god. I had been seriously worrying about continuing my war without funds. His new smaller clothes had nearly cleaned me out, and I was starting to worry that I'd have to get Darren's arsey brother to get me a job nude modelling to fund my war!

The problem was, I didn't want Neil to know that I had been snooping. If I took my cards back, at some point he'd notice they were missing. Shit, I don't think I've got the nerve for nude modelling. Never mind, I had a brainwave.

I put the box back down and went back to my own room. After rummaging through the wardrobe for a while I found my old handbag, which housed my old purse, which housed my old expired bank cards! I could switch them with the ones in Neil's box and he'd never know! Yes! I put all my things back away into the wardrobe and took my expired bank cards back to Neil's room. I pulled the box back onto my knee to swap the cards when a piece of paper fluttered to the floor. What was this then? There was my answer. It was a receipt for underwear. Ladies underwear! Big ladies' underwear! It was from Big & Bouncy, the plus size underwear shop in town.

He had a woman. A Big Woman.

With a little help from man's best friend

Discovering Neil had another woman shouldn't have come as such a shock really. The signs were all there. He'd evicted me from our marriage bed ages ago, claiming I was too ugly and useless to be privileged enough to lay my head next to his. And so I'd been unceremoniously evicted. I was relieved actually, he farted none stop in his sleep, and he was grossly offended by my nose peg.

I had noticed he'd been caring more about his appearance lately, but I just put that down to the effects of all the oestrogen I'd been pumping into him for weeks. True he'd starting buying new clothes, but I put that down to him gaining weight. All these weeks I thought I was so clever, getting one over on him, and all along, he's been getting one over on me!

I decided to take the pink dog out for a walk to clear my head.

After we'd been walking out for a while, I noticed he seemed to be having a problem peeing. He kept cocking his leg every two minutes and peeing a huge amount for such a small dog, it was a very funny colour too. He even whimpered a bit which sounded awful. I took him back home and thought I'd better give the vets a call; see if I should bring him in for a check-up. After speaking to the vet on the phone and describing his symptoms, she thought it was probably a urine infection. I was asked to bring in a sample!

For the next hour I chased a pink dog around the garden with a jug, trying to steal its urine! Christ, if the neighbours were watching they would've thought I was as barmy as Neil. I managed eventually, but me and the dog were no longer making eye contact.

The vet said she only needed around ten ml of fluid - which I syphoned off into an old clean tablet bottle, leaving me with a jug with a large amount of dog wee in it. Nice!

The poor dog did have a urine infection, and so I spent all afternoon in the vets with him, sitting in the waiting room for most of the time, listening to people sniggering about my pink dog. Did I tell you he was called Butch?

I had meant to spend the day catching up with May, filling her in on my discovery about Neil's other woman. I wanted to tell her in person, as it wasn't the sort of thing to say over the phone. I knew she'd go mad. But with the fiasco with the dog there wasn't time. I'd have to leave it until the next day. Anyhow, as me and a pink dog named Butch walked home from the vets I had started to think of another cunning plan!

That night, when I heard Neil's noisy fog horn sounding snoring start up, I quietly got up. Sneaking into his room, avoiding the creaky floorboard again, and his clothes on the floor, again.
I proceeded to pull the covers back very carefully. When I had enough sheet exposed, I poured the now warmed up dog wee onto his mattress. (Warm from me heating the jug up on the radiator in the box bedroom for hours.) I knew when he awoke; he'd think he'd had an accident. It really stank too!

With a satisfied smile I went back to bed and had a great night's sleep.

Neil was up and out before me the following morning. I was disappointed. I was hoping to see how peeing the bed would make him react. But no I was robbed. He'd already gone. I looked in the laundry basket, empty. I checked the washing machine, sure that he would have hidden the evidence, but no, it was empty. He wouldn't wash and dry his own sheets, such things were beneath him, but I thought he might at least put them in to the washer. But no. Mm.

Back up to his bedroom I went. He'd made his bed perfectly neat and tidy as always. Surely he hadn't made the bed with wet sheets? He couldn't have *not* noticed could he? It still stank of dog pee, though I noticed he'd opened a window. He had noticed, hadn't he?

I pulled his duvet off to find new clean sheets. He'd remade the bed. But where were the old sheets?

On my way out of the front door as I was setting off to May's I found my answer. He'd balled them up and hidden them in the dust bin. He was obviously embarrassed. Good.

And so off I went to May's.

On arriving at Davenport I pulled in, between Darren's tatty van and Matthew's silver Escort, hoping to god that this time Matthew would have some clothes on. If not he'd probably think I was a mental patient they way that I would be staring so intently at his eyes! Thinking all the while *DON'T LOOK DOWN!* I must be getting old, wanting naked young men to put some bloody clothes on! (Now I wouldn't.)

I found May seated at the kitchen table, along with Matthew and a young blonde hippy whom I presumed to be Darren. Thankfully both were fully clothed, phew!

I'd never actually met Darren before, and I'd only briefly spoken on the phone with him the day he thought May was having a heart attack, when in fact she was just laughing herself into the lino.

"Hello love, how are doing?" She gave me a hug before sitting back down again, and pouring me a cup of tea from the teapot.

"Not too bad, but I'll fill you in on stuff later". I didn't want to discuss this sort of stuff with two men in the room; I didn't think they'd be on my side somehow. I had a sip of my tea, ah, lovely.

"Now Sarah, I know you've met Matthew before." She gave me a knowing look. "But I don't believe you've met Darren have you?"

It must be said, both Darren and Matthew were looking decidedly uncomfortable in my presence. I wondered if aunt May had blabbed? They both said a half-hearted hello, and then said goodbye and quickly left. Strange.

I asked. "Are they both living here now then?" Curious as to what the situation was. After all, she had previously been paying poor Matthew by the hour! And Darren only looked about seventeen. I thought he was supposed to be working in the village pub?

"Well Darren as you know is standing in as gardener, and doing a few odd jobs around the place in exchange for room and board; Matthew was sacked from the art college last week after he was caught out 'freelancing' and so couldn't afford his flat anymore, so he's volunteered to help out here on the same deal as Darren." She sat back in her seat, taking a slurp of her tea.

I was suspicious. "Matthew got sacked for 'freelance' work? That was nothing to do with you was it?"

She looked shifty. "Possibly, I did let it slip in the pub about what an enjoyable hour I'd paid for with him. I didn't know it was the head of the art department sitting behind me, who completely got the wrong idea and thought Matthew was working on the side as a gigolo." She was definitely looking guilty. "Apparently they were worried that he was lowering the tone or something. Never mind. What sort of a job was that anyway, having people staring at your bits and pieces in exchange for money? It's not right."

Her hypocrisy was astounding!

I spent the next hour catching her up on the progression of plan B. She went from being delighted at the many things I had done to his car, and his 'cooling off' period from work; to being livid about his new woman.

"I don't believe it!" She stood up from the table, unable to sit still with annoyance. "I did *not* see this one coming. If he's got another woman why the hell won't he give you a divorce? It makes no sense."

"I know, it makes no sense to me either." I put my face in my hands; this thought had been troubling me for days too. I continued. "The only thing I can think of is that his parents won't approve of him getting a divorce. You know what they're like about any whiff of scandal, they think they're bloody royalty or something."

May looked thoughtful. "Yeah, and he'll be terrified they'll cut him off again won't he. Think about it, they own the house you live in, the car he drives, and they're responsible for him getting that posh job of his. They've got him by the balls haven't they?"

I was most annoyed at this 'new Neil'. Did he treat his new woman the way he used to treat me when we were first together? Did he hang off her everyway word, laughing at her jokes, telling her she was the most beautiful woman he'd ever seen? Probably. I suppose I should be jealous shouldn't I? But I wasn't. I was just annoyed. Not at his new woman, at him. Whoever this woman was, she didn't deserve an arse like Neil. But what to do about it?

May's thoughts went along the line of. "You ought to chop it off!"

I think she would have done too.

I said jokingly. "We should give the randy sod some bromide!" And laughed.

May looked up at me with delight. "Perfect!"

A Very Impotent Man

I had meant my comment about Bromide to be flippant. I wasn't seriously thinking about making him impotent, was I? Then again, if he was disappointing one woman in that department why not two?

But how to get hold of bromide? I could hardly march into the doctors and ask for it could I?

I could just imagine it. "So Mrs Pemberton, what can I do for you today?"

"Well Doctor, my erections are getting to be a nuisance."

I don't think so.

And it's not like I could claim it was for Neil, he wouldn't prescribe something like that without wanting to see Neil in person.

If only the internet had been around in those days it would have been much easier. But it was still the olden days so we had to get creative. In the end, May blackmailed poor little Darren into visiting the doctors with, and I quote, 'An overactive todger!'

Poor Darren. He was absolutely distraught. I was there with May while she gave him his 'pep talk' telling him exactly what to say. He was shaking, blushing and stuttering. He said in distress, "But I've never even dared to buy condoms."

She replied by punching him on the arm. "Well this'll make a man of you then won't it Darren. If you can get through this, you'll be able to buy condoms, and hemorroid cream without a second thought."

"But I haven't got hemorroids May."

"No but I have love and I need you to get me some Preparation H. while you're in the chemist getting the bromide."

Poor Darren. He didn't come back with Bromide or Preparation H. He came back with paracetamol and a new tooth brush. He'd been too embarrassed when the doctor was female, and so blurted out the first thing that came into his head, which was "I have a headache."

In the chemist his bottle went when he realised he knew the pretty young girl serving on the counter. He'd fancied her for weeks and couldn't bear the thought of her thinking he had a lumpy bum.

It was a very long time before he ever dare go buy his own condoms too.

So, back to the drawing board again. I went home empty handed. May said to leave it with her. She had another plan. Probably gonna rope poor Matthew into it this time I thought. But no, that's not quite how it went.

She went to the local vets, and gave them a long sob story about her poor horse (called Neil)
that was injuring himself due to him being 'over excited.' She never owned a horse in her life, but she came away with a huge supply of equine bromide. We were in business!

Meanwhile I had returned home empty handed (for now).

I spent the entire drive home plotting my next move while I waited for May to come through with the bromide. Driving has always relaxed me, letting my mind wander while my body is on auto pilot.

I thought about all that May and I had spoken about that day. She had come up with many more suggestions for torturing Neil a bit more, while we had been waiting for poor Darren to return from the surgery. She wanted me to up my game a bit more, try harder to make him appear as if he'd had some sort of mental breakdown, or mid-life crisis. If we could just get something written down by a medical professional that could discredit him for the purposes of a custody battle, we'd be laughing. After all, he was now having an affair too wasn't he? Surly that would be a mark against him. But then again, it would depend on what spin he put on it. He could play the victim, falling into 'sympathetic arms' of someone he loved deeply, helping him cope with the strain of living with a manic-depressive wife! I knew just how manipulative he could be, especially if his mother helped him.

Actually, his mother could be the lynch pin here. If I could get his mother to think he'd become unhinged, she'd probably have him shipped off to some private hospital (nut house) before his feet could touch the ground. After all, anything he said and did reflected on her, didn't it? Mm.

This new thought kept me company all the way home.

The next day, I couldn't wait for Neil to get home from work. I'd been plotting all day, and I'd come up with a corker. Every night it was the same routine for him, watch T.V. for an hour, have his tea, and then get a shower, before more T.V. and then bed. Although sometimes he went to the pub for a couple of hours, but not very often.

This particular night, he sat down at the table to eat his salad that I had prepared for him, when I exclaimed that he had something on the top of his head.

"Where?" he asked, wiping at the top of his head.

"Let me get it." I said. I wiped at the top of his head with my fingers, that were coated in *hair removal cream!*

"There, got it." I said, inwardly dying to explode laughing. "Looked like a little bit of bird poo." I managed to say it sounding quite normal I thought.

"Um." Was all he said as he continued shovelling his food into his mouth.

I looked at the clock, hoping I had timed it right. The hair removal cream was supposed to take five minutes to work, any longer than that and it might start to burn, then he'd notice and realise what I'd done. But no, the timing was perfect. With thirty seconds to spare he got into the shower. He didn't have a clue.

That night when he came down the stairs he had a nice shiny new bald spot. That should help his nervous breakdown along nicely!

I don't believe that Neil noticed his new bald spot until the following morning. There was an audible gasp from the bathroom when he went into brush his teeth and shave. I was dying to see his reaction, standing on the landing, waiting to see his face. I had to wait for about twenty minutes, so I made myself busy, picking up dirty clothes and putting them in the clothes hamper. Still no sign of the bathroom door opening. On to making beds then, still with an eye on the bathroom door. I was just hanging up my dressing gown on the back of the door when I heard the bathroom door open. Finally! He came out looking very pale and with a new comb over!

I didn't know what he was that bothered for; his bald spot was only as big as a five pence piece. I wondered if I could get it up to a fifty pence piece by Friday?

I also noticed his new boobs jiggling as he came down the stairs. Perhaps I'd been wrong assuming his visit to 'Big & Bouncy' was for another woman, he was certainly looking like he was in need of their services!

As soon as he finally left the house for work I had a good belly laugh.

Louise came up behind me looking bemused. "What are you laughing at Mum?"

"Nothing sweetheart, I was just remembering something funny. It doesn't matter. Come on let's find your shoes and get to school before we're late."

Car Trouble

On my way back from the school run, I made a stop off at the garage that was near the shops. There was something that I had been pondering for a while now, but was unsure how to proceed. Some professional mechanical advice was in order.

Half an hour and a sob story later, I had my answer.

I had left his beloved Audi Quattro alone for a while, fearing him deducing that it must be me that was messing with it. I could give you a long-winded excuse as to why now was the right time to pick up where I left off with it, but the truth was, I was bored. It was another four days before I would be able to go up to May's to see if she had managed to acquire the bromide. She'd seemed pretty confident that she'd pull it off somehow. So I was happy to leave it in her capable hands. Meanwhile I had plenty to occupy my time now.

When Neil finally returned later that night, I made my excuse that I needed to pop to the shops. I made my way out to his car, looking like a car thief as usual, the way I was skulking about on the lookout. I let myself in the driver door and began looking for the fuse box. Ah ha, there it was, just where the mechanic said it would be. I undid the cover and started looking through the fuses while holding up the diagram I had been given. Yep, that was the one there. I promptly removed the ignition fuse. Good.

I then took my self off to the shops feeling a foot taller.

The following morning Neil was livid. No matter what he did, the car would not start. He checked the battery, as this car seemed to have a history of unexplained flat batteries. (I wonder why?) He'd eventually had to invest in a battery charger. But no, it was fine. He had filled it with petrol the day before, so it couldn't be that.

This was the extent of Neil's auto skills, and so with heavy heart, he called the RAC, again. Sadly for Neil, I managed to replace the fuse before the RAC arrived.

The same man who had been called out so many times before looked very annoyed at Neil when he stuck the key into the ignition and it fired up straight away! Neil was positively stuttering with embarrassment...that day and the next two days.

His Raleigh Racer came in useful for the next few days. (Until the back wheel fell off!)

On day four, I got creative. I got up in the early hours of the morning, armed with masking tape, newspaper, and pink spray paint, I set about his car. I'd decided to 'customise' it. I didn't want to do anything over the top, just enough to wind him up, but not enough that the police could be called. I decided on what I thought was a fair compromise, and painted his lovely new alloy wheels 'hot Barbie pink.' Actually I thought I did quite a good job. Very nice spray work, no runs in the paint, I took a lot of care not to get any paint on the body work or the tyres. Yes, a job well done!

Neil was not at all impressed with my handy work. I don't think he appreciated the skill and care that was taken into the customising I had done. He went absolute bat-shit crazy. He was screaming and shouting in the street, calling all our neighbours everything he could think of, from cowardly vandals, eventually escalating into - "bastard-arse-shit-face-poggy-sister-shagging-wankers!"

As if to punctuate this sentence, he was swiftly punched in the face by the paper boy's dad. Again.

Unfortunately for Neil, a policeman was passing by, and happened to witness what he called, "an unnecessary breach of the peace." So a handcuffed Neil was dragged off kicking and screaming to the police station to be charged, while the paper boy's dad was forgiven for the punch he inflicted on Neil as the police man deemed it "mitigating circumstances."

That bit of customising was one of the best night's work I've ever done!

His mother was not impressed at all at being called out to rescue her son from the police station, again. I noted with delight that this time she wore dark glasses and a head scarf. When I went to collect her to take her to the station she wasn't very chatty at all. I tried making small talk with her, but soon gave up. For someone who thinks she's so posh and better than everyone else, she has no manners at all. She's like Neil with a wig on. (Oo that might be Neil as well soon the way his bald spot keeps getting bigger!)

She sat in my car, all stiff and uncomfortable, quite squashed in the tiny cockpit of my little blue Nova, looking distastefully at my orange fluffy dice. Incidentally I hated them too, but Neil hated them even more, so they stayed.

She didn't like my choice in music either. I thought everyone liked Oasis. She must be team Blur.

I don't know what she said to him when she went in to collect him, but it can't have been good. He came out like a meek little boy in trouble with his mummy. At least his mother might be starting to question his sanity now; after all, him being consistently in trouble with the police was completely out of character. He was also ordered to stay away from the paper boy's dad at all times. If not, a restraining order would be issued.

Once home I continued were I'd left off. I stole his tax disc. I wondered if he'd notice?

While I was in the car wrestling to get the tax disc out of the fiddly plastic wallet on the windscreen I noticed something odd -a big bare-foot, footprint on the inside of the windscreen. What did we have here then? Seemed like a pretty damming piece of evidence of infidelity to me.

Like I needed a reason to punish him.

Surely finding something like this should upset and shock me? But no, I felt nothing. I think he'd changed so much from the man that I fell in love with, that it just wasn't him anymore. Therefore, it was like someone else's husband that was the trouble causer. There was no reason to be jealous; the man I had married had been gone for years.

I decided to cause a bit of trouble between him and his intended though. I thought why have one woman mad at him when he could have two? So, I tucked a pair of knickers in the passenger side pocket, where anyone sitting in the passenger seat would see them. However, from the driver's seat they weren't on view. With a bit of luck that should scupper the randy sod's plans until I get the bromide!

The next day was Friday, the day I was to go visit May and collect the bromide. Neil seemed relieved when for the first time in days his car started first click, I swear he almost cried at the relief. He was so far beyond being mortified at the sight of the RAC man's furious face day after day let alone the crushing soul destroying fear of his Raleigh racer. Since his back wheel came loose on a roundabout leaving him almost riding a unicycle with sparks flying everywhere, he'd been terrified of it. Even after the wheel was put back on properly, he was frightened to death of it. (With good reason, as I loosened that back wheel again when he got home.) He'd never get on it again without his knees shaking.

The only reason his car started first click that morning though was because I was in a rush to get Louise off to school and then set off to May's.

I stood watching him drive off feeling quite proud, his pink wheels looked fabulous; you could spot him a mile off. I was pretty sure you could see them from space they were so bright. Hopefully the car would also stand out to traffic wardens; after all he was now without a tax disc.

Do I Really Dare?

All the way to May's house I was thinking. Do I really dare drug Neil with bromide? This wasn't just a practical joke with few consequences, this was serious. This was potentially go to prison stuff. I'd talk over my doubts with May when I got there, I'm sure she'd have plenty to say on the matter. Meanwhile I thought, I'd just enjoy the journey and worry later; after all I was driving through some breath-taking scenery. It was a glorious day, the sun was shining, the birds were singing, and the radio was playing some of my favourite tunes. And so I sang along with Blur, Oasis, and Terrorvision, all the way to May's.

Arriving at May's I pulled into her busy forecourt. I was growing accustomed to the extra vehicles that were always there. It was a bit of a relief really knowing that Darren and Matthew were now staying with her. At least she had them to keep her company, and to keep an eye on her. I hadn't liked the thought of her being all alone, rattling around that huge old building. I'd had many nightmares about her being taken ill, or having an accident, all alone with no one to hear her calls for help. Plus the company of young people was something she had always loved. I think it's because she'd never really grown up. I had no idea how old she was, as she constantly lied about her age. Even my mother could never get the truth out of her. Somewhere between sixty-eight and eighty we believed, but who knew? But despite the age of her body, her mind was still that of a mischievous, dirty-minded, teenager. She lived for causing mischief, causing many laughs and scandals within the village. She had many enemies, but they were outnumbered by her many fans. She was a real one off. (Thank goodness.)

I finally managed to shove the front door open. I hated that door; I wished to god that someone would take a wood plane to it. After shouting to announce my presence I heard a muffled call from the kitchen.

The kitchen truly was the heart of the home at Davenport. It was a huge room, built to cater for the demands of dozens of guests. One entire wall was taken up with the solid fuel burning stoves. There were six of these, but only one was ever in use since the Hotel closed in '44. Despite the kitchen now only running on its one cylinder, it was a warm inviting place to be. A huge scrubbed rectory table dominated the room, capable of seating twenty. It was easy to imagine the Hotel in its hay day, with the kitchen filled with servants, a veritable hive of activity, I was sure.

Today though the rectory table only had two people seated at it; Darren and Matthew, and it must be said, they were looking very rough. They both looked as though they must have slept in their clothes. They had stubble on their chins, or in the case of Darren, bum fluff, and very large bags under their eyes. They both looked up as I entered the room. Well, I say looked up, more squinted through blood shot eyes.

I gave them a nervous smile. "Hello, how are you both?"

Darren responded first. "Hi, and crap."

Next was Matthew who more or less just grunted. "Uh, and uh!"

Okay, not the warmest greeting in the world.

"Is May around?" I was starting to wonder what the hell was going on around here. I twiddled nervously with my bracelet, waiting for one of them to enlighten me. It was like getting blood out of a stone. They obviously didn't like me.

Matthew eventually responded. "She's not home yet, she'll probably be another couple of hours. She's been detained." At this they both looked at each other with a very knowing look. "She said to give you this though if she missed you." Matthew handed me a paper bag.

"Thank you, what is it?" I peered into the bag.

He gave me a dirty look. "The bromide you're going to poison your poor husband with!"

Okay, this was getting tense. "Did May tell you why I was thinking about giving this to my husband?" I was irritated with their tone.

"No" said Darren. "All we know is that she needed it to help you out. But Matthew overheard you talking with May about how you were planning more and more ways to torture your fella. We don't like it, it's not right." Darren shook his head and looked to Matthew for agreement.

"He's right it's not. And I don't appreciate you bringing my little brother into your games!"

I stared them down with disbelief. "Okay. Fine. You want to know why I've been reduced to such drastic measures? I'll bloody well tell you why!" I paused. "I thought May must already have filled you in on what was going on. But fine. I'll tell you everything you want to know!" I was *really* angry now and on the verge of tears. I took a deep breath, sat down, and ignoring their derisive glares, I told them everything. From the appalling way he had been treating me for years, through robbing me of my friends, confidence, job, money, and hair! Once I started, I couldn't stop. I told them all about him refusing me a divorce, denying me custody of my daughter, threatening to have me committed, the bloody pre-nup, and finally the affair. By the time I'd finished ranting, I looked up to two pairs of shocked but sympathetic eyes. The cold, judgemental expressions were gone. They sat staring at me in silence.

Matthew was the first to break the silence. "My god what an arsehole! I'm so sorry Sarah, we didn't know!" He looked to Darren who shook his head.

"I had no idea. May never said, and you know what she's like for practical jokes and winding people up, I thought you were just having a laugh at his expense."

Matthew followed on. "But then the bromide thing just seemed a step too far, we felt really uncomfortable with it." He paused and fiddled with his hands. "Now though I'm starting to think though that Bromide's too good for the son of a bitch."

Wow! They'd changed their tune. They no longer hated me! It was a relief that the tension that had previously dominated their presence was gone. Although I didn't like the thought that they now believed me to be a little powerless victim. I'm not a victim; I'm a warrior in a crusade.

"Okay, well now you know about all the awful things that Neil's done to me, let me re-address the balance a bit, and tell you just what I've done to him in return." I gave them a wide grin, which they both returned.

And so for the next hour they laughed and choked and spluttered through my many adventures. I told them all about sabotaging his cars, dying his dog pink, putting him on the pill, making him believe he was fat, bald and incontinent, and pretty soon impotent!

They roared with laughing over the clamping fiasco, until finally we were interrupted by the phone ringing. Darren did the honours, wiping the tears from his eyes as he answered. "Hello? Yep, I'll be ten minutes." He hung up. Turning back to Matthew and me, he smirked. "I can go and get May now. They've deemed her sorry enough now."

"Okay." laughed Matthew.

I was confused. "What the hell's going on?"

As Darren set off twirling his car keys in his hand, he turned to me, still laughing, and said "I'll let Matthew fill you in on May's adventure while I go and get her."

To cut a long story short, the previous evening, May and Matthew had attended the pub where Darren worked. After challenging Matthew to a drinking contest, she basically drank him under the table. Or so Matthew thought. After conferring with Darren the next day, they concluded that she had cheated. Every time Matthew bought a round, he bought himself a rum and coke, and a gin and bitter lemon for May. Every time May bought a round, she got herself an alcohol free bitter lemon, and a double rum and coke for Matthew. The crafty old bird. Despite drinking much less than Matthew, she was by all accounts 'rat arsed'. She demanded a deck of cards from the landlord, and proceeded to play strip Bridge (Badly) with her next-door neighbour, the doctor. His wife was livid, and after getting told to go away by her husband as he was 'having fun' she complained to the landlord.

On being told to put her clothes back on or she would be barred, May hit the landlord over the head with a tray full of cocktail sausages. Having had quite enough of her already, being hit over the head with a tray was the final straw, and so the police had been called.

She didn't go without a fight though, and had to be led out in handcuffs. She was taken to the police station for the night to cool off, and sober up. Darren and Matthew had been told by the constable that no charges would brought against her, (despite his split lip) but to teach her a lesson, he wouldn't let her out until she said sorry.

I couldn't believe my ears. I don't know what was more shocking, the fact that she spent the night in cells, or that she'd got the poor sensible, wouldn't say boo to a goose doctor, to play strip bridge! Who was probably now in the dog house with his wife!

Matthew and Darren had also been shocked, and amused. Matthew had giggled along with me as he told me the tale. I stood up after we had finished laughing and put the kettle on. May and Darren wouldn't be long now. I was sure May would be gasping for a decent cup of tea.

Mathew caught my eye as I sat back down. "I'm sorry I've been so rude to you."

"It's okay, you weren't to know. I didn't know how much you both knew." I rested my elbows on the table. "I told May to keep it to herself you see, but, I know she's not great with secrets, so I assumed that you probably knew."

"Only what I'd eavesdropped. Like we said before, we thought it was just a practical joke that had got out of hand. I mean, we could certainly see where you get your humour from!" He laughed. "I mean look at May, hiring me to model for her while she painted my portrait. She thought she was really clever getting one over on me, I knew what she was up to, she never even got her brushes wet. She was just perving at me." Fortunately he seemed to think it was funny.

"So you knew she wasn't really painting you then?"

"Course I did, it might have been a bit more believable if she didn't have a six-foot mirror behind her. I could see her swishing her brushes over that blank canvas." He rubbed at his tired eyes, still smiling. "Why do you think I bit your head off when you came in? I thought 'oh god not another bloody pervy woman come to stare at my wedding tackle.' Plus that sodding violin I was holding up was tiring my arms out." We both chuckled. He continued. "Jokes on her though really, she thinks that she got me sacked, bragging about paying me by the hour, when she was in the pub. I didn't get the sack; I just got Darren to wind her up. I just quit. I'd had enough, and I fell in love with this place and thought it might be nice to stay here with Darren for a bit till I figure out what I want to do next."

I was shocked; someone had got one over on May! Serves her right though, that little scam of hers bit her in the arse. I thought it was funny. "Don't worry your secrets safe with me."

We sat in companionable silence for a while before Matthew offered: "We'll help you, you know. Me and Darren. Now we know what's going on. You never know, it might be helpful to have a male perspective on things." His eyes sparkled with mischief.

And just like that I had found an army with which to fight my war.

Rallying the troops

It must be said, May was not looking her best. She staggered in on Darren's arm, one heel missing from her left court shoe. The right shoe missing completely, her foot was barely covered with a torn and dirty looking pop sock. Her underskirt was hanging below her crumpled dress, and an out of shape hat was jammed onto her 'dragged through a hedge backwards' hairdo. Oh and she had eyes that Darren later described as 'piss holes in the snow'.

I would have expected a scenario like this from a teenager. I looked at her with amusement. "Cup a' tea aunt May?"

"God yes, fill the teapot and keep 'em coming." She heaved herself down into a chair with Darren's help. Matthew raised his eyebrows at her. "Sleep well May?"

"Like a baby love." She lied.

"Hope they treated you well in there aunt May." I handed her a cup of tea.

"So you've heard about it have you? Don't listen to this pair of lightweights here, probably been exaggerating I expect." She took a long gulp of her tea. "Ah, that's better; these two missed most of the good stuff anyway. They were practically passed out before the police came. But yes love they didn't treat me too bad, I just didn't like having to apologise when I wasn't sorry. But it was no good, I had to bite the bullet and say it or they wouldn't let me out. Miserable buggers."

We spent the next hour catching up with each other's funny tales. It was during this conversation that I learnt about her trip to the vets for a randy horse called Neil.

I told her about my earlier conversation with Darren and Matthew, who both confirmed that they were now going to help me with my plans any way they could. She was delighted. I told them all about the car trouble I'd inflicted on Neil this week, the knickers, and his nice new bald spot. I liked having fellow conspirators, after feeling so alone for so long, it felt wonderful to have people on my side. People with new ideas for torturing Neil.

As I started getting ready for the journey home, I said my goodbyes to Darren and Matthew, and walked out to my car with May. She gave me a kiss on the cheek and handed me the bag with the bromide in it. There was a sticker on the front that said: -

'Equine Potassium Bromide for Neil. C/o May Fairhurst, Davenport Manor Hotel' - But nothing else, no additional information.

"Aunt May, have you got any idea what the dosage is on this? It doesn't say on the packet."

"Let me see, what did the vet say again? Oh bloody hell I can't remember." She looked deep in thought. "Mm, I believe this was a single dose for a stallion if I remember rightly." She stroked her chin. "Yes, that was it. They said if it didn't calm him down, I'd have to wait twelve days before I could give him a second dose."

"So how much should I give Neil then do you think? He's a lot smaller than a stallion, in all departments!" I added with a grin.

"I don't know love, a quarter of the dose maybe?" She shrugged.

"I don't know if this is such a good idea you know, I don't know if I dare." I sighed. "I might just keep this for now as a backup plan. See how our other ideas work first."

"Up to you love, I'd give him the full dose to kill the bastard, but that's just me. You do what you think's right. Keep us posted though. I must say it'll be a lot easier now that Matthew and Darren know. I was getting sick of lying." She grinned. "Actually that's a lie, I love pulling their legs."

I got into my car, and rolled the window down. "Bye aunt May."

"Goodbye love, see you soon."

And so I returned home, armed with some new little bombs to drop. Meanwhile, Neil had a bomb shell of his own to drop. After the fiasco with the paperboy's dad, he'd been in touch with the estate agent, and reduced the asking price of our house. I took it he must have run this by his parents, as the house was technically theirs. Shame he never thought to discuss it with me though I thought.

The house had been on the market for months, with nobody showing any interest. I didn't mind, I didn't want to move anyway. I liked my neighbours, and despite hating Neil, they seemed to quite like me too. After all, I used to join in with them slagging him off. In fact, on the previous bonfire night, I had 'donated' Neil's favourite suit for the guy on the bonfire that the neighbourhood was holding. Well, second favourite suit really, his best one went to clothe the scarecrow near where he worked; and it wasn't really a Guy on the bonfire that year, more like an effigy of Neil. (How many other Guy's had a briefcase?)

Apparently at its new reduced asking price there had already been interest in the house. Bugger.

There was a viewing booked for the following day, and as Neil was going out, it would be up to me to show the prospective buyers around. I was very annoyed at this, I had already planned to drop Louise off at his parent's house, and follow him to try and see who his other woman was. More importantly to see if she found the pink lacy knickers I had planted in his car.

The first thing I had done as I parked up next to his car was to peek through the window to see if they were still there. Yep. There they were. Good.

After preparing tea for Neil and Louise, I made a start on my new little plan. This one was the brain child of May, Darren and Matthew, I couldn't take credit for this one. Shame, 'cause it was brilliant. On asking Matthew and Darren on what their worst nightmare would be, after careful consideration they had agreed upon, the worst thing that they could think of to have inflicted upon them would be a prostate exam, BY A MAN!

We all laughed at the idea, knowing it wasn't really feasible. After all, how the hell could you get a man to voluntarily go for a prostate exam? It just wasn't possible. Was it? Apparently it was. May to the rescue!

We'd discussed all that we knew about prostates, which was pretty much limited to 'it makes you pee a lot'. After much deliberation that was the extent of our combined knowledge. But it was enough. May retrieved from her medicine cabinet the diuretics she had been prescribed after a nasty bladder infection a few years before.

She said. "They made me pee like a bloody race horse!"

Good enough for me. If Neil suddenly had problems with an over active bladder, what would be one of the first thing that a doctor would check? PROSTATE! Particularly if they asked him if he had any accidents while he was sleeping. What could he say; he already thought he pee'd the bed! Oh and did I mention Neil's doctor was a man? A gay man! It was brilliant. All that was needed now, was to figure out how to administer the diuretics without him noticing. In the end they only way that I could think to do it, was by slipping it into the foul looking, disgusting tasting 'health shakes' that he consumed throughout the day. He already held his nose to gag them down, it would be perfect.

After he disappeared off into the shower, I seized the jug of the foul looking mixture from the fridge. Thankfully I could rest assured that Louise wouldn't touch it, the smell of it every time she opened the fridge made her gag. It looked about a two-day supply, at three drinks a day. And so I put a dose in it that would be suitable for seven days. (Just to make sure it worked.) Oh boy it worked!

He was up and down like a yo yo all night. The sound of the toilet flushing would normally have driven me insane, although that night, it sounded like sweet, sweet music to my ears. I fell asleep with a smile on my face.

Not moving without a fight

The following day, after a last-minute toilet stop, Neil left the house, to 'play golf'. Mm. I'm sure it wasn't a complete lie; he would be playing with his balls after all.

At least he had taken Louise to his parents, so fortunately she wouldn't witness what I was about to do.

The couple who were coming to view the house were due to arrive at twelve o clock, it was now Ten o'clock, so I should just have time to nip to the *key and heel bar* down the road. I think I was keeping them in business actually that year, with the amounts I had spent getting keys cut and other such things. But what I wanted that day, was a nice new house sign. After all, it was the very first thing that could make an impression. I had seen the one that I wanted in the window. There were many types of signs on display, and many house names. Looking through them, I found the name plate that I wanted, a very pretty walnut surround with a brass plate screwed onto it, announcing boldly 'The Lawns.' It was perfect, and so I bought it.

I took it home, and after rummaging around for a while in the junk draw in the kitchen I found a Phillips screwdriver. I took it out to the front wall of the house and removed the old sign that had been there forever, replacing it with the nice shiny new one. Now the couple who were coming to view the house would see straight away that this handsome abode was 'The Lawns' which was a shame as our house was actually called 'Green acres'.

Hopefully it should confuse them enough to make them go away. Next, I pulled up the for-sale sign and hid it behind the garage.

At twelve o clock on the dot, I saw a couple wandering up and down outside looking lost. They hung around for about ten minutes before sulkily disappearing. Good. Mission accomplished!

I gave it a couple of hours before I put the for-sale sign back up, and took down the shiny new sign, reinstating the old one. After all I didn't want Neil to notice.

Neil returned later that day with a face like thunder. He and his ever-increasing comb over stormed past me, when I asked if he'd had a good day playing golf. I took it that was a no. He was storming past me to go to the toilet though, I noted with satisfaction.

After he'd had a shower he came back down the stairs to ask me how the viewing had gone.

"Waited in all day for them, and they never even turned up." I acted indignant.

"Bloody time wasters!" He grumbled, heading to the fridge for a 'health shake'.

Later on that night, as soon as I had chance to slip out, I peeped through the passenger side window of his car. The knickers were gone, and probably, so was the girlfriend.

I was just on the verge of falling asleep at around half past three in the morning, when I heard Neil creeping about. I listened to see if he was off to visit the loo again, no, he'd walked past the loo, he was heading downstairs. I peeped around my bedroom door, just in time to see him disappear down the stairs. He was fully dressed, in black! What was he up to?

I crept down the stairs a little way, in order to peep through the spindles. I could just see him trying to quietly ransack the kitchen junk draw. Suddenly he seemed to find what he was looking for; he turned around, looking at it with a childish glee, and actually giggled. I ducked quickly before he saw me, but not before I saw what he held in his hands….superglue.

He had one last look around the kitchen, before quietly 'ah ha' ing to himself. He stole the lid off his deodorant. What the hell was he doing? Had I finally tipped him over the edge and into madness? Next he pulled on a balaclava. Now I *was* getting worried. He's never worn a balaclava in his life. He'd certainly never owned one; he must have bought it with something major in mind.

Once he'd put on a pair of forensic looking rubber gloves?!? He quietly left the house. I shot back upstairs to try and see what he was up to from my bedroom window. I pulled a corner of the curtain back carefully; I didn't want him to know I was watching.

There he was, creeping down the side of next doors front fence. He kept stopping at every little noise, and looking around him, before resuming creeping down the fence. He stopped in front of the paper boy's house. Okay, this could get interesting.

He walked around the lovely cherry red, new Vauxhall Cavalier that they had just bought that day. Taking the superglue from his pocket, he poured superglue into the keyholes on the front doors. Oh my god! He was standing back with his hands on his hips, I could tell that underneath his balaclava, he would be doing his constipated grimace that he called a smile. But he wasn't finished.

Next he poured the glue into the boot lock. But what he did next at least explained why he stole the lid from his deodorant. He held it up, painting a line of glue all around the rim. I was fascinated. He then stuffed the superglue soaked deodorant lid into the exhaust pipe. He stood back, probably admiring his handy work for a minute, and then sauntered home.

Meanwhile I shot back into my own bed before he heard me moving about.

I lay in bed quite shocked. Neil had sabotaged the paper boy's dad's car! He obviously thought the paper boy's dad was responsible for the pink wheels and the racy knickers. I lay there, quietly digesting it all. 'My god' I thought to myself, 'I'm contagious!'

The following morning, Neil was up very early for a Sunday. He was looking for any excuse to look out of the window. He'd also been outside to the bin four times. I watched him discretely with fascination, this was interesting!

To be honest I was also dying to watch out of the window too, wondering how events were going to unfold. Surely this would bite him in the arse?

I thought I'd throw Neil a bone for once in his life, and asked if he would mind cutting the front lawn. He looked positively delighted, and then tried to cover his enthusiasm. "Well, I suppose it does look a bit untidy. Might as well give it a quick go over."

I helped him out. "Plus, it'll look that much nicer to any potential buyers won't it."

"Yes." He rubbed his hands together with glee. "Yes it will. I'll get straight on it." He shot out to the shed to get the lawnmower. A few minutes later I could see him looking puzzled at it. He couldn't get it to start. Then it dawned on me, he'd never actually used a lawn mower before. Feeling generous, as he was entertaining me no end with his new vendetta, I went out to help.

"Bloody thing won't start." He said as he was pulling the starter, to no avail. He got petulant and kicked it.

"Let me have a quick look. Ah, you need choke on." I slid the small lever on the handle to 'choke'. "Once it starts, you slide this lever back the other way." I pointed.

I stepped back to allow him another go at starting it, noticing that his attention had wandered back over his shoulder to the paper boy's house. "Erm yes, right."

He pulled the string and this time it fired up. He looked happy enough, so I left him to it. It normally took me twenty minutes to cut the front lawn, but Neil dragged it out so much that it took him three hours! All in an effort to desperately see how his handy work would be received.

He had just given up, and was putting the lawnmower away when the PBD (paper boy's dad, I can't remember his name.) decided to take his new car out for a spin. He didn't get very far; He spent ten minutes desperately trying to unlock it to no avail. He shouted and swore, kicking at his tyres; I thought he was going to start shouting 'bastard-arse-shit-face-poggy-sister-shagging-wankers' as Neil had done a few days previous. But no, his wife dragged him into the house to calm down.

Neil locked up the lawn mower shed and sauntered into the house whistling. He also 'casually' remarked later that there was a tow truck outside PBD's (Paper boy's dad's) house, biting the smile off his lip as he said it.

The following day, the estate agent called to say that the couple who had previously booked a viewing, had called to apologise for not turning up on the Saturday, as that they couldn't find my house. Would it be possible for them to come this morning at eleven o clock? I said fine, and asked if they now knew where it was. I was told yes, the estate agent had described it to them now, and they would surely find it this time.

They didn't.

Peeing for England

To Neil's obvious disappointment, there were no more outbursts from the PBD (Paper boy's dad.) Either he didn't suspect Neil, or he was biding his time. But then again, perhaps he thought it was just kids playing a practical joke. Anyway, all was quiet on that front. Although I did see Neil smirk when the PBD had a courtesy car dropped off. It was a hideous yellow Lada.

However, my plans were working spectacularly! Not one potential buyer that the estate agent sent to our house could find it, much to their annoyance.

Neil's man boobs were coming on a treat, closely followed by his ever-increasing bald spot,
and thanks to the diuretics, he was peeing for England! Wouldn't be long now before he'd be having that prostate exam!

Neil started off that week in a great mood. I suspected he was probably upset over losing his girlfriend, but I was sure that getting one over on the PBD had cheered him back up again. But by Wednesday he was back to being his old miserable lemon-lipped self. He kicked the dog, threw his dinner at me because I'd forgotten and put mayonnaise on his salad, he bent over to pick up a stray potato (presumably to throw at me) and split the seat of his trousers. Well that was the final straw. He burst into tears, crying. "I just want something proper to eat!" and then stormed out of the house.

What a bloody woman. I thought.

I'd just started to clean some stray mayonnaise from my face, when he stormed back in. He'd remembered his arse was hanging out.

I had a theory about his sudden bad-tempered aggressiveness. After reading up on diuretic medication I discovered that it is often given to people who had taken too much medication, or have had an overdose. The diuretic would flush their systems of toxins. Shit. Neil was on a huge dose of the pill wasn't he? Perhaps not anymore. It seemed the massive dose of oestrogen he had inadvertently been taking was being flushed away with every trip to the toilet. Which must mean…. he had testosterone again! Oh well, at least he'd lose weight again I suppose. Maybe he wouldn't keep throwing food at me once he'd shed the pounds again. Plus, once he'd had his prostate exam I could knock the diuretics on the head and reinstate the pill anyway.

Neil's week went from bad to worse when he tried to get into his car on Thursday morning to find that the locks had been super glued shut. But more to the point, it wasn't me!

Neil was shaking with a silent rage when he came back into the house. I didn't dare speak. I had seen him trying to get into his car from my spot at the window, and had deduced what had happened. PBD had retaliated in kind.

But remember, I couldn't let on that I knew what was going on, and Neil didn't know that I knew. He vented his rage by breaking every object that he could get his hands on. He absolutely smashed the place to pieces. Louise came in crying, I pulled her behind me quickly. I had no idea if he would try and hurt us. He was like an animal. Once he was finished he straightened his tie as he assessed his handy work and turned to me. "This had better be cleaned up before I get home!" And left.

At least he had to leave on his Raleigh Racer though. He only got to the end of the drive before the wheel fell off! (Both me and the PBD clapped.)

According to witnesses Neil didn't act much better at work either. He sacked five people before lunchtime, threw a jug of water over his secretary, and for some reason that nobody quite understood, he threw a chair at his boss. He was sent home on 'sick leave.' Obviously people were starting to notice his erratic behaviour.

His parents learnt very quickly about his atrocious behaviour and blamed it on me. His mother said that it must be the stress of living with an 'eccentric'. She even did the bastard air quotes when she said it, the snotty cow.

Their solution was to take him away on holiday for a week skiing, they had been going anyway and had wangled an extra ticket, the holiday would do him good, they said. So, they affectively rewarded his despicable behaviour with a treat.

I had been desperately hoping they'd have him committed. At least then he'd have no chance at all of winning custody of Louise.

But looking on the bright side, at least he was out of my hair for a week. Thank goodness. Only problem was, with Neil away, how could I continue dosing him with the diuretic? I'd come this far with my plan, and after his earlier behaviour, I had no intention of abandoning it now. His arse was mine! (Or rather the lovely doctor's.)

The answer came to me as he was packing. He had packed altitude sickness pills. I smuggled these out of his hand luggage while he was at the toilet, (again), and after opening the bottle and having a peep at the pills, I noted they looked similar enough to swap with the diuretics. Good, problem solved.

Another little thing I added to his hand luggage was some of Darren's pot. Darren had given it to me before I left May's, after we had giggled at the thought of Neil getting caught with wacky-backy. But, I couldn't do that. Neil would know it was me that planted it, and I couldn't have that.

I took it back out of his luggage, and then had a thought. Sniffer dogs would still smell where it had been wouldn't they? That would probably still result in him being pulled out and searched wouldn't it? Even if they didn't find anything.

Just to be sure the dogs would smell it; I rubbed it all over the outside of the bag. Poor Neil, looked like a cavity search was on the cards for him.

What a way to start his holiday to de-stress. At least it might prepare him for a prostate exam though. Every cloud 'eh?

It must be said, I had a quite an enjoyable week while Neil was away. I ignored the estate agents calls, as our phone had caller i.d. I could avoid them like the plague. No more having to take down the bloody name plate every other day, the screw threads were wearing out and it was getting more and more difficult to change every day.

Neil's friend from the RAC came out to collect the pink wheeled Quattro, and towed it away to have the locks fixed. He said it would only be a couple of days before it could be returned to me. I'd put money on it though, that if it had been Neil talking to him and not me, he would have said it would be with the garage for a month. He hated Neil. I commiserated with him, and agreed that yes, Neil was a stuck-up toffee-nosed wanker.

The day that the car was towed away was the day that Neil finally rang home. He wasn't having much fun at all. For some bizarre reason, the sniffer dogs had sniffed him out at the airport, and so armed security guards had dragged him out, interrogated him, and searched him.

I asked. "How thorough was the search?" Stifling a giggle.

"VERY thorough. If you did that to someone in England you'd go to prison for it."

Oo I was so dying to laugh.

Apparently it didn't get much better after that either.

His mother had gotten drunk and thrown herself at a waiter. A waiter who was gay, and wanted nothing whatsoever to do with her. However, he did quite like the look of Neil's father, who thought the young waiter was 'a marvellous chap, good fun and very friendly.' In fact, he went so far as to invite his marvellous new friend in for a night cap. When Neil's father excused himself to slip into something more comfortable, he had meant 'excuse me why I go take this bloody girdle off that my wife makes me wear. My back is killing me.' However, the waiter assumed that this meant 'party time', and proceeded to take all his clothes off and got himself comfortable on Neil's father's bed. While Neil's father was in the bathroom, his wife entered the chalet via Neil's connecting door. Suffice to say, there was much confusion all around.

Neil's mother had seen the naked waiter on her bed with his back to her, (looking towards the bathroom for some reason,) and believed he was there for her. She had been delighted, and so slid the zip down from the back of her dress and stepped out of it. The waiter turned around at the noise of the zipper, and screamed. Neil's father came out of the bathroom, saw the naked waiter and screamed. Neil's mother realised the naked waiter was for her husband and screamed. Neil came through the connecting door after hearing the commotion and at the sight of his father with his shirt off, his mother in her underwear, and a naked waiter in the bed, he had screamed too.

They all left the ski lodge the next day to look for alternative lodgings.

Oh my god how I managed to keep my composure on the phone while Neil was telling me all this I don't know! By the sound of his voice he was not at all amused.

Wait till I tell May, Matthew and Darren!

A Good Gossip

As soon as the Quattro was returned to me by my new good friend from the RAC, (thankfully this time it had two keys. Though Neil would never know that!) I decided to take it for a run up to May's. I had a lot of things to get my troop up to date on.

Despite the pink wheels, that car was amazing. How could Neil trundle along at five miles below the speed limit? This car was built to go fast!

Despite being an automatic - which I usually despised, this car was like shit off a stick, and I loved it! I was doing about seventy miles an hour on the duel carriageway, when I got annoyed at the car in front of me that kept tapping its brakes constantly; I checked all was clear, and hit kick down and swung out past it, thrown back in my seat with the G force, it was AMAZING!!! I checked my mirror to see how far I'd got passed the annoying car I'd been stuck behind. I couldn't even see it anymore, it was gone! Ha! I checked my speedo, bugger a hundred and thirty, that was a little excessive, and so I eased off the accelerator. God, another ten minutes and I'd be at May's, I think that was the quickest I'd ever done that journey. I flew around the hair pin bends like a rally driver; the only thing that could make this car better would be a manual gearbox. But hey, couldn't have everything could you?

Arriving at May's I noticed Darren's camper van was missing. Hurting my shoulder shoving at that goddam front door again, I shouted my Hello's.

Matthew popped his head round the kitchen, door. "Hey Sarah, Alright? I've got the kettle on."

"Brill, I'm gasping." I followed him through into the kitchen and sat down.

"Where's May and Darren?"

"Ah, well, May decided that Darren needed to learn how to play bingo! She's dragged him down to the community centre; apparently they have OAP bingo there twice a week." He was obviously delighted at the prospect of poor Darren playing bingo.

"Poor Darren, she does wind him up doesn't she. I just hope she doesn't start playing strip bingo up there". I giggled.

Matthew put a cup of tea and a plate of biscuits down in front of me.

"Oo thank you very much, don't mind if I do!"

"I reckon they won't be too long now anyway. How's things being going then since I last saw you?"

"Eventful!" I laughed. "I might as well wait till the others come in to tell you, I think I just heard a car pull up." The sound of the gravel crunching on the drive was unmistakable. I strained my ears for the creak of the front door.

"We've been dying to know what's been going on. It's better than a soap opera." He paused, "We've been thinking up new ideas all week." He grinned at me.

I couldn't believe this was the same arsey person from last week. Now he was practically my best buddy.

I replied smiling. "I can't wait to hear."

I could hear May and Darren laughing before they even got to the kitchen. "That bloody car of his looks wonderful with pink wheels!" May was chuckling as she pulled a chair out. "Darren love, put the kettle back on."

"Hey Darren, how did you like bingo?" I teased.

"Never again. I never knew old ladies were so dirty minded. I've had my bum nipped more times than I could count."

May joined in. "Plus that bloody Doris tried to sit on your knee didn't she love? I thought it was ever so funny when she fell off."

"Well she was twice the size of me, my knees were buckling. She was 'two fat ladies' rolled into one!" He was very indignant.

Matthew pointed out the lipstick on Darren's cheek, who then furiously rubbed it with his sleeve. Bless.

With a cup of tea and a plate of biscuits in front of her May finally asked. "So then love, what's been occurring? We've been dying with suspense all week haven't we lads?"

Darren butted in. "Not half, me and Matthew have been plotting all week while we've been waiting for you. It's all we've been able to think about."

Matthew nodded. "Yep, actually it's become a bit of a hobby." He reached for one of May's biscuits, who smacked his hand away from them.

"Well it's been eventful." I spent the next hour filling them in on all that had happened. It took me a while to think of all the things that had happened, there'd been that many things to remember. I told them how well the diuretics were working, and the plan was on track for his prostate exam. I had them snorting and chuckling about making it impossible for any prospective buyers to find my house. I was particularly smug about that little gem I must admit.

They were as stunned as I had been about Neil 'doing a Sarah' as they put it. His new vendetta against PBD was surprising to them too. Not quite as surprised as Neil was though when his bit of vandalism bit him in the arse. They agreed with me, I must be contagious!

Their humour turned to outrage though as I told them about him trashing our house and scaring both me and Louise. I ignored their outrage and sympathies and ploughed on with the story. How he had a meltdown at work, sacking employees, terrorising his secretary, and throwing things at his boss. They were shocked.

May broke the stunned silence. "Surly that's gonna get him locked up now then? He wants bloody sectioning!"

"No that isn't what happened. It's what should have happened 'cause he was a bloody maniac, but no, his parents took him skiing instead to cheer him up a bit!"

They were horrified. Matthew shook his head. "Neil isn't the only one who wants his head testing. I can't believe his parents took him skiing. They all want a smack!"

I couldn't agree more.

"Right, I've told you all the horrid stuff, now let me cheer you up."

During the next hour the atmosphere went from tense to euphoric as we all entertained at Neil's expense. I started with the pot smelling luggage and him getting pulled out by the security guards for a cavity search, and then launched into how much he'd been humiliated in Switzerland by his parent's bedroom antics. After we'd all supped our body weight in tea and gossiped the afternoon away, with Matthew and Darren coming up with more and more ideas for me to get Neil with, Matthew got a serious look on his face, looking deep in thought, May asked him. "Penny for 'em?"

"Sorry I was just thinking." He turned to me. "Did I hear you say Neil sacked a load of people from the factory?"

"Yes, about five I think. Neil's boss Mr Hemsworth tried to get them to come back after Neil went nuts, but they told him to stick it. They wouldn't work for an arse like Neil. Why?"

"I was just thinking, I could see if I could get a job there, couldn't I? Then you'd have someone on the inside, wouldn't you?"

Oo this was a new angle that hadn't occurred to me.

He turned to May. "What do you think May, could you spare me for a few weeks while I go undercover?" He crossed his fingers and looked at me while she formed a reply.

"Course I can love, you're neither use nor ornament to me anyway." She winked at him, and looked at me expectantly.

"I couldn't ask you to do that Matthew; it's too much to ask." I was very flattered, but I didn't care for taking advantage of people.

He retorted. "I think it's brilliant, you get someone on the inside to report things back to you." He was getting excited now. "And, sabotage things from the inside! Plus, I'd be getting paid for my troubles wouldn't I. It's perfect!"

"Well, when you put it like that it is hard to say no." I paused. "It's only a job in packing though."

"So what, it's better than getting naked in front of strangers." He laughed.

I was starting to like this. "If you apply for an interview, I'll put a word in with Mr Hemsworth; I'll say you went to school with me and my brother's or something."

May was looking impressed. "Sounds like a plan then!"

The Enemy Within

The following morning a very tired and rough looking Neil came in through the front door. He was two days early! He looked terrible; he had huge dark bags under his eyes and a serious five o clock shadow on his chin. His normally immaculate hair was unwashed and un-styled, and displaying his new bald spot beautifully. I sniggered at my own pun, his 'immac-ulate hair'. Ah I kill me sometimes.

His clothes were crumpled and he smelt very ripe. Something was amiss. I cautiously asked him how he was.

"Shit!" He grunted.

Okay obviously in a mood. "Did you enjoy your holiday?"

"No."

"Why are you back early?"

"I DON'T want to talk about it!"

I was stumped. I tried once more. "Are your parents back early too?"

"Go away and stop quizzing me for Christ sake!"

And so I was pretty clueless. But something major must have happened. He wouldn't come home early like that, in such a state like that too, it was un-thinkable. I was dying to know what had happened.

He grunted that he just wanted a cup of tea, followed by a shower and then sleep. I obliged him with a cup of tea; all the while my brain was whirling with possible scenarios, as to what had happened.

As he finished his tea, I said. "Hang on, you've got something stuck in your hair, let me get it." I rubbed my hand over the top of his head. "There, got it." I had a sneaky feeling that fifty pence piece on his head was about to increase in diameter.

After showering I heard him go in to his bedroom, and then a few minutes later, a deafening
BANG!!!!

I forgot I'd loosened his bed legs again. Welcome home Neil.

I received a telephone call from Neil's boss Mr Hemsworth around dinnertime, asking me to give a character reference for Matthew Barton. He had turned up that morning in a suit and tie, armed with his C.V. and a smile. Mr Hemsworth had been impressed with his C.V. and was willing to hire him on the spot pending my reference.

I told him that Matthew was a fine and upstanding member of society, whom I had known for years, as he went to school with me and my brothers. He was a very conscientious and dependable person, I gushed.

Mr Hemsworth wanted to know if Matthew would cope with such a menial position as he was obviously very over qualified. Apparently he had an honours degree in English, seven A levels, and ten GCSE's. He had previously worked as an assistant Manager in a bank, he lectured at the local university, and he had once worked for John Major. I bit my lip, and rolled my eyes, agreeing with all the things I had just been told, with my fingers crossed behind my back. I later learnt the C.V. had been written by May. At least she didn't mention the nude modelling.

The job was his. He'd start the following day.

It was many hours later that Neil finally emerged from his bed, looking much cleaner and more like himself.

"Would you like something to eat?" I asked, trying to gauge his mood.

"I'm going out; I'll get something while I'm out. Don't wait up!"

As if I would?

He then picked up his car keys and sauntered off. He never even acknowledged that his car had been repaired in his absence. Arsehole.

As soon as he was safely gone, I went rummaging for clues through his luggage that he was yet to unpack. First I tried the hand luggage. Un-zipping the lid I was greeted first with his travel documents. I opened his passport just to laugh at his picture. It was a belter that never failed to cheer me up whenever I was down. He looked like an escaped mental patient about to go on a killing spree.

Under his passport was his plane ticket. I almost tucked it to one side before I realised what it said. He'd arrived at Heathrow airport, and his ticket was for 'economy class.' Some serious shit must've gone down. Never ever in a million years would Neil fly anything less than business class. He also would never fly to Heathrow as he despised the place, it was too busy. He only ever flew in to Humberside Airport or at a push, Leeds/Bradford Airport. Anything beyond that he wouldn't entertain. I must reiterate, *something major must've happened.* He'd cut his holiday short, flown home in economy class (something he said would happen over his dead body), and landed at an Airport he hoped would one day be bombed! Mm.

What I found next really made me question if that had actually been Neil that came home and not an imposter.........BUS TICKETS!!! He had seven of them! He had used public transport! It had taken him seven buses and coaches to arrive home!

I sat back down on his mattress, which was still on the floor where it fell. My brain was hurting trying to work out what could have happened. I was completely stumped. I rummaged further down the bag but couldn't find anything else of interest, just a few receipts for massages and ski lessons. I put everything back in the bag, and was just zipping it back up when I felt something further down the bag. I slid my hand down the side and felt a small cylinder. I pulled it out careful not to disturb anything else in the bag. It was a used film cartridge. Mm. This little cartridge could explain a whole lot of what had happened to Neil this week. But dare I steal it? Of course!

The brand of the film was Kodak, and I happened to know that I had a brand-new Kodak film in the dining room draw. I could swap it! I shot down stairs to find it.

I was concerned that the chemist might tell Neil when they developed it, that it had been a blank unused film. After thinking about it for a while I knew what I had to do. I pulled the new film out of its canister and inserted it into my camera. I left the back of the camera open, and held it up to the dying sunlight out of the window, camera lens still on of course, and clicked away. I then wound it all back in to the canister, still in full sunlight. Hopefully now it would just look like a duff film.

I got my coat on ready to drop the film of Neil's mysterious holiday, off at the chemist on the way to Louise's school, I was worried about both of us dropping our films off at the same chemist, in case there was a mix up and Neil got the holiday film back. In the end I chose the chemist along the route of the school run. Neil would never try and get his film developed at that chemist. He'd been forced to buy me tampons from there and had never got over the shame! It would be a long five days waiting for my film though.

Undercover Agent

The following day Matthew started working in Neil's factory. I was dying with suspense all day as to how he was getting on. He'd agreed to give me a ring at one o clock when he had his dinner break. All morning I'd been pacing up and down looking at the clock. Still only ten o'clock, I huffed. I decided that I would make myself useful, doing all the laundry, after all I had all of Neil's holiday clothes to wash. I loaded up the washer with the wools first, wondering how my life had turned to such crap. I had always had high hopes for my life, often dreaming of the adventures I would have one day. I was meant to *BE* somebody. I wasn't meant for a life of drudgery like this. At least I had a hobby now though, I supposed, it gave me something new to think about every day.

Operation prostate was going well though. I had snuck into Neil's room again in the night, armed with a jug of warm, very diluted orange cordial. I had put a flask of orange cordial in Louise's lunch box the previous day and was struck by how much it looked like wee. Well I've never been one to waste an opportunity.

I bumped into him this morning when he was coming up the garden path from the bin, obviously getting rid of the evidence again. At the rate he was throwing away his bedding pretty soon he'd be in a sleeping bag. Which got me thinking.

I headed to the airing cupboard where we kept all the bedding, and pulled out the last remaining change of bedding. I pulled down the loft ladder from the hatch over my head, and hid the bedding in the loft. I knew Neil had never even been up there so was unlikely to venture up there any time soon.

There, I wiped my hands, a good job done. Now if Neil wanted a change of bedding he'd have to wash his own bedding or change his duvet and sheet for Louise's old My Little Pony bedding!

I pottered about all morning trying to keep busy until one o'clock. I hoovered the house top to bottom, polished everywhere, swept and mopped, polished the windows, and cleaned the bathroom. Smiling as I opened the bathroom cabinet, Neil had hidden a bottle of 're-grow' at the back. I toyed with the idea of messing with it, possibly replacing it with immac or something. I shelved that idea for another time.

I looked at my watch. Ten to One, time to go and wait by the phone. After fifteen minutes that felt like an hour, the phone finally rang. I picked up on the first ring.

"Hello?"

"Hey Sarah it's me Matt",

"Hi how are you? How's everything going?"

"Interesting!" He sniggered. "I keep hearing from everyone here that Neil is a stuck-up arsehole that nobody can stand! I mean it, *EVERYBODY* hates him."

"I knew it! It isn't just me is it? Have you spoken to him yet?" I twirled the phone cable around my fingers.

"Briefly, I introduced myself when he came into the warehouse and I went to shake his hand, he just looked at it. He looked as though a cockroach had just said hello to him. I thought he might actually swat me! He's horrible, he's worse than I expected him to be!"

I don't know why I was surprised. "I'm really sorry; he's got no right being rude to you. He's vile!" I paused. "Did he question how you knew me?"

"No, never mentioned it. Everyone else here is nice though. A woman from the canteen was just telling me about the time he turned up here with three feet of toilet roll hanging out of his trousers. Was that you?" He laughed.

"Guilty!" I laughed too, it was a good memory. "I must've forgotten to tell you that one. Anyway, I don't know if you realised or not, but Neil shouldn't even be there today. He got back off holiday last night, two days early, filthy and stinking. Something must've happened to him, but he won't talk about it. It must've been something major though."

"Yeah I was surprised he was here, I was told I wouldn't meet him till Monday. I wonder what happened to him? I'll keep my ears open anyway."

"Thanks. I found a film cartridge in his luggage, and I've stolen it and took it to be developed. Might give me a clue."

"Hopefully." He paused. "Anyway, I did find out something interesting. You're gonna love this. You aren't the only one with a vendetta against him."

"Really? I'm intrigued!"

He continued. "Every day for the past three months, a young lad called Craig who works in the canteen has been messing with his coffee." He paused while he stopped giggling. "So far, he's been spiked with, amongst other things: - toner from the copy machine, his dog's ear wax softener, and get this... his mother's menopause tablets what is it? H.R.T?"

I gasped. "My god I can't believe it. He brings this out in people doesn't he?" I paused digesting it all. "I wonder how that reacts with the pill that he's on?"

"I don't know, but I can't believe all along there's been two of you at it." He sounded highly amused. "I think I'm gonna enjoy working here, I've laughed no end, and I've only been here four hours!"

"I'm really grateful you know, I owe you massively for this. It'll cost a bomb for petrol money back and forwards from work to May's. I'll have to chip in for it."

"No need, I've got a mate around the corner from the factory who said I can crash there a few nights a week, so it won't be an issue. I wouldn't take your money anyway, don't be daft."

"I can't thank you enough."

"No sweat, I wanted a change anyway, this is turning out to be fun! Anyway I've only got a minute before I'll have to go, I just wanted to let you know I've started undercover duties already. I snuck out to the car park five minutes ago and let two of his tyres down! Don't expect him home on time. Think he might be back on the phone to the RAC again!" He laughed.

"Brilliant," I smiled down the receiver. "Keep me updated then."

"Will do, Bye for now."

"Bye." I replaced the receiver.

Wow! I had an accomplice! Two of them if you count Craig in the kitchen with the HRT. (Oo that sounds like Cluedo doesn't it?) What an interesting morning. At least I had the rest of the day to myself now; after all, Neil wouldn't be home for hours.

After twiddling my thumbs for half an hour, bored out of my brains, I decided to call May and fill her in on all that I'd heard from Matthew. She was as surprised as I was to hear that I wasn't the only one sabotaging Neil, and spiking him with hormones.

"Who knew he had so many enemies?" She sounded shocked.

"I know! I swear he brings it on himself doesn't he. But, Neil shouldn't be back off holiday yet. He's come home early. You should have seen the state of him when he got back. He was filthy and stank to high heavens."

"I can't image that of Neil. He's always so well-groomed isn't he? Too well groomed, I don't like it."

"Something major must've happened to him but he won't talk about it. I'm dying to know."

"Who knows with that sly bugger." She coughed.

"I've stolen his holiday film and took it to get developed. That might tell me a bit more. I can't pick it up till Tuesday though."

We chatted a while longer. May came up with a good point about Plan B.

"You should encourage the feud between Neil and the PBD as you call him. If you do something to wind PBD up, Neil would get the blame, PBD would then retaliate on Neil and it would escalate into a war. That'd be sure to tip Neil over the edge."

She had a point.

I agreed with her. "All I'd have to do was annoy PBD with something. Mm. I'll give it some thought." (Ah ha. I've remembered PBD's name, it was Mick. That was it. I can't believe I'd forgotten that, especially after what happened.) I just had to think what to do to wind up Mick. But what?

Stakeout

Neil finally returned home from work an hour late, and he had a face like thunder. "Some bastard," he said, "let his tyres down, Again!!!!" He was not happy. He'd put a request into logistics about them buying him an air compressor so that he could blow them back up himself so that he wouldn't have to keep facing 'that condescending bastard from the RAC'.

He'd now sworn that when his policy is up for renewal he was going with Green Flag!

I faked sympathy and concern but nearly blew it when he added. "And the penis drawn on my windscreen was very inappropriate."

Whoa that nearly made me laugh. I pretended to have a coughing fit. Nice one Matthew could've warned me about that! I composed myself and asked. "How was your first day back? Well apart from the car trouble?"

"Mm terrible. Wish I hadn't gone back. Lot of bloody incompetent fools! None of them can do anything right, they're all a bunch of lazy shirkers. God only knows where my secretary's been all day, hardly seen a glimpse of the woman. Anyone would think she was hiding! I got lectured off old Hemsworth with something about 'staff morale' or some such rubbish, load of cod's wallop, treat 'em mean keep 'em keen I say. Lucky they've got a bloody job." He went over and peered into the fridge. "Is there any of my health shake left?"

"I've just finished making you a new one!" I smiled and produced a jug full of the stuff from the blender.

"Good, it's very good for you know. Helps keep a man's brain active."

And his bladder, I mentally added.

This was the most he had spoken to me since before his holiday. I tried pushing my luck. "So, you haven't said how your holiday was?" I asked sweetly.

He almost choked on his shake. "It was dreadful, you know about how awful I was treated at the airport, I was positively violated. Then the fiasco with my parents and the waiter. Then the other thing with the......No it was dreadful. I don't want to talk about it anymore; I'm off to watch T.V." He almost ran out of the door.

He almost slipped up there though didn't he? The less he told me, the more I had to know!

Meanwhile I had to come up with something to wind up Mick the PBD and blame it on Neil.

When I got back in bed at around three o'clock after having ensured that Neil wasn't having a 'dry night', I came up with a plan. I decided to keep it simple. But I would need a trip to the art supply shop in the morning.

The following morning was a Saturday and so both Neil and Louise were home. Me and Lou were up first and in the middle of making pancakes when Neil came in looking cagey. He looked about him, looking unsure of what to do, and then left. He was obviously wondering how to get rid of his wet sheets without me and Louise seeing.

I kept half an eye on him as I finished making Louise's breakfast, I heard the front door go and the dustbin rattle. Ah, I inwardly smiled; there goes more sheets to the tip. I wondered if he'd found the My Little Pony bedding yet?

Louise told me her breakfast wasn't fit for a dog, and could I please drop her off at her grandparents as they were bound to have brought her a gift back, if not, she told me, she would demand money instead! I'd had just about enough of her caustic comments for one day and so obliged her. She was never like a normal child, I even thought for a while that she may be autistic, but according to the school doctor that tested her, she wasn't autistic at all, she was just greedy and selfish. Wow. I was shocked that he'd be so blunt! But he was only blunt because she'd spent the last hour telling him, amongst other things, how awful his clothes were; whoever cut his hair should be sacked. Poor people should be shot, and how much money would she be getting for this? I had never been so embarrassed! She was only seven when she was tested!

And so, this particular morning I dropped her off at her grandparents' house. I was hoping to be invited in so that I could ask about the holiday, they should only have been back a few hours, but I was kept on the doorstep while Neil's mother blocked the doorway and gave me a pointed look. I knew where I wasn't wanted, and so I left. Their loss I thought. Well, actually they lost more than me; I stole their hanging basket from the end of the drive on my way out. May would love it. (Petunias were her favourites.) And so off to the art shop I went.

I did a little detour first though just to see if Neil had snuck off to Weightwatchers. I pulled into the car park where I guessed he'd be. Yep, there was his car. I had a shifty look about for him, no sign. I unlocked his car with my spare key, and took his parking ticket out of the window and locked it back up. I sauntered back over to my own car and put my newly acquired ticket in the window. There, waste not, want not!

I set off towards Weightwatchers trying to blend in as much as possible; I didn't want him to see me. I stopped across the road and peered from behind a post box. Yep, that was definitely his comb over going through the door. He was still going after all. I wondered if he'd go anywhere after that, if he had anywhere else to go? I popped into the café next to the post box and prepared for a stake out.

After two teas and a cream scone, he finally exited. He looked like he was chatting with a big fat woman as he was walking….towards me! Oh shit! I better hide. I bobbed down behind a table but it was no good, they were coming into the café. I shot into the door marked 'Gents' (I know but I panicked). I just got off view in the nick of time as they entered the café…HOLDING HANDS!!! My god! Was this the woman? THE woman? She obviously wanted her head testing if she was going to forgive him over the knickers thing.

I hadn't had chance to get a proper look at her as I'd dived into the gents. I got curious, and so cracked the door open an inch to peep. I looked across at their table, noting how happy Neil looked, holding her hand and gazing into her eyes. I couldn't see his woman very well from this angle, but she was obviously smitten with him as she had her foot wedged in his crutch. I was seething!! I didn't think I would be jealous. But I was!! No, not jealous MAD!!!!!

She threw her head back and laughed, mocking me no doubt, and turned her head slightly towards me. Oh My god, it couldn't be! No, it isn't, it can't be! But it bloody was...Fat Wonder Woman!!!

I couldn't believe it. How the hell? He'd been devastated when she descended on his office all lasso and Lycra. I could hardly imagine him saying, "Now you've finished humiliating me by bursting into my board meeting dressed up as wonder woman, making me a laughing stock and breaking my boss's nose, would you mind going out for dinner with me sometime?"

I don't think so!

Plus, (and I do feel like a cow for saying this,) she was far and away more common than me. She wasn't a working-class girl, she was working-girl class! I didn't get it. But then, it suddenly dawned on me, they must have bumped into each other in Weightwatchers.

Oh, yes, makes sense now. Her apologising for embarrassing him, him apologising for being rude. Ah yes, I could see it all. "Would you like a coffee while we laugh over such a misunderstanding?"

But to start an affair with her? He hated me because he thought I was beneath him in intelligence and breeding, as well as class. So, what the hell? But, how many times has he said he wanted a REAL woman with CURVES. Oo what would his mother say? I'd love to see her face! Oh my god they were coming my way. Shit!

I hadn't really looked at my surroundings before - three urinals two sinks, and two cubicles. I shot into the right-hand cubicle as they burst through the door. Oh god I'd just realised what that meant. They were BOTH in the GENTS! That could only mean one thing.

I jammed my fingers into my ears as they tried to squeeze into the cubicle next to me. I'll spare you the horrific details of what I heard next, but on the plus side I only had to endure it for forty-one seconds, yes, I counted.

At least she had the good grace to sound disappointed. One *small thing* worth noting however, was that she'd apparently named his penis Colin.

Finally, after they had wriggled back into their under crackers, (which can't have been easy while wearing a cubicle), they departed.

I sat back down on the toilet lid, which was incidentally very clean for a public toilet. Who knew men's toilets were cleaner than women's? I sat there in shock; surely I must've imagined that? That didn't really happen. did it? Bloody Nora! Well at least I knew for sure now that there *was* a woman, a Wonder Woman.

I thought I best get my breath back before I went to the art shop, try and get my hands to stop shaking. I snuck out of the Gents as discretely as possible, and ordered a cup of tea to steady my nerves.

As I sat down at my new table I thought to myself, 'Know thy enemy'. I did, and his name......was Colin.

Criminal Shenanigans

I sat in the café for about an hour, stunned from what I had witnessed. I could just have run away, gone back to May's crying, again. But no, I had known for a while that there was another woman, I shouldn't be so shocked. But I really was.

I think it was because suddenly it was very real. It was no longer a hypothetical woman, it was a real one, and if memory serves me, she was called Vicky.

I finished the last swig of my tea, and stood up. Onward and upward. Can't let the bastards grind you down can you?

I set off back to the car park to retrieve my car.

As I was walking into the car park entrance I could hear a commotion coming from the other side of the car park. It sounded like Neil. I'd better get a closer look.

Oh yes, there he was, having a tantrum, shouting at the top of his lungs and kicking at the clamp that was now wrapped around his back wheel. His face was so flushed with anger that he matched his wheels beautifully. I peered out from behind the hedges that formed the divide between sections of the car park, and smiled. It's nice to see your handy work so well received isn't it? Another five-hundred-pound fine I believe.

I trotted over to my own car, unlocked it and slid behind the wheel. Leaning across to the windscreen I pulled Neil's stolen parking ticket off it, cheers Neil. I crumpled it up and threw it out of the window. I'm not usually a litter bug, but that day I couldn't give a stuff.

I looked in my rear-view mirror as I left the car park, yep, he was still going nuts. It looked as though he was trying to prise the clamp off with a stick. Nope, back to hitting it with the stick. No wonder his boss called him Basil Fawlty.

So, after an eventful and enlightening morning I finally parked up outside the Art supply shop. After looking up and down all the aisles, looking at the endless opportunities for winding up Mick the PBD and in return Neil, I made my choice.

I purchased my items and headed home to hide them before Neil and Louise returned.

It must be said, it was a very long day. I spent all day with my mind racing with all that I had seen (and heard.) I had to just keep my head down and get on with the plan. No more time for self-pity, time to get even. I shook myself out of my black cloud and went off in search of the bromide.

May said this was one full dose for a stallion, surly a quarter of the dose would be about right then? I could always give him more if it didn't look like it was working. I spread the powder out on the clean counter top, and using a knife split it into what looked like about a quarter. I thought that looked about right. I put a jug under the lip of the counter and scraped the quarter into it. The rest I scraped back into the veterinary bag, and hid it at the back of my knicker draw. I then made him a new batch of his 'health shake'. There. That felt better. It's good to be pro-active isn't it?

Soon after that I got a call from Neil's mother, informing me they would be keeping Louise for the weekend and would take her to school on the Monday morning. 'Charming' I thought, nice to be asked. She also wanted to know if I had seen anything suspicious while I had been at her house earlier.

"Suspicious like what?" I asked innocently.

"Somebody has stolen my hanging basket from off the driveway. Sometime between your departure and the gardener arriving ten minutes later."

I got her inference. "Sorry Penelope didn't see a thing. But while I've got you on the phone, how was your holiday?"

"I've got to go; I don't have time for chit chat!"

She hung up on me. "Bye then!" I said to the dial tone. I cannot bear that woman. Wait till she meets her new future daughter-in-law, then she might remember me fondly! Oh well, at least Louise was in good company for the weekend.

Next time the phone rang it was Neil, barking at me to come to the impound lot at the police station; and bring the cheque book. Now!

I had a cup of tea and a sandwich, did the crossword in the paper, then thought I might have a little mosey on down to the police station and see what he had his knickers in a twist about.

On arriving at the police station, and announcing myself at the desk, I was told by a very sympathetic police woman that Neil was currently in cells after becoming abusive to the arresting officer. After refusing to pay the five-hundred-pound clamping fine, the car had been impounded. It had also been noticed that Neil wasn't displaying a tax disc, and, according to a police speed camera, he'd been captured on film doing a hundred and thirty miles an hour on duel carriageway the previous Thursday. Despite his protests that he had in fact been out of the country at the time, after checking official airline records, it was proven that he was actually back in the country Thursday morning.

Also, after having his finger prints taken, they were found to be a match to a finger print taken from an item that had been wedged into the exhaust of his neighbour's car. So vandalism was also added to the charge sheet.

So altogether he was being charged with failure to display a tax disc, dangerous driving, vandalism and assaulting a police officer. Bail was set at four thousand pounds. Plus, the five-hundred-pound clamping fee of course.

All in a day's work, I thought.

I swapped a cheque for four and a half thousand pounds for a very shocked and stressed looking Neil.

Once we were back home, I asked him what the hell was going on? (Like I didn't know.)
He seemed pretty bewildered. He was SURE that he put his new tax disc in the window. It couldn't have fallen out, could it? He asked himself more than me. And he remembered *specifically* putting a parking ticket in his window. He wondered aloud if the ticket had fallen into the heating vent on the dash board. (Mm.)

I asked about the speeding on the duel carriageway next. On that he was livid. There was no way in hell that could have been him; he'd been trapped on a coach full of Christians happy clappers at the time. I asked why, and was told, "doesn't matter".

He said he'd even thought it must have been me driving at first, until his stressed-out brain had remembered that I couldn't drive an automatic. (Phew.) It must've been a joyrider he thought.

"Ok, well what about this alleged vandalism?" I had asked.

"Load of rubbish. They can't prove a thing. All they've got is my finger prints on a deodorant lid. Anybody could've been through our bin and stolen it to frame me. As for assaulting a police officer, that's rubbish. I only slapped him."

Oh dear.

He headed for the fridge, hopefully for his 'health shake'; he did seem to live on the bloody things. He continued. "Just got to wait for a court date now. I'll have to arrange a decent solicitor, that one I was given today was useless. He was trying to make me believe that there was a chance I could go to prison. Bloody rubbish. They don't send people like me to prison." He paused for a sip of his shake. "Apparently because of that little incident with the with the bloody paper boy's dad when I lost my temper, I've already got a criminal record. It's a bloody lie. I could sue him for slander!"

I thought someone was in denial. But it looked as though Plan B was melting back into Plan A. Either way soon I'd be free.

Love thy Neighbour

After the events of the day, I almost decided to call off my planned attack on Mick the PBD. Right up until I was getting my nighty on and brushing my teeth, I was having second thoughts. The day had been eventful enough hadn't it? It seemed like an age ago that I had dropped Lou off at Neil's parents. It was hard to believe it had only been that morning. But Neil never knew when to quit though did he! He burst into my bedroom as I had just got into bed, without knocking. He crossed the room towards my dressing table, and began ransacking my jewellery box.

"What the hell?" I asked. Sitting up in bed.

"It's no good you having all this jewellery just sitting here collecting dust, I need to raise some money to pay for a solicitor. That fine today cleaned me out." He said as he was picking up the necklace that he bought me as a wedding present. He stuffed it in his pocket and carried on rummaging.

"Give me that back." I grabbed at him. "It's mine."

"Not anymore it's not." He slapped my hands away as I tried to make a grab for the box, I was seething, I'd only just got it back from the bloody pawnbroker.

He turned to me and snarled. "Get back in that bed and keep quiet or I'll give you something to whine about!" He looked demonic. It was the first time I had been truly scared of him. He looked like he'd throttle me given half the chance.

I begrudgingly got back in bed, glaring at him. He took another few items from my jewellery box, and then left slamming the door behind him.

I was SEETHING. That's it I thought. The plans back on.

I had set my alarm for three o'clock, late enough that no one would be around, and early enough that no one would be up yet. As it happened I didn't need the reminder as I couldn't sleep anyway.

I quietly dressed (in black, perhaps Neil had been right about that.) and even borrowed Neil's balaclava, from the hall cupboard. Armed with my supplies I slinked my way down the block to Mick's house.

I carefully pulled off the cover that Mick had used to cover his newly returned car. I set it down on his driveway looking surreptitiously about me. Good, nobody seemed to have heard me slide it off. I opened my carrier bag and pulled out the large folded up piece of paper. I put the paint to one side for now while I found the masking tape in the bottom of the bag. I unfolded the large stencil that I had purchased and spread it out over the bonnet. I took care to make sure that I had it perfectly central and symmetrical, and taped it in place. Next came the paint. I'd already shaken the spray paint a few hours earlier and was hoping that it would still be alright. Fortunately, with the car being red, I only had to use black and white paint, as the red was already there.

I carefully unstuck the masking tape and slowly removed the stencil. Luckily the paint had dried almost instantly. I folded the stencil back up, and put it back into my bag along with the tape and paint. I stood back and admired my handy work. Mick's car now had a lovely new decal that covered the whole of its bonnet. Micky Mouse grinned up at me as I replaced the car cover. I hope Mick thinks it's a fitting tribute!

Next, I had to get rid of the evidence. I had taken heed of Neil and worn gloves throughout. I walked into the next street to ours, and taking a cloth out of my jacket pocket, I wiped my fingerprints off the spray paint tins and dropped them into the first dustbin I came across. The grinning Micky Mouse stencil and the masking tape went into the canal. I doubted any finger prints could tie it back to me now. Satisfied that my work here was done, I set off for home.

The following day, I waited with baited breath for poor Mick to uncover his car and discover what he thought would be Neil's handy work. I was dying with anticipation. I took a leaf out of Neil's book the previous week and decided to cut the front grass. I was out there for an hour before I ran out of lawn to cut, how Neil had managed to make it last three hours I had no idea.

Speaking of Neil, he'd been keeping his head down that morning. Not because of any guilt, I thought, just probably worrying about his new legal problems. Wait till his parents found out, they'd probably disown him again.

His mother had phoned me later that morning to tell me that they were having a garden party the following Saturday. It was formal dress, and I was to make sure I wore something 'suitable'.

Snotty cow. I was dying to tell her about Neil, but I'd rather she found that out for herself, which she would. She moved in the same circles as the Chief Constable after all.

I agreed that we would be there. On hearing her invitation had been accepted, she promptly put the phone down on me. I blew a raspberry down the phone before I replaced the receiver and then went in search of Neil.

I found him in his study with a large glass of brandy in front of him. A little early I thought but then again, he had had a tough few days - and hopefully a few more to come too!

He looked up at me warily as I entered. "That was your mother on the phone." I explained.

That made him sit up straight.

"Don't worry." I said before he had chance to speak. "I never said anything."

"Good". He replied with a grunt. "What did she want?"

"She was ringing to invite us to a garden party on Saturday."

"Oh. Was there anything else?" He obviously wanted rid of me.

"No. That was all."

"Good."

I then left; I know when I'm not wanted.

I resumed my watch through the curtains waiting for Mick to uncover his car. He didn't. Not until the following morning anyway.

The next morning I had slept in, after all Louise was still at Neil's parents - who would be taking her to school. Neil would sort himself out with breakfast (health shake) and get himself off to work, and so after such a rubbish night's sleep I thought I'd have a lay in - that is until the shouting woke me up!

Mick had uncovered his car, getting ready to go to work. I think the sight of that grinning Mickey Mouse had finally tipped him over the edge. He was screaming and going ape-shit pointing and gesturing at our house while his wife and sons were holding him back for dear life. They finally managed to drag him in through the front door and get it closed. Oh dear. Poor Mick, I felt very sorry for him. But as May had said, he'd gotten himself involved by punching Neil, twice. Every war had its casualties.

It didn't make me feel any better though. Mick was a nice man.

One thing I knew, that Mick didn't know though, was that the paint I'd used was water based. With soap and water, it'd be gone in minutes.

He came back out of the house half an hour later with a face like thunder and drove his Mickey mobile off to work.

At ten past one I got a phone call from Matthew. He had news! Apparently, an hour ago the police had turned up demanding to speak to Neil immediately. Matthew had heard from Neil's secretary who had been eavesdropping, that Neil was being questioned over a second case of vandalism against his neighbour. The police had been very adamant that he was currently the only suspect, and unless he could provide an alibi he would be charged.

"Oo." Matthew quizzed me. "Was it you?"

"Might be." I laughed. "Did you hear what the vandalism was?"

"No but I'm dying to know."

And so I filled him in on the previous night's activities. Plus the day I'd had with Neil and Wonder Woman, and the police.

"I don't believe it!" He said. "I could punch the son of a bitch! Who the hell does he think he is? Treating you like that! Having an affair, shouting at you, stealing from you, threatening you. I'll kill him!"

This was new! I've never had a man defend my honour before!

"Don't go doing anything daft, Matt, he's just not worth it. He's getting what's coming to him anyway, with a bit of luck he'll be locked up soon." I paused. "But thank you for defending me, it's really nice."

"That's what friends are for. You just say the word though and I'll have him."

"You're an angel Matthew, thanks."

"No problem. Okay." He paused and cleared his throat. "Do you still have a spare key for that car of his?"

"Yes why?"

"Can I borrow it?"

"'Course, what ya' planning?"

"It's a surprise." He sounded mysterious, I was intrigued.

"How can I get the key to you?" I wondered.

"I've been thinking about it, when Neil gets home tonight, do you think you could cellotape the key under the front bumper? Then I'll have access tomorrow when he gets back to work."

"'Course, no problem. I'm dying of suspense though." I laughed.

"I promise it's worth the wait." He sounded dead smug.

After that we chatted about this and that, until Matt had to get back to work. Once he'd gone, I couldn't help but wonder what was going to happen with Neil. Would I have to give him an alibi? I don't think so.

At four o clock the police rolled up.

I invited them in, asking innocently what the problem was. Despite my calm exterior, inside I was shaking. They informed me that another complaint of vandalism had been brought to their attention, by my neighbour. They believed the culprit to be my husband, again, *and* did I know his whereabouts between midnight and seven o clock that morning.

I answered that I assumed he must've been in HIS bed. This made the constable's ears prick up. "So, you don't share a bed madam?"

"No constable."

"Do you share a bedroom madam?"

"No constable." At this he and his colleague exchanged a knowing look.

"So, madam, would you say it was possible that Mr Pemberton could have exited the house without your knowledge?"

"I suppose it's possible." I shrugged meekly.

"That will be all for now Mrs Pemberton, thank you for your time."

This was getting better and better. I hoped they didn't keep him locked up overnight though.

I wanted to get that spare key cellotaped to his car so that I could see what Matthew had planned the following day.

Tuesday's Revelations

Neil finally arrived home at around seven o clock. His previous cockiness was gone. He was extremely pale, and was visibly shaking. I tried to question him as he came in but he shot past me to the toilet, where I heard him peeing for five minutes solid.

"What's going on then? The police were here earlier asking where you were last night."

He looked up frowning as he sat down. He sighed. "What did you tell them?"

"The truth, you were in bed between midnight and seven o clock."

"Well it wasn't a strong enough alibi, I've been charged with criminal damage. Again." He dropped his head and rubbed his tired eyes.

"Did you do it?" I asked timidly.

He bellowed. "Course I bloody didn't! It's some sort of conspiracy! I've been framed!" He was on his feet now shouting. "I'm going to get to the bottom of it though. No more mister nice guy!"

My god his previous behaviour was him being nice? Christ what was I in for next then?

"Did they keep you for long?" I queried.

"About four hours. At least I got a break in the middle while they let me go to my doctor's appointment. Although in hind sight I wish I'd have missed the bloody thing."

This made me prick my ears up. "What doctor's appointment?"

"I had to go for a general check-up, nothing important!"

"Well it was important enough to interrupt a police interview for." I argued.

"Fine. I'm too tired to argue. I've been having problems with my er, waterworks. I had to take in a sample, and have a….an…a prostate exam."

RESULT!!! I was dancing inside with joy. Yes! Yes! Yes!

I feigned ignorance. "What's that?"

He looked up sharply, trying to gauge if I was being sarcastic I think. He stared at me for a few seconds then seemed satisfied I wasn't mocking him. "It's a, it's, it's a special erm, procedure, for, well, erm, for men." He looked away.

I wasn't gonna let him go that easily. "What sort of procedure?"

He finally lost it with me. "God, it you really *have* to know, the doctor stuck his finger up my rectum. There! Satisfied?"

I was.

"Right, I've had a long day being interrogated by police, doctors, and now you. I've had enough. I'm going out. Don't wait up!" He slammed back out the front door. Probably going to cry into the arms of his mistress, I thought. At least he'd only be cuddling though, thanks to the bromide!

But, we had done it, hadn't we? We had done the impossible and gotten him to voluntarily go for a prostate exam...by a man. By a gay man at that! By god me and my team were a force to be reckoned with weren't we?

I was straight on the phone to May to fill her and Darren in on it all. They both were laughing like mad at the thought. It was mission accomplished. We were all shocked that the plan had worked; I had no idea that he'd even booked a doctor's appointment!

May was very pleased to hear all my news, from my little stunts, to the trouble Neil now had with the law. She already knew all about Neil's woman as Matthew had been home and told her. I was glad; I didn't really want to talk about that anyway. She was livid, but ultimately glad that I could really see him for what he was now. The blinkers were off.

I told her I'd given him the first dose of the bromide to her amusement. Darren interrupted then. He wanted May to tell me that he and Matthew had a corker planned for Neil the following morning. He wouldn't tell me what either. I couldn't wait! I rang off, promising to ring them the following day. May was waiting to go out anyway. She was taking Darren ballroom dancing. Poor Darren.

Neil didn't come home until after midnight. As soon as I heard him start to snore I slipped out of the house to cellotape the key under the front bumper where we had arranged. I cellotaped a package containing the key and a note: -
Dear comrade,
Target has been prostated! Mission accomplished! For further information, please call me at thirteen hundred hours, Love from, a comrade in arms.

I didn't dare put either of our names just in case Neil found the note.

The following morning was Tuesday, the day that I could collect Neil's holiday photos.
I couldn't wait! I got up feeling on top of the world, everything was coming together nicely. I was no longer a victim, I was the winner, the succeeder. But I was also the breakfast maker, so I better get my arse moving. I got dressed and headed downstairs to start preparations.

I made my way into the kitchen to put the kettle on before I got Louise up. Surprisingly Neil was already up and making both of us a cup of coffee. That's right, BOTH of us! I couldn't remember the last time he'd done anything thoughtful for me. He looked dreadful. The huge bags under his eyes betrayed a night of little sleep, I suspected.

"Thank you." I accepted the mug that was offered to me.

"I've had about six cups already this morning." He stated morosely.

"Well, I suppose you've got a lot on your mind I expect." I offered.

"Yes, well, all this rubbish with the police, and that bloody fool Mick, it's all just got a bit much." He looked down at his coffee cup, swilling the brown liquid around and around.

"Don't you think you should ask your mother to help with a solicitor or something, otherwise I don't know how you're going to afford private council, I mean there's no way you'd get legal aid is there?"

He got to his feet and snarled at me. "You are *not* to mention this to my mother! If I even get a *whiff* that you've told anybody about this, I'll knock you into next week!" He pointed at my face as he spat the words at me. He threw his mug at my head, narrowly missing me as I ducked. He glared at me for a moment and then left slamming the door behind him.

What a tosser, I thought. For a minute there I had felt sorry for him. Nope. Not anymore though.

I got down on my hands and knees and picked up all the pieces of pottery and swept the mess into the bin. A quick run over with the mop, and it looked fine again. Once I was satisfied that it looked neat enough, I went upstairs to get Lou up.

She was already up and dressed when I got up there. She gave me a dirty look as I came in. "What did you do this time to make Daddy mad?" She stood with her arms crossed waiting for an explanation.

I couldn't believe her. She really hated me didn't she? No matter what I did for her, however much I tried to get close to her, she simply didn't like me. Yet Neil could act as disgracefully as he wanted in front of her, and her view of him never wavered. If she was capable of loving anyone it was Neil. Perhaps because they were so alike? But anytime she *did* disapprove of his behaviour, she blamed me for it. I truly could not win with her.

"Don't speak to me in that tone of voice Louise. I had quite enough for one day. Go brush your teeth. Your breakfast will be ready in five minutes."

She stood there looking scornfully at me.

"NOW!" I shouted. With that she skulked off to the bathroom.

God what a day this was turning out to be.

Once *madam* was finally ushered through the school gates and into class, I felt a huge weight lift from my shoulders. God, she could be hard work.

Right then, now the fun bit, off to the chemist to pick up Neil's photographs! I was so excited and worried about what those pictures contained, that my hands were shaking as I handed over my ticket to the chemist. It could be nothing, I thought, it was probably just a load of photos of scenery like he normally took when on holiday. But you never knew did you?

As soon as the package was handed to me and I had handed over the money, I shot home as fast as I could.

I let myself in through the front door, and went straight through to the kitchen. Pulling my coat off and throwing it on the stool beside me, I pulled out the stool in front of me and sat down. I took a deep breath and…the bloody phone rang! I shot across the room, annoyed at being interrupted. "Hello?" I said impatiently.

"It's me Matt."

"Hi Matt, how are you, did you get my package?"

"I'm fine, better than fine." He stopped whilst he composed himself, I could hear the laughter in his voice. "Yes, I got the package. I knew about the prostate exam already, Darren rang a friend of a friend who came to give me the message last night. I have to say, I laughed all night. I can't believe it worked!" He sounded thrilled.

"I know! I don't know how I kept a straight face when he told me!" I sniggered.

"Anyway, what I'm really ringing for, and I know it's earlier than I normally ring, but do you think you could come down here and have a quick look at what me and Craig have done to Neil's car? I need you to see it." He exploded laughing again. Once he'd gotten his laughter back under control he continued. "I know that I could describe it to you, but you *really* need to see this, trust me a picture is worth a thousand words."

"Oh my god," I laughed. "What have you done?"

"I don't want to spoil the surprise."

"What if Neil sees me?"

"He won't if you're quick, can you be here in fifteen minutes?" He was really excited.

"I can be there in ten."

"I'll keep an eye out for you." He added "You might want to use the loo before you see this though; I refuse to take responsibility if you can't hold your bladder."

"Fine, I won't embarrass you I promise. See you in ten."

"Can't wait." Then he was gone.

So much for the photos, they'd have to wait till I got back.

I took Matt's advice and went to the loo first, after all one incontinent in the family is quite enough.

With a minute to spare I pulled my car up around the corner from the factory. I slipped through the side gate into the car park, and spotted Matthew as he stepped out from behind a skip; he waved at me and beckoned me towards him. I returned his wave and quickly made my way over there.

"Hi Matthew, I'm dying of suspense." I panted, out of breath from the quick sprint.

"Hiya, come on over here and have a look at who's hiding from the big bad wolf in Neil's car." He was grinning like a Cheshire cat. I followed his eyes over to my right, were I noticed Neil's car was parked. I couldn't see anything wrong with the car at first. I had no idea what he was laughing at.

I walked a little closer, and that's when I saw what was sitting in the car. It was sitting upright in the driver's seat, wearing what looked like Neil's grey suit, and with its seat belt securely fastened. A huge pink DEAD PIG! A huge pink dead pig wearing a suit! It was even wearing a wig with a comb over! A little pair of spectacles sat on its dead snout. It was a *dead* ringer for Neil though! I couldn't believe it!

Matthew had really outdone himself on this one. I put my hand to my mouth trying to stifle the belly laugh that was about to explode out. Then I caught Matthew's eye, and all thoughts of keeping the laugh in, went out of the window. We howled, holding on to each other laughing, coughing and snorting, desperately trying to be quiet, we each put a hand over the other one's mouth as the door opposite us started to open. We shot behind a fiat panda and ducked just in the nick of time, as Neil came out.

"Shit," Matthew whispered, "He's not supposed to go for his dinner for another forty minutes."

"Looks like he's going early." I whispered back. "How the hell did you pull this off?"

He looked at me with glee. "Darren's mate works at the abattoir, and he owes us a favour."

"How the hell did you get hold of Neil's suit?" I was impressed.

"His secretary stole his spare one from his cupboard in the office. I thought she was gonna blow the whistle when she came in while me and Craig were planning it. But she was more excited than we were! The suit was her idea, and she was our lookout!" He sniggered quietly.

"My god, all this time I thought it was just me that hated him. It's the whole bloody factory too!"

We peeped through the fiats passenger window, watching as an unsuspecting Neil made his way over to his car, waiting with baited breath.

He sauntered over to his driver side, without really taking any notice, until he opened the driver door and the dead pigs head rolled towards him.

"AGGGGHHHHHH!!!!!" Was Neil's petrified cry.

He tried to back out of the way of the horror in front of him, and promptly fell over his own feet, which just increased his proximity to the pig. He landed nose to crotch with it. The pig had - since it had been man handled into the car, let go of the remains of its bladder, and this was also the precise time that Neil let go of his too.

I was so glad that Matt had told me to use the loo before I got there, or I think I would have lost control of my bladder too! It wasn't so much the sight of Neil weeing himself in terror; it was more the sight of the pig. It looked SO comical! Its head had wobbled to one side as Neil had opened the door, if it hadn't been wearing a seatbelt it would have fallen on Neil. With its head lolling to one side, tongue hanging out, and a little pair of John Lennon glasses balanced on its snout it was the most comical sight I had ever seen. But, what *really* killed me was that its wig had slipped, showing off its comb over beautifully!

Me and Matt were rolling round behind the little fiat panda, crying with silent laughter. Meanwhile Neil had just realised that the pig was wearing his suit. He screamed out far more expletives than I could possibly recall, but the gist of it was: - "SON OF A BITCHIN, BASTARD, SHIT-FACE, ARSE-WIPE, BOLLOCKING WANKERS!"

He put both hands behind the back of his head, now whimpering looking at the scene before him. He paced up and down, hopping from one foot to the other. Obviously clueless at what to do about the pig. Suddenly he looked down horrified as it dawned on him that he had a very large wet patch on the front of his trousers. A little sob escaped his throat as he quickly took off his jacket wrapping it around his waist to hide the evidence. He took one last bewildered look at the pig, and then charged back into the factory like his arse was on fire.

"That's my cue to leave." Matt smiled up at me from the tarmac where he was still laid from laughing.

I grinned down at him, offering my hand to pull him up. "I'll never forget this Matthew as long as I live." I looked down at my feet and laughed again." I can't say I owe you one, because I could never repay you for this!"

He heaved himself up off the floor, with my help. "No sweat, I can honestly say it's been a real pleasure, comrade." He mock saluted me.

"At ease soldier." I joked.

He laughed. "Right come on then, we better both scarper before he calls the police."

"Right, good point, I'll speak to you soon then, take care Matt."

"You too Sarah." He leaned in and gave me a quick hug, and was gone.

Phew what a morning! And so exhausted from laughing, I made my way home. Time to look at some holiday snaps.

A Picture's Worth a Thousand Words

I arrived home, still laughing at what a sight I'd seen, I hoped desperately that someone had thought to take a photo. I'd pay any amount for a copy. God only knew how Neil had reacted after I left. Would he call the RAC or would he call the pigs?

I hoped that Matt had covered his tracks well; I didn't want him to get into trouble. But he wasn't daft, I'm sure nothing would be able to be traced back to him.

Oo I had been wondering what to give Neil for tea, now I had the perfect idea. I went over to the freezer and pulled out a pack of pork chops and put them on the draining board to defrost. Perfect.

I made myself a cup of coffee and sat down at the breakfast bar to finally have a look at Neil's photos. I opened the packet and pulled out the wad of photos, and began flicking though them. Okay, the first few were photos of snowy mountains, I impatiently skipped past those. The next few looked as though they had been taken in a ski club bar or something. One of Neil and his parents grinning like the posh twits that they were. I noted that whoever had taken the photo had cut the top of their heads off. Best thing for them!

The next one was of his parents stood in front of a stuffed Bear. But the next one made me chuckle. It was of Neil's father standing with his arm around a very attractive and very camp looking waiter. Now that's a keeper!

I started flicking through the rest of them a bit faster, getting impatient. More scenery, more posh people trying to ski, and then it suddenly got interesting. A photo of a blonde Scandinavian-looking girl standing at a bar. An innocent enough looking photo, yet it bothered me. I think it was something in the way she was looking at the camera, rather lustily I thought. Mm. I put that one aside and carried on. Next was a photo of a very drunk looking Neil half naked laid on a bed with his tie around his head, like a geeky insipid-looking pigeon-chested Rambo. Oh dear. The next one looked like it had been taken by Neil at arm's length, it was a slightly out of focus, much too close, headshot of Neil and the mystery woman kissing. My god, the son of a bitch was at it again! He was cheating on both me *and* Wonder Woman!

I was seething! What an absolute arse hole! He was completely beyond belief wasn't he? I felt like I'd seen enough, but there was one more photo to look at. I had a long swig of coffee and brought out the last photo. I almost spat my coffee out. It showed the pretty buxom blonde from the earlier photo, sprawled out on a bed, wearing tight white shorts and a pink halter top that had slipped a little, leaving a pink nipple protruding. But, what stood out to me the most from the picture, was the very obvious erection in her shorts! She was a HE! My god! Had Neil known? Was he now into lady boys too? Goodness gracious me! What a week for surprises.

I put the photo down. Staring into space, trying to get my head around what I had just seen. Still baffled, I picked it back up again. Nope the bulge was still there. I hadn't imagined it. I looked closely at the date stamp in the corner. It was taken the very day he had suddenly flown home in a panic! I think I now had my answer as to why he'd suddenly gone to such extreme lengths to get home. If he had known 'She' was a 'He', he wouldn't have fled like he did would he. He must have thought the beautiful blonde was a woman. Probably met her in the lodge bar, bought her a drink, got chatting, and invited her up to his room for night cap as his father had unfortunately done to the poor waiter. He probably couldn't believe his luck, attracting a girl that good looking. Probably thought his luck ran out though when she suddenly got very pleased to see him!

Oo I stifled a laugh. I wonder if the girl was transgender and had tried to hint to Neil about her 'situation'. Neil was never very quick on the uptake, I could just imagine it, if he had been told that she was waiting for gender surgery, he'd probably think she meant 'women's troubles'. He truly was that dense.

I picked up the earlier photo of the blonde, taking a closer look this time. She was a very convincing woman, I'll give Neil that. On closer inspection though I thought I could see a trace of an Adam's apple.

I put the photos back down on the counter in front of me, laughing to myself. Neil's father had pulled a gay waiter, Neil had pulled a lady boy, and all Neil's mother pulled, was the zipper down of her dress amidst a lot of screaming!

No wonder none of them had wanted to talk about it. But what made it such a fitting punishment was that they had always been such a bunch of bigoted homophobes. Serves them bloody well right!

I wonder how long it had taken Neil, in his drunken state, to notice the very obvious bulge in his bed buddy's pants? God I was so dying to ask him. It would be hell only knowing half of the story. I was pretty sure that the version I had concocted in my head wouldn't be far from the truth though. I wonder what Wonder Woman would think? I was quite tempted to send her a copy. I think I would have done if I could, but Neil would guess what I had done, he'd put two and two together and deduce that I had stolen his film. Shame it couldn't be done. Or could it? I have been known to work miracles the last few months.

I made myself another cup of coffee while I had a think about it. After all, I had been handed a golden opportunity here that shouldn't be squandered. A cup of coffee later and I had a plan in mind.

Back to the art supply shop I went.

I couldn't resist taking a route that took me past Neil's factory though. I slowed down as I approached the main entrance straining my head trying to look in. I thought I could see two men in white suits trying to lift the pig out of the car as I went past, but I couldn't tell who they were. Shame the men in white coats were there for *that* pig and not the other one! I thought.

Smiling, I sped up again and continued on my way.

Once I got to the art supply shop, I ended up having to ask the girl on the counter for help, as my requirements were a little different to the many variety of kits that were on offer. I told her all about my cheating husband (naming no names of course) who desperately needed to get his comeuppance. She was *very* helpful. Her previous boyfriend had been a cheating scumbag - so she said, so she had every sympathy for me. She even went so far as to help me construct the very thing that I went in there to purchase, and so after paying for my item, and leaving the sales girl a hefty tip, I set off for the photocopy shop.

Once I was satisfied that I had a nice little portfolio of Neil and his 'friend,' I set off back home.

Once I got back in, I went straight in to Neil's study to look for a large manila envelope. Finding one in the top draw of his desk, I inserted the photocopies into it. I then wrote 'Vicky's' work address on the back of it - with my left hand, so that the writing didn't look like mine. Next came the Swiss stamp that I pilfered from Neil's old stamp collection. Then finally I brought my new handy work out of the paper bag that I had brought in with me. The lady in the art supply shop had been kind enough to help me make a rubber stamp such as was used in post offices. Except mine was one for Switzerland. I opened the ink pad, smugly, and pressed in my new rubber stamp. Once it was adequately coated I pressed it down firmly over the Swiss stamp. It looked perfect. Even I was impressed. Brilliant! Now I could grass the little toe rag up to his mistress without him being able to trace it back to me.

I was sure it would completely drive him mad trying to work out who in Switzerland could have stolen his film and found out about his mistress in England. All in a day's work for me, I grinned.

My last job of the day before collecting Louise from school, was to pop the manila envelope through the letter box at the company address from which Wonder Woman worked from, that had been listed in the yellow pages. Perfect. Now off to pick up Madam.

Not Pigging Funny

Neil arrived home ten minutes after Louise and I arrived home from school. He was very early for once I noted. Ah, he couldn't very well stay at work all day in a suit with a wet patch on the crotch, could he? He seemed to have cleaned it up a bit, it wasn't as obvious now that it was dry, I wondered if he had stood in front of the hand dryer in the gents desperately trying to dry his crotch. I hoped someone had walked in and caught him. It would add to the rumour that he was a pervert.

I had to bite my lip so as not to laugh and blow my cover. "You're home early." I innocently observed. As he trundled past me with a face like thunder.

He barked in return. "Day from hell, off to get in the shower." He then barged up the stairs leaving a pungent aroma of urine behind him.

I smiled and put the pork chops into the oven. I then sat down at the breakfast bar to help Louise with her homework.

"What are you smiling at?" She asked me suspiciously.

"Nothing, just thinking about something funny that I saw earlier."

"What?" She asked snottily.

"It was just a funny episode of porky pig on the TV." I snorted.

"Cartoons aren't for grownups." She whined petulantly.

"Never mind. Let's get to grips with the Norman invasion before tea's ready."

When eventually Neil did come down the stairs he smelt much better, although his face was still a thunder cloud. As Louise sauntered off from the kitchen to go watch TV Neil sat down in her place.

"So, what's this day from hell then?" I asked with my bested straight face on.

He huffed loudly, looked down at his fidgeting hands and began. "Well, today my car was vandalised again. They went too far this time though, too, too far. When I find out who put that d…." He trailed off mid-sentence, before getting his rage under control and starting again. "When I find out who put that dead bloody pig in my car I'm going to murder them. I'm going to murder them with my bare hands!" He thumped the table for emphasis. He then took a deep breath and slowly exhaled, looking up at me. "Somebody put a dead pig in my car!" He said it meekly this time, more asking me then telling me. Completely bewildered I thought. "It was wearing my spare suit."

Whoa I nearly lost it there. I had to turn and fidget with the oven dials while I swallowed my laughter.

Once I was composed again, I turned back to him. "Somebody put a dead pig wearing a suit in your car?" I asked incredulously. He nodded. "Why would anyone do such a thing?" I questioned.

Quietly he replied. "I don't know, but it wasn't funny. It scared the living day lights out of me when I opened the door and it almost fell on me!"

Whoa nearly laughed again there. "What did you do about it?" I was genuinely curious.

"I got two of the newbies from packing to get rid of it. After they'd finished laughing at the bloody thing. I threatened to sack them on the spot if they carried on with such unprofessional behaviour."

"Well, I don't suppose moving a dead pig dressed up in a suit is part of their job-description, is it?" I countered, hoping Matt wasn't going to lose his job. He seemed to have settled in nicely there.

"They tried that 'not in our job description' nonsense, I said in that case, pack the damn thing. That is your job-description isn't it? That had them stumped. Once they had it packed up in a box, I sent them off to the abattoir with it. Might be of some use to them up there."

I smiled inwardly. Neil thought he was so bloody clever didn't he. He was nothing but a bloody pawn!

"Did it make a mess of your car?" I asked as I started straining the veg I had been simmering while we talked.

"A right bloody mess! It had spilled 'fluid' all over the driver seat." He grumbled.

"What fluid?" I asked as I started spooning out mash potato. "Blood or something?"

"I believe it was urine."

Okay I couldn't let this one go. "I thought I caught a whiff of wee as you came past me earlier, must've been from the pig then." I smirked into the oven as I pulled out the tray of meat.

"Must've been." He said very quickly. I noticed he didn't look me in the eye either.

"Have you cleaned the car then?"

"Got one of the lads who got rid of the pig to do it."

I hoped it wasn't poor Matthew.

I put the food onto the plates and placed one in front of Neil. "I'm sorry I'm sure you've had quite enough of pork today but I'd already started cooking your chops before I knew." I fibbed.

He glared at me. "I suppose you think this is funny do you? Mocking me like this? You're a disgrace!" He then threw the plate across the room. It hit the far wall and sent meat and veg flying everywhere. Lovely!

Louise looked at me in disgust. "You've done it again Mummy!"

He pulled his coat out of the hall cupboard, and shouted. "I'm going out. Don't wait up!"

Yeah well, I thought to myself, enjoy it while it lasts, 'cause it's not going to!

Sending Louise off upstairs to get her pyjamas on, I turned to the mess of meat and veg that was cascading down the wall. Great! I opened the door and let the dog in to help clean up. At least he seemed to enjoy my cooking.

Once the kitchen was clean and Louise was tucked up in bed, I gave May a call and filled her in on the events of the day as I promised I would.

She was delighted at hearing that the pig scenario had worked out so well. I described it all to her in great detail, from the pig's hilarious comb over, to Neil weeing himself. She howled down the phone as she related it all back to Darren. They had already heard a bit about it from Matt who had called them earlier while he was on his break, but not in as much detail as they did from me.

Matthew had also told them that he had been the one instructed to dispose of the pig and clean the car, which he did, except for the pig's trotter that he hid under the rear seat! It should be nice and fragrant in a few days he had laughed.

"Hopefully it should attract a few flies too!" I laughed with May. We both knew Neil had a pathological fear of creepy crawlies. We wondered what he would think to a few hundred maggots in the back seat of his car? I just hope he didn't have any romance planned for in the back of there! No that's a lie. I hope he did!

Once I'd got my breath back from laughing I asked if it would be okay to call down the following day as I wanted to show her Neil's holiday pictures. She was intrigued, but I wouldn't even give her a clue as to what they contained. I was doing to her as Matthew had done to me.

"Trust me." I had said to her. "A picture is worth a thousand words."

And so it was arranged, after taking Lou to school in the morning, I'd be off to May's for a giggle with her and Darren. I couldn't wait!

Matthew's Little Secret

The following day was a beautiful sunny day, not a cloud in sight and the temperature was already in the mid-twenties though it wasn't even yet ten o clock. I had dropped Louise at school an hour earlier, and then loaded up the stolen hanging basket into the boot of my car before setting off to May's.

I was now pulling up the pot holed driveway at Davenport, watching grey squirrels darting out of my way and charging back up into the trees. The oak trees looked magnificent gently swaying in the late summer breeze. It was like a little piece of heaven out here. You could almost feel as though you were the only person in the world. There was no traffic noise; no voices carrying on the wind, and no pollution. I could hear a cuckoo somewhere up above my head, as I got out of my car. It sounded so peaceful, I loved Cuckoos. (Trust me that changed!)

I went around to the boot and lifted out the stolen hanging basket. A bit wilted but it'd be okay after a good drink. I hung it up on the empty hook beside the front door, and went over to the outside tap. Underneath it was an old watering can that had been here almost as long as the house looking at the state of it. I filled it up and gave the newly brought petunias a good drink. There, May would be pleased with that, I thought. I turned the handle on the great front door and charged it with my shoulder.

"Whoa shit!" I shouted as I went flying through the door way and landed on my arse in the hall.

"Hello love, I see you've noticed Darren's planed down that bloody door at last!" May stepped over me as if nothing remotely funny had happened. "Come on then, I haven't got all bloody day, are you coming for a cup of tea or what?" Her eyes were laughing at me even if she was keeping a straight face. Crafty bugger, she knew I'd charge the door. "Darren! Come and give Sarah a pull up, she seems to have fallen down!" May went through to the kitchen still smirking.

"Don't bother on my account Darren I'm fine!" I bellowed back sarcastically. I got up and made my way to the kitchen, where aunt May and Darren were both sat sniggering.

"Very funny!" I said as I sat down at the table.

"Ha ha. We've been dying to see you do that for a week haven't we Darren!" She laughed throwing her head back.

Darren rolled his eyes at May and looked at me shaking his head. "Sorry Sarah, it was May's idea."

"It's okay." I grinned. "Whilst you were laughing aunt May did you see that I had brought you a present?"

Her eyes lit up. "Did you love? Oh, you shouldn't have. What is it?"

"I stole a hanging basket full of petunias from Neil's parent's house after they were rude to me. I thought it might look nice next to your front door."

"Oh lovely my favourites! I'll go and have a look." She shot out of the kitchen heading towards the front door belying her age. Me and Darren looked at each other shaking our heads as we followed after her. It was a good job we did follow after her, as when she came back in through the front door she forgot it no longer stuck any more either, and so when she gave it a hearty shove she came flying towards Darren like a little grey haired bowling ball! Fortunately, Darren caught her.

He turned his head to me and said "That's the second time she'd done that today!"

May shook herself down, and straightened her dress, trying to look dignified. "Yeah well that door's been sticking for sixty years, takes a bit of getting used to." She stuck her nose in the air and made her way back to the kitchen.

After we were all seated I asked. "So then, do you want to see some lovely holiday photos or what?" I grinned at them as I brought the packet of photos out of my bag.

Darren was first to reach for them. "God yes, we can't wait to see what all the mystery is about."

May slapped his hands away as he tried to grab them. "Look with your eyes Darren not with your hands. Give 'em here love!" She reached for them.

I held them up in the air out of the way of her snatching hands. "Look with your eye's May not with your hands!" Darren taunted her laughing.

I put the photos down in a stack between them so that they could both see. "Bon appetite!" I laughed as they both made a grab for them. "Careful". I said. "They're in a specific order.

In the end they compromised and kept the photos between them, slowly turning each one over so that they could both see.

"Oo is this Trevor's waiter then?" May asked, holding up the photo of Neil's father and the waiter.

"I'm pretty sure it is." I sniggered.

"Nice looking boy, but not a patch on my Darren!" She said grinning and ruffling his hair and making him blush. "All the girlies round here are after our little Darren."

"Give over May, let's see the next photo." He was clearly inwardly pleased, bless him.

Next came the photo of the blonde in the bar.

"Now who's this then?" Darren asked.

"That was my first question too. Keep going." I gestured for them to turn over the next photo.

"Ha ha, what a pasty skinny excuse for a man!" May was laughing.

"So, this is Neil then? You know, he looks exactly as I imagined he would." Darren stated while staring at the hideous image of Neil's skinny white chest and blood shot eyes with that dopey grin on his face, as though having a tie on your head meant you were cool!

"Keep going!" I grinned.

They looked at each other and shrugged and turned over the next one.

"Ugh, who the bloody hell would wanna kiss that ugly mug? So, it was another woman then? I should've known, the dirty bastard." May shook her head in disgust.

"One more photo to go yet!" I stated, on tenterhooks waiting for the shock that was to come. Finally, they turned over the remaining one.

Darren was the first one to notice. He looked closer at the photo, puzzled; then, realisation came into his eyes as he covered his mouth with his hands trying to stop the laugh from escaping.

May looked up confused. "What? What am I missing?"

Darren pointed to the blonde girl's shorts. "It's not what's missing May; it's what is very much there! He said tapping the very obvious bulge.

May pulled her glasses up from the chain around her neck and slipped then on her nose. Peering down at the photo, she now saw what Darren and I had noticed. "My Goodness!!! It's a man!" She looked up in shock.

And so I spent the next hour telling them all about my theory as to how they may have met, and more importantly pointing out the date stamp on the incriminating photo. How it looked like it might have been the reason Neil legged it home like he did. They were pretty much in agreement with me; it seemed like the logical conclusion.

After we had all sniggered at Neil for a while, I told them how I had sent a copy to Wonder Woman via a fake Swiss stamp.

"Oh god I wouldn't like to be in his shoes when she opens them photos," said May. "She's a big girl isn't she? She could do a lot of damage to a skinny little thing like Neil."

"Hopefully!" Me and Darren both said at the same time.

"Matthew hates him you know." Darren said getting up and putting the kettle back on.

"Everybody hates him! I can't believe how many people at the factory have been sabotaging him nearly as much as I have!" I exclaimed.

"No, I mean Matthew REALLY hates him." He looked at me meaningfully. "It's driving him mad how Neil treats you and gets away with it. He'd knock his head off given half a chance. He's always been the same, can't bear to see injustice, always trying to fight other people's battles."

"I can see that. I can't believe how much he's gone out of his way to help me like he has."

May chipped in. "That's 'cause he fancies you pet."

"He does not!" I blushed.

"I've seen the way he looks at you. I might be old but I'm not daft." Her eyes were shining.

"Tell her Darren, does Matthew fancy her or not?"

Darren looked decidedly uncomfortable. "It's not for me to say."

"Go on Darren, we're all friends here does he or doesn't he fancy her?"

Darren conceded. "Probably! But I know for a fact that he would never do anything about it. He still hasn't got over what his wife did to him!"

"Wife?" Me and May exclaimed.

"Oh god now I'll be in trouble." Darren dropped his head down on the table and banged it.

May was falling over herself with curiosity. "Wife you say? Matthew's married?"

"He was, well, still is I suppose." He looked up shiftily.

"Well I never!" Exclaimed May. "Come on Darren, out with it. You don't keep secrets among friends."

Darren looked up and rolled his eyes. "Fine, I'll tell you, but don't tell Matt I caved so easily." He huffed. "Have either of you ever noticed the bumper sticker on my van?"

May looked at me puzzled. But I looked back at Darren and nodded. "Actually yes, it was the first thing I noticed. I thought it was good and wondered where I could get one from." For May's benefit I explained. "It said 'I still miss my ex but my aim is getting better!'"

May snorted at that. "Yes, very good, but get to the point Darren."

He continued. "Well that van along with its bumper sticker belonged to Matthew before he gave it to me when he left. He bought the sticker before he gave me the van. That should give you a clue that he had 'issues with his ex."

"What issues Darren?" I was intrigued.

He swallowed and looked down. "Well, her name was Mary, is Mary I should say; and she's crazy. They went out a few times, Matthew didn't really like her all that much to be honest. He thought she was a stuck-up snob. But, she was obsessed with Matt, and chased him till he gave in. One night Matt got drunk, and they had a one night stand. She said they didn't need condoms because she was on the pill. Matt was too drunk to question it. He said it only happened the once, and avoided her like the plague afterwards. He couldn't stand her. She was such a stuck-up smart-arse, and nobody liked her. She was so superior and snobby thinking she was better than everyone else.

Anyway, six weeks later, she brings a positive pregnancy test around to our flat and tells Matt the baby's his. He really freaked. He'd always been so careful you see, it was a complete shock out of the blue. Plus, she'd told him she was on the pill, which turned out to be bollocks. Anyway, the day she turned up at our flat, she said her parents had thrown her out for bringing disgrace to the family, or some rubbish like that. So, Matt invited her to move in with us. We'd only just got our first flat after moving out of our parent's house, so we didn't have a lot of room.

Well, she made herself right at home in Matt's room, and crawled and crept around him, manipulating him, until he gave in and married her. It was just a quick registry office thing, wham bam you're married man." Darren paused for a moment. "A week after they were married, Matthew overheard one of her friends in the pub gossiping to somebody else about 'her friend Mary' who had drawn a blue line with felt tip pen onto a pregnancy test, in order to make the poor fella' who she fancied marry her! Well Matthew was livid. He went home and confronted her, and she burst into tears straight away, saying she just did it because she loved him. Matt threw her out, and then had to leave a while later after she kept stalking him. I didn't see him for six months. It was only after I heard he was modelling for the art classes at the college that I got in the campervan he'd given me the day he left and drove out here to find him."

Wow! Matthew had kept that little secret to himself hadn't he? No wonder we got along so well. We were both saddled with a crazy spouse!

"Well I never!" Exclaimed May.

"I know!" I agreed.

"Oh well, I can't be expected to keep secrets," said Darren sighing. "He knows I'm rubbish at it."

I cleared my throat. "So, is he divorced?"

"No. She won't sign the papers. She's an absolute cow. That's why he's avoided women like the plague for the last six months. She's put him off for life."

"I don't blame him; Neil's pretty much done that to me too." What a day of revelations this was turning out to be!

We spoke for another half an hour about Matt's fear of crazy women. I thought to myself, 'no wonder he hated me when he first met me and he thought I was torturing my husband for kicks. It all made sense now.'

Once we'd exhausted the subject of crazy ex's we got on to discussing 'the pig'. That lightened the mood immensely as we laughed over Neil weeing himself, at the suit clad bespectacled, comb overed, wigged pig.

"One thing I wanted to mention aunt May," I began. "The bromide that I gave Neil doesn't seem to be having any effect. Well I assume, I don't *know*." I said, raising my eyebrows. "But shouldn't he be more docile or something, less aggressive at least?"

"The vet said it would calm him down no end. Maybe you need to give him a bigger dose?"

"Mm, I've been wondering that myself. Yes, if he starts getting aggressive and arsey again, I'll re-dose him, see if that works."

After a few more gags at Neil expense, I finally bid my farewells and set off for home.

Legal Problems

All night last night when I should have been sleeping I was thinking about Matthew and his wife Mary. I thought I was the only person that I knew, that had to deal with a crazy manipulative partner. It just goes to show, you never really know what people keep behind closed doors do you? Poor Matthew. At least I knew now why he'd been so sympathetic and helpful; he'd been in the same boat. I felt very sorry for him. How awful to be tricked like that. At least I had loved Neil when we married, or rather loved the person I believed him to be. To marry someone you didn't even like must be terrible.

This was pretty much my train of thought for the whole sleepless night. Well, that and wondering about when Wonder Woman was going to lasso Neil for real this time.

Once it was finally morning, I got up and got dressed. I ran my fingers through my hideous Princess Diana hairdo, willing it to hurry up and grow back. Next it was the usual routine of getting Louise up, dressed, breakfasted, teeth brushed and off to school.

Neil seemed quiet all through breakfast I observed. He looked like a man with the world on his shoulders. Good.

After I got back from the school run, I was surprised to find Neil still at home. "Are you going in late today?" I asked, as I was wiping away the toast crumbs from the work surface.

"I've got the morning off while I go to see my solicitor." He sighed looking quite crestfallen.

"So, you've got a solicitor organised then?"

"Yes, but she's hardly the best. I'd rather be defended by a man but she was all I could afford." He sighed again deeply.

Sexist pig! I thought. "What time are you due there?"

"Ten thirty. I'll only be there for an hour and it's going to cost seven-hundred pounds." He sulked.

I rolled my eyes as my back was to him. "I wouldn't be too long before you set off then, traffic's crazy already." I wasn't bothered about him being late; I just wanted him out from under my feet.

"I'm going now." He said morosely. He finished the last swig of his coffee, and put his coat on. Picking up his briefcase, he headed for the door.

"Bye then!" I shouted after the slamming door.

Half an hour later I got a phone call from his mother. Had I ensured that I had 'something suitable' to wear to the upcoming garden party? She wanted to know.

Yes, I answered, after all I had a killer skin tight, tie-dyed mini dress I was dying to embarrass Neil with.

She also wanted to know if I would be going to a hair dresser first, as something had to be done about my unruly hair. Cheeky cow! I responded by asking her if she'd 'auditioned' any waiters for it yet, inwardly laughing. She seemed to sense my sarcasm and put the phone down on me.

What was it with that family and their inability to say bye?

The rest of my day was pretty un-eventful. Just the usual mundane housework, so I was quite excited to receive a phone call from Matthew later on that afternoon.

"Hi Sarah it's me."

"Hiya Matt, how are you?"

"I'm okay, I had Darren come over and stop with me last night. He wanted to come and tell me, he'd been blabbing all my deep dark secrets."

"Oh, I'm sorry. He really didn't mean to tell us, it was May goading him, and he sort of burst out with it."

"It's okay, I was gonna tell you both myself anyway, I just couldn't seem to bring myself to bring it all up again. I've spent nearly a year trying to forget about it all. But I'm glad you know now, it's quite a weight off to be honest." He did sound quite relieved.

"Well, anytime you want to talk about it you know where I am."

"I know, thanks. Anyway, what I'm really ringing for, I've got some good news, it looks like I'm getting a promotion already! I'm being promoted to supervisor! Can you believe it?"

"That's brilliant news, well done." I was really pleased for him.

"I know! Apparently it's due in part to the fast and efficient way I solved the problem of the pig in Neil's car. The boss was very impressed with me keeping a level head in a crisis, and being able to solve the problem quickly and easy without a fuss!" He sounded very pleased with himself. "Plus, he still thinks my CV is genuine."

"That's fab, what a brilliant idea that pig turned out to be wasn't it." How funny I thought. Neil's tantrum over the pig had only served to make Matthew look good. Serves Neil right.

He continued. "I also wanted to find out if you know Neil's been to his solicitors this morning?"

"Yes, he mentioned it briefly this morning."

"Ah, okay, just checking. We've got a new ally in Neil's secretary. She spied into his Filofax last night before she left and saw it in there. Just thought to keep you updated."

"That's great, thanks Matt, and thank Neil's secretary too."

"Will do. We're both dying for him to hurry up and get back. I snuck into his office earlier and loosened the nut under his chair. As soon as he leans back in it he'll go flying." He laughed.

I laughed too. "I'd love to see that! He'd be so embarrassed."

"Oh god" Matt exclaimed loudly. "I can't believe I nearly forgot to tell you. Yesterday Craig from the canteen put a slug in Neil's salad sandwich, and he ATE it!" He laughed again. "The entire factory knew what was in that sandwich, and we were all waiting with baited breath when he started to eat it. You could have heard a pin drop in that canteen!" He paused to regain his composure. "He ate every last bite."

I giggled. "Serves the son of a bitch right doesn't it!"

We chatted some more for another few minutes before Matt had to go. Neil was back and he wanted to watch out for him sitting in his chair. So with a smile I hung up.

After collecting Louise from school, I spent an hour helping her with a collage for art class.
She had to pick a subject that was close to her heart for the theme of the collage; and so we spent an hour cutting out photocopies of ten and twenty pound notes that we printed off in Neil's study. She added to this cash stash, cut outs of treasure from the National Geographic magazine, and spent ages scissoring around a photo that she found of the crown jewels. I was sure that the other children would probably be handing in collages of their family and friends, or perhaps horses and ponies. God only knew what her teacher would think when Lou handed in her treasure haul.

Just as I was tidying her thing away while she went to watch her program on TV, Neil arrived home.

"You're back early." I commented as I was picking up hundreds of tiny slivers of paper.

"Bad day! Had enough. Left!" Was the blunt retort.

"How did it go with the solicitor?" I asked.

"God, it was awful." He sank down onto the stool at the breakfast bar. "She was a complete bitch. You know the type, stuck up snotty career girl, a complete man hater, you could tell. Probably a lesbian come to think of it."

My god he was a bigoted arse! But I kept my trap shut and let him continue. After all, I needed to know what was going on.

"She spent the whole time trying to persuade me to plead guilty to all charges. She must be joking I told her. No way on earth will I plead guilty. Then she said, if I didn't I could be looking at a long prison sentence. Between the two counts of vandalism, dangerous driving, failure to display a tax disc, and assaulting a police officer, and with a previous criminal record, she tried to make out that I could get up to two years in prison! I told her she was out of her mind. But then she went onto say that if I plead guilty I would be lucky to get a sentence of maybe three to six months!" At this he looked like he started to hyperventilate. He took several deep breaths before resuming. "I need a better solicitor. I don't have any faith in that woman's competence at all. I need a more experienced legal team. I'm just going to have to raise the cash somehow; I don't care if I have to rob a bank. I can't go to jail!" He banged the counter top for emphasis.

I thought his last statement was a bit counterproductive; after all, robbing a bank to avoid jail as a plan seemed a little flawed. But instead I said. "How are you going to raise the money? Are you going to ask your parents?"

"Absolutely not! I do not want my parents to know about any of this! If they knew about this, they wouldn't believe I was innocent, they'd cut me off again! I'd be out of a job; they'd take this house, not to mention I'd lose my inheritance! No. Under *no* circumstances can they know!"

"Okay, I didn't mean to wind you up. I was just trying to understand." I tried placating him. "I promise I won't breathe a word to your parents."

He looked at me trying to size me up. He seemed to accept me at my word, and so relaxed a little. "I'll think of something, time is of the essence though. I have to go to the magistrates court on Tuesday to be given a proper court date for crown court. I'd rather turn up with a proper legal team and try and quash this thing there and then without having to wait for another court date."

He put his head in his hands. "Why is this happening to me? I haven't done anything to deserve this. I'm a model citizen, a good boss, a good son. I've been a good father and a loving husband. I just don't understand!"

I almost lost it when he said that! He thinks he's been a loving husband? And a good boss?

Good god he's delusional! I thought. I pretended to have a coughing fit while I composed myself.

"You ought to get that cough looked at you know. I've noticed it's getting worse."

I took a deep breath, cleared my throat and through gritted teeth I said. "Yes, I think you're right."

He nodded at my agreement. "Well I'm going to go and have a shower, get changed, and go down to the pub for a bit, try and clear my head. I'll get something to eat while I'm there. I don't know what time I'll be back but I've got my key. Don't wait up."

I had had my head in the cupboard below the counter pretending to be looking through for something. I stood up just as he was starting to get up. "Hang on," I said, "you've got something in your hair, let me get it." I swiped at the top of his head. "There, got it!" I said sweetly. That should give his comb-over a stretch.

The Getaway Car

Neil looked an absolute fright when he got up that morning. I possibly had overdone it with the hair removal cream the night before. His fifty-pence piece had more than doubled in diameter. I hoped he would blame it on all the stress of all the legal problems he was having. He had very big dark bags under his eyes, and he looked like he was getting a nervous rash. (Either that or it was the caustic soda that I had rinsed his flannel out in).

He was definitely looking like a man falling apart at the seams. He was already up before me that morning and I could hear him having a heated debate over the phone with someone who I presumed to be his bank manager. The gist of it seemed to be. "Can I have a loan so that I won't go to prison?"

"No, if you lose, working in the prison sewing room won't earn you enough in a week to buy me a stamp to put on your bankruptcy notice. Please go away and stop pestering me." I'm putting my own translation in there, but that was pretty much the thread of it.

When the bank manager finally lost patience with him, he hung up. Neil was left clinging to the receiver like a drowning man clinging to a life raft. He looked completely desperate. Part of me felt bad for him, but then I reminded myself about his mistress, and his mister, and the guilt went flying out of the window.

He finally seemed to pull himself together, in body but not facial expression, for he looked like someone had shot his puppy (or dyed it pink.) and simply said. "Going to work." It sounded quite robotic. He then left, as though in a trance and on auto pilot.

Perhaps he was finally cracking up? I wondered. All of this would never have happened if he had simply given me a divorce.

191

I spent the morning washing and ironing my new hooker dress ready for the garden party the following day. It was very short and very revealing. (Actually, I had better be careful or Neil might suggest I go out and earn the money for his legal team the old-fashioned way.) I briefly wondered if fat Wonder Woman would get tapped up for money too. Did he dare go riffling through her jewellery box looking for things to sell?

I also was curious as to if wonder woman had received the holiday snaps yet. I think if she had, she would have confronted Neil and if she had confronted Neil, I'm pretty sure he would at least have gained a black eye and a testicle retrieval operation. Hopefully as soon as she goes into the office headquarters to receive her wages she'd be given the envelope.

Once my dress was ready I hung it up on the back of my bedroom door -along with the six-inch heels that made me walk like a drunken drag queen, it should be an outfit to make Neil's mother twitch.

As usual just after one o clock I got a phone call from Matthew. I looked forward to our afternoon chats; it was the highlight of my day. He was calling to tell me that he'd sabotaged Neil's car yet again.

"What did you do this time?" I laughed.

"Well, I noticed that he'd managed to park in quite a tight spot this morning. It took him about fifteen manoeuvres to get in it, and about ten minutes. Well, it got me thinking. I've still got the key to it haven't I? I kept forgetting to send you it back. So, while Neil was out of the way, I borrowed a turkey baster from the kitchen and did a little mischief with his car. I popped the bonnet up and used the turkey baster to empty out all of his power steering fluid. You should have seen him huffing and puffing trying to get that car out when he left a little while ago. It wouldn't steer properly. He took his left-hand mirror off, with the right-hand mirror of his boss's Bentley. The Bentley's alarm went off straight away, so the whole factory looked out of the window to see what was going on. He noticed everybody watching him, looked like he panicked and floored it trying to get away and nobody's seen him since."

"Goodness me Matt, you're worse than me for inventing evil little pranks. With you I do believe I've met my match!" I was very impressed.

"All in a day's work comrade." He sniggered back.

"Is everyone there going mad that he stormed off after crashing?"

"I think they will be when the current crisis is over." He said thoughtfully.

"What crisis is that?"

"Ah well, it looks like there's been a robbery. Mr Hemsworth got Neil's secretary Brenda to call the police, because someone's been in the company safe and stolen ten grand."

"Good god." I paused. "Oh shit." I said with a sinking feeling. "I think it might be Neil."

"Neil? Why would he steal from the company? I would have thought ten grand was a drop in the ocean for him?"

"It was before all these legal bills wiped him out. He's desperate for money to pay for a lawyer that'll get him out of going to jail!" Oh dear, he was no master criminal robbing from his own workplace was he?

"It hadn't occurred to me that it was Neil. God no wonder he was in such a panic trying to get away. I had sabotaged his getaway car!" He started laughing.

"I can't believe he could be that stupid." I was bewildered.

"Oh, hang on, I'm going to have to go, the police have just arrived, I'm supposed to escort them up to the office. Take care; I'll see you soon, bye Sarah."

"Yes bye Matt."

I put the phone down in shock. Neil was now officially a thief!

I was in shock all day, thinking it can't be Neil. He wouldn't do such a thing, would he? I was starting to think that yes, he probably would. He was pretty desperate when he left the house that morning wasn't he? Surly he must know he's going to get caught. After all, there were probably very few people at the factory that had access to the safe, let alone the combination. Didn't he think he was in enough trouble already?

I drove myself crazy with it all for the remainder of the day. I half wondered if he would actually come home, or if he would've gone on the run with FWW (Fat Wonder Woman). I don't suppose they'd get far with ten grand and a highly recognisable Audi Quattro with pink wheels that smelt like rotten pork and couldn't steer round bends!

Fortunately Louise had gone home with a friend from school for a sleepover, so she didn't have to witness the state Neil was in when he finally came home.

He fell in the door around ten o'clock that night, stinking of whiskey and cigar smoke. I had just been getting ready to go to bed when I heard the tapping on the front door. As I opened it, the drunken Neil fell through it and landed on the floor in a heap - with his door key in his hand. I deduced that he had been knocking on the door with the key as he was too pissed to find the lock. When he finally staggered to his feet and leant up against the wall to get his breath back, I saw the lipstick stains around his mouth and noted his shirt tails sticking out of his half-opened flies. It didn't look as though FWW had opened the photos yet, and apparently the bromide hadn't worked. I later confirmed this when an empty condom wrapper fell out of his jacket pocket when I hung it up.

He threw up everywhere before I finally managed to get him into bed. He told me to go and clean it all up pronto, 'cause that was all that I was good for, cleaning up his puke! He then passed out cold.

It took me hours to clean all the puke out of the carpets, I was seething! I'd actually been starting to hope that maybe he had gone on the run with FWW. I did not expect to be on my hands and knees all night cleaning up his disgusting whiskey smelling vomit.

It was his parent's bloody garden party the following day; I hope he had a hangover for it, the son of a bitch. One thing was for certain, he was getting another dose of bromide for breakfast!

Bromide for Breakfast

I got up early this next morning, still fuming from the night before. I had barely slept all night listening to him snoring and farting through my bedroom wall. He'd gotten up in the night several times to vomit, at least managing to get to the toilet this time. Thank goodness, I couldn't face cleaning up any more puke.

I slid my dressing gown on, I wouldn't be putting my dress on until five minutes before we left, after all I didn't want to give Neil time to kick off about it. If he thought we were in danger of being late he wouldn't care if I was wearing a bin bag as long as I was in the car on time.

I went downstairs wrinkling my nose up at the smell of stale vomit and disinfectant. I had to work quickly before Neil got up. I had brought the remaining bromide down with me in my dressing gown pocket. When Neil had been in a state like this before he had always drunk a hangover cure, his friend from university had taught him. It consisted of orange juice, a banana, and two raw eggs. It was vile, but Neil had always sworn by it. I poured the juice into the blender, along with the peeled banana, and cracked two eggs into it. Next I added what I thought was around a third of the remaining bromide, then after thinking about how little effect it had last time, I thought, what the hell and in went the whole bag. After blending the hideous mixture for a minute, I poured it into a tall glass, and took it up to Neil.

I knocked and shouted "Neil, breakfast!"

"Ugh!" Was the reply.

Good enough I thought, and so I went in. "Good god it smells like a brewery in here!" I set the hangover tonic down beside him on his bedside table and made my way across the room, picking a path amongst the previous day's clothes that were scattered everywhere. I opened the window and gulped in the fresh air. "There, that's better." I turned to look at Neil and almost jumped at the horror that was squinting back at me from under the duvet. Good god he'd aged twenty years in the last few days! This half-bald, sickly, grey-looking old man was looking back at me with blood shot eyes.

"What do you want?" He whispered.

"We've only got a couple of hours before we have to go to your parent's garden party."

"Oh god!" He collapsed back against the covers. "I can't go, I'm dying." He pulled the covers back over his head.

"Fine, I'll go get the phone then and you can ring your mother and tell her you aren't going." I pretended to leave.

"Wait. Hang on. Just let me wake up a bit."

I smiled as I turned back to him. "This might help." I offered him the hangover cure.

He wrinkled his face up at the sight of it.

"Come on." I said. "You know this works, hold your nose and throw it down and you'll be fine in twenty minutes."

"Oh god!" He sat up in bed a bit. "Give it here." He held his nose and gagged the hideous concoction back. He was braver than me I'd give him that. Nothing on earth could make me drink raw egg with a hangover.

"There." He said handing me back the empty glass. "I'll just have another half-hour nap, and then I'll get up and get showered and ready." He slid back down under the duvet. That was it. I was dismissed.

I went back down the stairs feeling smug. I called Louise to check that she was having a good time at her friend's house, which she was. Her friend had very rich parents, and Louise delighted in telling me about the large indoor swimming pool that they had just had built, and how they were going to have a pool party there later that afternoon. I told her I was pleased that she was having fun and arranged that I would collect her later on that night. It had been quite convenient her friend asking her over, as I had been under strict instructions from Neil's Mother, that the garden party was adults only. I don't know what mischief she thought Lou would cause. She was usually pretty well behaved when at their house. But never mind, at least I hadn't had to hire a babysitter.

I spent the rest of the time getting my make up on and sorting my hideous hair into a sort of Marilyn Monroe 'do.' It wasn't brilliant, but I'd rather be a Marilyn than a Diana. Lastly, I slid into my skimpy tie-dyed hooker dress. With a quick look at my watch I saw that there were only fifteen minutes left before we would have to set off. Good. Time to go wake Neil up and put him in a panic!

"Shit! Shit! Shit!" Was his response on hearing that he had less than fifteen minutes to get showered and dressed. "How could you let me sleep this late?" He was ranting.

"You said you were just going to have half-an-hour. You never said you wanted me to wake you up. Plus, I thought I could hear you moving about up here." I reasoned.

At least he was too stressed to notice my arse almost hanging out of this bloody dress. I sauntered back down the stairs smugly, or at least I tried to. I tripped over my bloody drag queen shoes half-way down; I almost thought I would be okay as I flayed my arms out almost catching my balance. But no. I teetered and went down arse-over-tit and landed in a heap at the bottom with my dress wrapped around my head. I had just remembered why I stopped wearing these bloody shoes. I picked myself up with as much dignity as I could muster and continued towards the hall closet to try and find my light summer coat.

Ten minutes later and a very rough but clean looking Neil appeared. I had *really* out-done myself with his bald patch. He was going to have to seriously grow the sides in order to cover that monster with a comb over. His eyes still looked terrible, he looked very spaced out, still probably drunk. His chin was hilarious though. I loved it when he tried to shave in a rush. His jaw was peppered with little dots of toilet tissue where he had tried to stem the bleeding. My, his parents would be proud. Oh oh! I think he just finally realised what I was wearing. He was staring at me like I had two heads. "What?" I asked.

He shook his head. "Doesn't matter we haven't got time." He reached into the hall cupboard and grabbed his suit jacket. "Come on woman we haven't got all day!"

"I'm coming!" I said fiddling with the bloody shoes. "Whose car are we going in, mine or yours?"

"Mine. I won't be drinking today my head hurts too bad. Might as well travel in comfort than be cramped up in that bloody thing of yours."

"Fine by me." I was wondering if I could operate pedals in these sodding shoes, at least I wouldn't have to find out.

He ushered me into the passenger seat of his Audi, almost trapping my fingers in the process as he slammed the door after me. I had noticed the wing mirror hanging off as I had got in. I was going to innocently ask what had happened, but Neil silenced me with a stare.

Good god! The smell in here was horrific!

Neil got in the driver's side and threw his jacket on the back seat. He almost gagged too. "It's that bloody pig left that stench in here." It doesn't matter how many air fresheners I hang in it, or how long I leave the windows open, the bloody smell won't go!"

I bit my lip to stop the smile that almost slipped out. I had remembered the pig's trotter that Matthew had left under the back seat. God with the summer heat it must be really rotten by now. It sure smelt it.

Neil started the car up and tried to set off. He really had to fight to turn that wheel to make it move though. What a good idea it was to drain the power steering fluid. I never would have thought of that. It looked like he was almost going to throw his back out just trying to turn out of our road. Good.

And so, we were finally on our way to the party!

The Party

We finally arrived at the house on time with a stroke of luck. Neil pulled the car into the driveway with a little help from me. I had to lean over from the passenger side to help him pull at the steering wheel. I really had to fight not to giggle when I noticed Neil already had pit stains on his shirt just from the effort it had taken to steer the car. Eventually we finally steered it into the parking court between us. I got out of the passenger door, carefully as my bloody shoes were sinking into the gravel. Neil got his jacket out of the back and slid it on, hoping to cover the sweat stains. Smoothing his hands over his comb over he said to me "Come on then."

I looked back at him, and did a double take. My hand shot to my mouth in shock. "Good god Neil, you're covered in maggots!"

"What?" He looked down in puzzlement. "AGGGHHHHHHH!!" He started flapping his arms and screaming, swatting at his coat that was alive with maggots.

The coat had been on the back seat above where the rotten pig's trotter housed its new inhabitants. It seemed as though they had decided to move home!

Neil screamed like a little girl, flailing his arms and trying to get the coat off, but in too much of a panic to coordinate his arms properly. He started running in a blind panic, through the side gate and into the garden where his mother was just proposing a toast with her posh guests. He was still screaming and trying to pull at his coat desperately trying to get it off when he canon-balled into his mother as she had just raised her glass. She fell forward and emptied her glass of wine over the very expensively dressed lady in front of her. It was priceless.

Eventually a man stepped forward who had seen what was covering Neil's coat, and rugby tackled him to the ground. Once Neil was immobile and crying, the hero of the hour peeled the offending coat off him. It was brilliant.

I wished Matthew was here to see Neil being hoisted up by the armpits, sobbing, with a snot trail hanging from his nostrils, I'm sure it would have made his day.

Neil's mother Penelope was mortified! She did not see the funny side whatsoever, and the sight of her maggot ridden son careering through her posh garden party was too much for her. Added to this was the fact that she had just emptied a glass of champagne over the Lady Mayoress! Things were not going well for her. But at least it had distracted her away from my hooker dress.

Neil was then dragged inside the house on his father Trevor's instructions to be cleaned up and to pull himself together, while his mother tried to repair the damage with her guests. None of them seemed *that* bothered to me. It had given them something exciting to talk about. Better than the usual mundane topics such as "I like your shoes", or "nice handbag". Incidentally it was these two statements that became my own repertoire later on when I couldn't think of anything else to say. It's served me well over the years.

Eventually Neil came back out looking very pale and ill. I'm sure he would have rather gone home, but his mother would never allow it. He had to repair the damage he had done with his entrance.

I, on the other hand, was having a marvellous time. I had enjoyed the entertainment immensely, and was now on my third cocktail, the shoes were off and the hair was down. Penelope had finally noticed my dress and was silently giving me daggers. Good. Mission accomplished!

Next on my agenda was to have a little fun.

I awaited Penelope disappearing off to 'the powder room' as she put it. (She thought she was being posh by saying that but I just thought it made her sound like a coke head.) Once she had finished doing her business, I slipped into the now vacant toilet, and deposited into the toilet water, a sausage that I had stolen from the buffet table. It looked like a lovely little turd floating there. I slipped back out of the door checking that the coast was clear, and then removed the tiny glass vial from my clutch bag, and threw it at the wall across the toilet as hard as I could. (I had been so relieved a few days ago when I discovered that stink bombs could still be bought at joke shops.) Instantly the vile smell filled the toilet. I shouted in my loudest voice. "Ugh who was the last one in here? They've left a stinking turd in the toilet!"

Everyone who was in the huge hall where the buffet was laid out looked up at me as I shouted and then turned to look at Penelope who had just made a big deal about going into the 'powder room' because she thought she may have a wine stain on her blouse.

It's surprising how many of these so-called posh people actually went into the toilet to see the turd. They soon came out though balking and holding their noses. One of the guests called over to Penelope and shouted. "Good god Penelope what did you eat?" Holding his nose.

Penelope looked at me, purple with rage and embarrassment. I smiled sweetly back at her and joined the cue for the buffet.

Yes, I was having a wonderful time.

After I'd eaten a few vol-au-vents and a couple of sandwiches, I had a wander back out to the garden. It was a huge lawn that had been filled with tables and chairs; there were probably around a hundred people out here already. Some had joined the queue for the barbeque which smelt delicious, and some where gathered around what looked like a projector in the shade of the car port. I wandered over for a look. Oh god. It was Trevor showing his holiday pictures to his very bored looking guests. It was just another excuse to show off, look at us, we go skiing to Switzerland, aren't we ever so posh! Yuck!

I sniggered as I wondered if he'd show them a picture of the waiter he pulled.

I moved on to the next crowd of people that I saw congregating around a chocolate fountain. Yum. This one I liked. I stuffed myself with all manner of things dipped in chocolate, before I finally had to give up before I threw up. I decided to make my way back to the house to see if I could cause anymore mischief.

There was no sign of Penelope, but there was a very prominent 'out of order' sign on the 'powder room' door. I could still hear people whispering about it and chuckling.

I did find Neil though. It must be said; he didn't look very well at all. He was deathly white and trembling, I knew he was terrified of maggots but I thought he'd have calmed down by now. He was sat on the second step of the staircase; I asked if he'd seen his mother since 'maggot gate'.

He said. "She's not speaking to me, but she's over there."

As he nodded over to where Penelope now stood, I noticed his face drop. I followed his gaze to see Penelope deep in conversation with the Chief Constable. Oh dear. I got the impression that Neil's little secret was out of the bag. She looked back at Neil with a face like thunder, and started heading over to us.

Fortunately for Neil, the man who had saved him earlier from the maggots (who I later learnt was called Bob) whispered in Neil's ear. "Come outside right away."

I had heard too as I was sitting next to Neil.

As we stepped out of the side door, we heard the shouting. There was a large crowd of people gathered around the car port. Bob took Neil by the arm, and led him towards the crowd. I followed as quickly as my bare feet would allow, and to my shock and delight I saw the image being projected onto the back of the car port wall was one of the pictures I had sent to Fat Wonder Woman. She was here.

She was shouting at the top of her voice to the curious onlookers describing each photo in minute detail. She even had a pointer that looked suspiciously like a car antennae; which she was currently using to point out the very obvious bulge in the blonde 'lady's' shorts. Suffice to say, she was NOT happy!

She spotted Neil just as his mother had wandered over to see what all the fuss was about.

"YOU!" She bellowed, as she fought her way through the audience, trying to get to Neil. "You cheating lying son of a bitch! I'm gonna kill you!"

Penelope asked me in confusion. "Who is this person?"

"Meet your new future daughter-in-law Vicky!" I paused. "She's a stripper you know!" I was loving every minute of this.

Neil turned and started running, obviously terrified of the huge woman thundering after him. Unfortunately for Neil, he ran straight into the arms of a uniformed police man.

"Neil Pemberton?" He asked, still holding on to Neil's wrist.

"Yes," replied a bewildered Neil.

"I'm arresting you in connection with the robbery yesterday at the Flinton Factory. You have the right to remain silent. You do not have to say anything, but it may harm your defence....."

He never got a chance to finish reading Neil his rights, as Neil had fainted.

"Goddam it!" Uttered the police man. He turned and spoke to his colleague whom I had only just noticed. "Best get an ambulance, he's out cold."

What a day this had turned out to be! I think it was fair to say that Neil's parents would definitely never live down the scandal of today. Neil had showered their guests in maggots, I had stink bombed their toilet, they had found out Neil was going to prison, discovered he had a fling with a lady boy...which was revealed to them by their new daughter-in-law to be...Fat Wonder Woman! Who was a stripper! And if that wasn't enough, their son was then arrested for a robbery in front of all their guests, before being carted off in an ambulance with their drunken, shoeless, hooker-dress wearing daughter-in-law! You just couldn't make stuff like this up could you!

Not That Clever After All

Once Neil was taken (handcuffed to the stretcher) to the hospital, I was led off into a side room to wait for a doctor's diagnosis. I was told by the arresting officers who were on guard outside Neil's door, that they had had quite a few fainters in their day, it wasn't that uncommon apparently.

I was kept waiting for hours, wondering what was going on. Why didn't they just stick some smelling salts under his nose I wondered?

Eventually I had to bite the bullet and call Neil's parents to ask if they could collect Louise from her friend's house for me. It was Trevor that answered and I think it's fair to say that he was very short with me. I was definitely not in favour! But he did agree to collect Lou. He never asked after Neil though.

After what seemed like hours, a doctor came out to speak to the police officers on guard outside of Neil's room. They went back into the room with the doctor, all speaking in hushed tones. I wanted to know what was going on, and tried to follow them in, but they had locked the door after them. What was going on?

Eventually I found out.

The police came out from Neil's room and gestured for me to follow them into the side room. After we were all seated, the older officer gave me a long look. "Mrs Pemberton, your husband is suffering from acute potassium bromide poisoning."

"Oh my god!" I felt the colour drain from my face.

The officer continued. "Now you wouldn't know anything about that would you?"

I shook my head; I didn't trust my voice not to squeak.

"Now it's my opinion Mrs Pemberton, after overhearing at the garden party of Mr and Mrs Pemberton senior about Neil's infidelity, that you indeed knew of your husband's affairs, and had decided to do something about it. That something was to dose your husband with bromide."

Again I shook my head, looking away from the probing eyes of the two officers. Eventually I found my voice and asked meekly. "Is Neil going to be okay?"

"According to the doctors he should be okay in a day or two, but he's had his stomach pumped and they are currently flushing his system. You've been very lucky this time. You could very easily have killed him!" He pointed at me accusingly.

"I'm sorry; I didn't mean to hurt him. I just wanted to erm, calm him down a bit." I paused. "I asked him for a divorce you know, but he said he'd take my little girl if I left."

The police man's eyes softened a little. "You know we're going to have to arrest you, don't you?"

I nodded.

I was then read my rights and taken to the police station to await my fate.

I was told I would be charged with poisoning Neil, and a warrant had been issued to search my house for evidence. I was devastated, and had sobered up immensely.

I had felt very lonely all night in my little cell at the police station, I wasn't treated badly or anything, I was just in shock. I didn't know how May could be so nonchalant about being behind bars that time she was arrested for playing strip bridge. An hour later I could ask her myself as she was locked up along with me. The police having raided my house had found the bromide bag in the bin with May's name and address on it, and the words 'for Neil' written across the top. (Bloody vets).

One little twist in the tale though, was what the police had found in Neil's study. A small quantity of marijuana that was hidden at the back of a cupboard in there. (I'd forgotten I'd put it there out of the way of Louise's prying eyes until I could give it back to Darren.) But what really made the police pat themselves on the back was the 'forgeries' that they discovered in the tray of Neil's printer. These were the ten and twenty pound notes that Lou and I had photocopied for her art project. So, all in all, Neil was going to be charged with: - two counts of vandalism, failure to display a tax disc, dangerous driving, assaulting a police officer, robbery, leaving the scene of an accident, (crashing into the Bentley) possession of marijuana, and forgery!

May and I were released on bail the next day thankfully. When Neil recovered he was sent to prison on remand until his trial.

Eventually May was let off with a caution, she played the part of a dotty old lady who didn't know what she was doing, and the gullible police believed her and sent her on her merry way.

I on the other hand was charged, and found guilty. But due to the 'mitigating circumstances' my solicitor had highlighted, I was given a suspended sentence. (It was brilliant at my trial when the photos of Neil's lady boy were introduced as evidence. The jury got told off by the judge for laughing.)

Neil's parents severed all contact with both Neil and I, and applied for custody of Louise. As I now had a criminal record for being a husband poisoner, the social services sided with Neil's parents. It didn't hurt their case either that they were friends with the judge who oversaw the case. When Louise was questioned on who she would prefer to live with, she wouldn't even look at me, she just stated she'd rather stay with her grandparents who could better provide for her. (Louise's words). I was given visitation rights, but as she went off to boarding school the following year I only saw her through the holidays.

Everything I had planned for had gone up in smoke. Everything I had done was for Louise, to keep her with me, to stop her from being influenced by Neil and his stuck up snotty parents. I couldn't believe after everything that I'd been through I had lost.

I missed Lou dreadfully, although I eventually came to accept that this was a one-way street. She didn't miss me at all. This was the point where I had her tested for autism, and was told that she was just selfish. I didn't believe that though. Not at first anyway. But after a while even Neil's parents had started to notice that she only loved them for their money.

After losing Louise, the next blow was when Neil's parents sent the bailiffs round and had them throw me out. Bastards.

I went to live with May permanently after that, along with Neil's dog. Although I never forgot what those people did to me, and after all, you may have realised by now, I DON'T TAKE THINGS LYING DOWN!!!

Part Two
Back Home to Davenport

May was delighted when I came to live with her and Darren. Despite how miserable I was, I was glad to be living there too. Plus at least now Darren had an ally with which to fend off May's advances! She was forever trying to drag him off on some caper or another. As I've already told you, she took him to play bingo and ballroom dancing regularly. Poor Darren, he was only eighteen, most lads his age would be out at the pub with their mates, or clubbing, looking out for girls. But no, Darren would be holding May's handbag while she furiously tapped away with her pen on the bingo card.

Darren told me much later, that she once took him shoplifting too. Apparently he had taken her to an electrical shop to buy a cd player. She was sick of her tapes getting chewed up and so Darren had persuaded her to upgrade to a cd player. On arriving at the shop, May had tutted at the hefty price tags, and changed her mind.

"Come on Darren, let's go home." She said. "I've changed my mind. Too bloody dear for a poor old pensioner like me love."

So, after rolling his eyes and tutting, he headed for the exit with her. As soon as they got through the doors, all the security alarms started going off and Darren was promptly jumped by a security guard who dragged him off to the office to be searched.

The security guard ignored the little old lady who had also been heading through the door. By the look of the hippy looking lad who followed her, she probably would've been mugged once she was outside. Good job he'd caught the bugger.

She was a crafty old bird. She knew what would happen.

When Darren finally got back to his camper van that was parked up in the car park opposite the electrical shop, May was sitting in the passenger seat like butter wouldn't melt.

She smiled sweetly at him. "What kept you?"

Darren was too shocked to speak.

"We haven't got all day you know. I've got this lovely new cd player to play with." She grinned removing it from inside of her duffel coat.

Poor Darren.

May and Darren did their very best to cheer me up after I lost Louise to Neil's parents. I appreciated their efforts, and I did eventually come around. It was hard, but I just took it one day at a time. After all, Lou was happy where she was, I could go see her three times a week, and I could call her every day. I did eventually come to accept things, but I could never ever forget what Neil's parents had done to me. They would pay for it.

After the trial, I'd not really known what to do with myself. I moped around the grounds trying to take my mind off things, but my mind just kept coming back around to thoughts of revenge.

Matthew came to visit often, and he cheered me up no end with his visits. He's always make me laugh with something. He had decided to stay on at the factory after the whole Neil-gate thing. After all, everybody there was much happier now that Neil was gone. There was nobody more surprised than Matthew though when he was given another promotion. He was given Neil's job. I wrote to Neil in prison to tell him!

But whenever Matthew got any days off, he was back up here like a shot to stay with us. We had some great times that first year I came to live there.

One weekend he came up on a motorbike, I was quite surprised; he'd never mentioned that he liked bikes. Matthew and Darren spent the weekend trying to teach me how to ride the thing. I have to say, for the first day I was TERRIFIED of the bloody thing! But nothing on earth would have made me admit it to them. I plastered a fake smile on my face and pretended it was fun.

It wasn't. I fell off three times, and took a fence out when I couldn't find the brake. Matt and Darren were holding their bellies laughing at me. (Bastards). The only thing I hurt though was my pride.

By day two, after finally getting the hang of the clutch, I LOVED IT! I rode round and round the grounds for hours. I wanted one!

When it started to get dark, and I could no longer see properly, I joined the others in the kitchen. It was lovely and warm in there; I pulled my chair towards the stove to try and warm up a bit. I could tell they must have been talking about me as they suddenly went very quiet as I came in.

"Get this cuppa down you love, you'll soon defrost." May said, handing me a cup of tea.

"Thank you, I'm ready for that now."

"Good, tea won't be long either; I've got a nice casserole cooking in the oven."

"I can smell it, it's making me hungry."

I looked up to find Matthew grinning at me.

"What?" I asked.

"You love that bike now don't you!" It wasn't a question.

"Maybe." I smiled slyly.

"I knew you would if you gave it a chance. It's the first time I've seen you really smile in weeks." He was quite concerned wasn't he? Ah.

"True, but there was a lot of screaming before the smiling started." I laughed.

Darren chipped in. "When you took that fence out I couldn't help you for laughing. It just looked so comical." They were both sniggering now.

"Glad to hear I amuse you!"

"You've been amusing *me* since the day you were born love." May said, joining in.

"Yeah well, I think it's done me good the last few days, I feel more like myself again, stronger, able again. And I've been thinking, I'd better start looking for a job. I can't keep scrounging of you aunt May." I waved away May's protests and continued. "But while I've still got time on my hands, before I get a job, I'm going to get my own back on that pair of bastards Penelope and Trevor. They've took something away from me that I love, and now I'm going to take something away from them that they love. I've been thinking about it all day. What do they REALLY love? And then it came to me, they only thing they really care about is their precious reputation! Well, I'm gonna take it away."

May looked concerned. "Are you sure that's a good idea love, don't you think you've been through enough? Maybe time to put it all behind you now, and start again. A fresh start."

"I will have a fresh start." I replied. "But first I need a little retribution."

Darren was the first to speak up. "Well I for one am in!"

I smiled at him gratefully. I looked up at Matt; he shook his head. "Oh what the hell, count me in." He rolled his eyes at me with amusement.

We all looked at May. "Oh bloody hell, in for a penny in for a pound."

There. I had my troop back.

Phase One of Getting Even

We spent most of that night plotting and planning. Going over all the things we had previously done to Neil and laughing at it all over again, before discounting any of it as we didn't want to repeat ourselves.

May chipped in with some cracking ones before retiring to her bed at half past nine. Both Darren and I had noticed she was disappearing off earlier and earlier each night. We were a little concerned; she wasn't getting any younger after all, despite her juvenile behaviour. Whenever we broached the subject of her health we were told off.

"There's only the good die young, and nobody could ever accuse me of being good could they?"

We conceded she had a point. And so, after offering a few good suggestions, she departed leaving me, Matthew and Darren to laugh on our own. We came up with a few more ideas but nothing that really felt right - until the whiskey came out, then we got inspired with all kinds of wonderful and creative ideas. Fortunately for us, Darren had thought to get a note pad and write them down, which was a good job, as the next morning none of us could remember a thing.

We were all surprised the following morning with the ingenious plans we had made. By god that pair of bastards were going to suffer!

Once I had bid Matthew farewell - as he had to go back to work that morning, I started phase one of the plan.

I went to the Pemberton's local post office, where their mail was dispatched from, and asked for a post re-direction form. Wandering over to the little table at the back of the post office, I filled out all their details on the form as if I were Penelope. I ticked the box that said mail re-direction to last for six months. (It cost a bit but it would be worth it.) Next, I pulled the address I had written down earlier out of my pocket, and copied it down onto the form. The new address that I wanted their mail redirecting to belonged to...The Lady Mayoress.

I read on the form that a confirmation letter would be sent to their current address, just to confirm that all the details were correct. That would be the day after tomorrow, I worked out. I had put the commencement date for the mail to be redirected for three days' time. That was phase one complete. Next I had to intercept the redirection confirmation letter.

On the Wednesday, (the day I had worked out that the letter would be sent out); I was hiding behind a rhododendron in the Pemberton's garden waiting for the postman. Fortunately for me, the Pemberton's didn't have a letter box; all their letters went into a little post box at the end of their drive - which would make my job much easier.

Both Pemberton's were out for the day, and Louise would be at school, so this little operation was quite straight forward really.

Their garden wasn't overlooked by any neighbours, and so I didn't have to worry about being mistaken as a burglar. (Which was a good job as I had a suspended sentence remember?) As soon as the letters had been posted, and the post man was out of sight, I slinked around the shrubbery and began picking at the lock on the post box. It was a piece of cake; it only took a pen knife slid between the little door and the frame to pull the catch open and I was in business. I flicked through the handful of letters and thought to myself, mm it might be a while before they get any more of these! Ah ha. There it was, a letter from the post office. I stuck this in my back pocket, and put the rest back in the box, locking it back up.

I drove back home very pleased with my handy work. From tomorrow, all their mail would be sent to The Lady Mayoress, and I knew exactly what I was going to send.

Darren and I giggled like mad as we parcelled up the large box on the kitchen table. The box was empty but its contents were of no consequence. It was what was on the outside that mattered. We stood back and admired our creation, the large cardboard box proudly boasted on all four sides "CAUTION BULK ORDER SEX TOYS" underneath was a list of contents: -

4 BUTT PLUGS
4 RAMPANT RABBIT VIBRATORS
1 BOTTLE OF LUBE
1 PAIR OF HANDCUFFS
1 INFLATABLE SHEEP
1 RUBBER FIST
'Thank you for being a repeat customer.'

The Pemberton's home address was listed on the label, along with - 'F.A.O. Penelope Pemberton'.

But of course it would be redirected to the Lady Mayoress by 'mistake'. I would *love* to see their faces when their friend the Mayoress returns the package obviously meant for them. We got the feeling they might not be getting invited to socialise with the Mayoress anymore!

Me, May and Darren laughed for hours at the box sat on our kitchen table. The only problem was, we were all too embarrassed to take it to the post office to post. In the end, we drew straws for it. Darren lost.

We also subscribed them to Neil's former magazine, Bums, butts, nobs, and nuts. That would also end up at the Mayoress's. And for the sheer hell it, we rang a promotional company we saw advertised in a magazine, and asked for a free sample of vagisil.

It was such a shame we couldn't be a fly on the wall to see how our handy work would be received. But god it made us laugh.

May's secret

The following day was a Thursday, which meant I was allowed a visit with Louise after school. The Pemberton's weren't happy about it, but it was part of the custody deal so they were stuck with it. I don't know what they thought *they* had to complain about!

All day I was excited, I drove May mad with my pacing up and down, and so I was evicted from the kitchen and ordered to go make myself useful elsewhere.

I didn't mind. I thought as it was a nice day I'd get my wellies on and go and feed the chickens. It'd save Darren a job later I thought.

Once I was booted up, I made my way out of the back door and out through the kitchen garden towards the chicken runs. The rest of the gardens might be a wilderness, but Darren had kept the kitchen garden immaculate. The cobblestone floors were swept and free from weeds. There were planters set up full of runner beans, peas, sweet corn, potatoes, and goodness knew what else in the first section. Then there was the herb section, full of mint, parsley, rosemary, thyme, and basil. I made my way past all these wonderful sights and smells, picking a pod of peas as I went past. I went through the archway at the end that led me past the greenhouses that looked bursting at the seams from tomatoes. There was no wonder we all ate so well was there?

I meandered down the little path past the greenhouses and round the back to the hen houses. I was surprised by the sight that I saw. Darren had certainly earned his keep while he'd been here. I'd never seen it looking so nice. The chicken wire had all been replaced, all the timber had a fresh coat of paint, the lawn inside had been trimmed, and the hens looked perfectly fat and happy.

I spotted Darren through the window of the feed shed. I could also smell what he was smoking in there. I thought I'd wind him up seeing as I was bored. I banged on the door as hard as I could. "OPEN UP! THIS IS THE POLICE!"

I ran around the side and peeked through the window. He was in a right panic looking around for somewhere to hide the evidence. He gave up and was just about to try and swallow it when I burst in laughing.

"That's not funny." He fumed. "Good god my hearts racing!" He was holding his chest being dramatic.

I was still belly laughing at the look on his face.

He was starting to smile now too. But trying not to. "It's not funny."

"It is!" I gasped between laughs.

"No it's not!" he started laughing now too.

I think it was the fumes in the shed because we both laughed for ages after that.

After we'd composed ourselves he asked. "So, did you actually want me for something then or did you just come out to wind me up?"

"I came out to feed the chickens; I thought it'd save you a job, but you'd already done it. Plus, May threw me out for driving her mad." I was sat on a bag of compost that was quite comfortable I thought. I shuffled my bottom and got even comfier.

"She let you believe she threw you out for driving her mad?" His eyes were twinkling.

I was curious. "Darren, what do you know that I don't?"

He smiled and looked away shiftily. "Well after that little stunt you just pulled on me I don't know if I feel like telling you now." He pretended to be fascinated by a packet of seeds on the shelf.

"Oh, pleaseeee tell me! I'm sorry I wound you up. Tell me what she's up to?" I gave him my best pout.

He looked at me teasingly. "Fine I'll tell you." He looked down at his watch. "No, actually I'll go you one better, I'll show you." He hopped down off the compost bail. "Come on then, we'll have to be quick."

I chased after him dying of suspense.

He stopped a moment waiting for me to catch him up. He was heading back in the direction of the house, but not going back through the kitchen garden, he was going the long way around, heading to the dense shrubbery that hid the foundations of the old east wing. "Come on." He whispered, beckoning me to creep alongside of him quietly.

"Where are we going?" I whispered back.

"We'll have to hide behind this hedge so we won't be seen spying."

What the hell was going on?

He pulled me down beside him as he whispered. "Duck quick."

I did as was told. Trying to see where Darren was looking. After a few moments I realised there was someone coming. I watched fascinated as a figure started creeping down the side of the east wall.

"Who is it?" I whispered.

"Shh wait and see."

As the figure walked slightly out of the shade, I realised who it was, it was May's next-door neighbour, the doctor. "What's he doing?" I was puzzled.

"God! Shh. they'll hear us!" He whispered back.

"They?"

"Yes, they. Look."

I looked up to see a second figure joining the first. It was also sneaking down the side of the wall towards the doctor. Just what the hell was going on? I was fascinated. As the second figure reached the first, the pocket of light that had illuminated the doctor, now lit up May's face too. She placed both hands gently on the doctor's face, and gently kissed him on the lips.

What the Hell?

Then they both turned towards us. Bugger. We both ducked quickly.

When we heard no commotion, and it looked as though we hadn't been spotted, we peered back over again. They'd vanished.

"What the hell?" I said standing up. "Where did they go?"

They had absolutely vanished into thin air! I turned to Darren, expecting him to look as baffled as me. He was smiling knowingly.

"Darren, what the hell?" I was thoroughly confused. "Where did they go?"

"Come on, but be quiet, they might still hear us." He took my arm gently and lead me across the undergrowth to the point where May and the Doctor had vanished.

"Look." Darren said, parting the privet that had grown up against the wall.

I looked a little closer. It was an old wooden door.

Darren shushed me again and beckoned me to leave back the way we had come.

Once we were clear out of hearing range, Darren smiled. "Come on, I've got a flask of coffee in the shed, I'll tell you everything I know."

I was dying of suspense!

A Bit of Snooping

Once we got back to Darren's shed, he poured me a cup of coffee from his flask, and sat back down on a bag of compost. I sat back down on my own bale and got comfy too.

"So?" I asked. I was getting impatient.

"Okay, well, I've been here for months now right?"

"Right."

"Well, I started to notice a pattern after a few weeks of being here. On Tuesdays, Thursdays, and Sundays, come twelve o clock; May would be doing absolutely anything in her power to get rid of me. She'd send me off on errands, have me grass cutting, send me out on a wild goose chase. Anything at all to get rid of me. Well, I got suspicious, so I started going out of my way to make sure I was *always* here at twelve on Tuesdays, Thursdays, and Sundays.

It drove her mad. If she tried to send me out, I'd be back after five minutes because I forgot my wallet. If I was out doing jobs around the grounds, I'd think of some ridiculous question to come back and ask her. The madder she got, the more curious I got. *Then*, she had a word with my boss at the pub and tried to have my hours changed to..."

I finished for him "Tuesdays, Thursdays, and Sundays."

"Yes. Fortunately my boss said no, but, now I REALLY wanted to know what was going on. So I started leaving the house of my own accord at ten to twelve, and watching from a distance. I was as surprised as you were when I saw her kissing the doctor. I mean, he's married, isn't he?"

I nodded.

"After that strip bridge stunt perhaps I shouldn't have been so surprised. But then when they disappeared I was gobsmacked. It wasn't till the time after that I found the door that they had disappeared through."

I jumped in. "I didn't even know there was a door there. It looked like a cellar door or something didn't it?"

He nodded. "I'm sure that's what it is."

"I never even knew there was a cellar here. I explored every inch of this place when I was little, and I never saw that door before." I was perplexed.

Darren offered. "Do you think she'd had it put in recently then?" He too looked puzzled.

"No way, that door looks ancient, it's definitely part of the original east wing. I don't get it. It didn't used to BE there!"

We sat in silence for a while each with our own thoughts.

After a while Darren broke the silence. "What do you think to May having a boyfriend then?" He was finding it funny by the smirk on his face.

"I'm shocked." I said laughing. I really was! "Have you asked her about any of it?"

"No. You know what she's like, with most things she's an open book, but other things, she's really private about. I figured she's old enough to deserve to keep her secrets." He paused for a swig of coffee. "Doesn't mean I'm not dying to know though."

"Me too." I agreed. "I'd like a closer look at that door though. Have you ever tried the handle, see if it's locked?"

"It *is* locked. May must have the key somewhere, but like I said, I figured she's entitled to her secrets." He shrugged.

"Mm. Well I for one want to know. How long are they normally down there?"

"All afternoon."

"Bugger. I'll have to leave before then, I can go see Louise later you see, it's my day. But tomorrow, I want a proper look at the door. What do you say comrade? Do you fancy checking it out with me?"

"Curiosity killed the cat you know?" He was smiling.

"Yes, but satisfaction brought it back. Are you in or not?"

"Oh I'm in." We shook on it.

I went back to the house and made myself a cheese salad sandwich; all that snooping had given me an appetite. I decided to take it up to my room to eat up there while I pondered all that I had learnt.

I ate my sandwich and paced up and down my room thinking. Me and my brothers used to build dens in that shrubbery; it was our favourite place to play - off view from all the adults, plenty of wood lying around to build dens and forts with. I swear that door was *not* there! I once asked aunt May years ago when we were children if there was a cellar to explore. She said no, the water table out here was too high for houses to have cellars. I had been confused at the time, how could water be in the shape of a table? Bless. But if that door didn't lead to a cellar, where did it go?

I tried to work out the layout of the house in my head. The house front faced north, the east wing was to the left of the house if you viewed it from the front. The furthest point on the left-hand side of the house was the parlour at the front and the library at the rear, with a small sitting room in between which used to be the entrance to the now bricked up east wing.

I went to investigate.

I started in the parlour first examining the panelling for clues. It was a huge room that we hardly ever used, it was too big a room to heat in winter, and too warm to use in summer. We only really used it if we were trying to impress somebody. It was a stunning room, walnut parquet flooring under foot, maple panelling on the walls. A huge Stone fireplace that dominated the room was sadly covered in soot and cobwebs from years of neglect.

I tapped at the wall panelling listening for hollow spots. Nothing. Every tap sounded the same. I couldn't see any obvious seams in it either. Okay, not in the parlour then.

Next I tried the library. I tried not to come in here if I could help it. It must have been a beautiful room in its hay day. Hundreds of bookcases covered the walls reaching right up to the fourteen-foot-high ceiling. The only part of the walls *not* covered in books was the dirty leaded floor-to-ceiling windows. An old wooden ladder used to be here years ago, that slid around the shelves on a little track, but sadly it had rotted away with the damp. Most of the books in here were ruined. The once stunning plaster ceiling was now black with mould and mildew which had seeped down the walls too. When the bomb dropped on the east wing, a small fire had broken out and unfortunately the water used to put out the fire did more damage than the fire itself. None of us ever came in here if we could help it. It was too depressing.

I made my way over to the far wall to look for any sign of the mystery door. I parted the soggy books on the shelves and banged on the wall for hollow spots. But no. Nothing at all, it just sounded solid.

With one room remaining, I closed the door on the depressingly sad and beautiful library.

The last room to try was the small sitting room. I had to turn the light on in there as there were no windows or natural day light. To be honest none of us ever liked this room, it gave everybody that came in the creeps. I was terrified of it as a child, but now I'm older I think it's just the lack of natural daylight that makes it seem creepy - that and the millions of cobwebs in here. You could tell this room was never *ever* used.

It was a fairly modest room, around fifteen-foot by maybe eighteen. Small compared to the parlour. It had some pretty furniture in here, chaise longues, Gainsborough chairs, little tables dotted about, all covered in dust sheets though. I made my way through the cobwebs and around all the covered furniture to the far wall.

Originally this wall would never have been there, instead there would have been an archway with big double doors marked 'Private'. This marked the entrance to the east wing. I had seen the photographs of it. Once again I knocked all over the mildew covered wall, finding no hollow spots whatsoever, and so my conclusion was that the only place that outside door could go to was down. But to what?

Sadly today I didn't have time to investigate, but tomorrow was another day.

The Gods Must Be Laughing

I checked the clock in the hall as I left the little sitting room. Yikes! It was later than I thought; I'd better get my arse moving! I pulled my slippers off and slid into my boots, grabbing my coat and handbag off the coatrack on my way out. I just had a little errand to run on the way to see Louise.

I fought my little Nova through the busy school-run traffic and pulled up outside the pet shop. I went inside, looking into the various cages and fish tanks full of potential pets. I wanted something in particular to take with me to collect Louise. I had been assured by several people that this shop would have what I required. After asking the pet shop owner if he could help me, I was provided with what I wanted.

I slotted the small cardboard boxes into my handbag, and set off to get Louise.

On arriving at the Pemberton's I was told by a very unfriendly Trevor, that Louise wasn't ready yet, she would be another ten minutes. I was shown into the living room to wait - on my own! Perfect. It was just what I was hoping for.

I reached into my handbag and pulled out the larger of the two boxes. But where to open it? I looked about me. I didn't want what I had done to be too obvious, but time was of the essence. I opened the bottom drawer of the antique bureaux that was on the far wall, and emptied the contents of the box into it. Five-hundred crickets were very excited to be out of that tiny box! I shut the draw quickly. They'd soon find their way out of the back of the drawer anyway, but hopefully not until I was far away.

The second box might not be quite as easy. I cracked the living room door open and peeped out. I couldn't see or hear anyone, so I crept out and across the hall to the umbrella stand that lived below the coatrack. In it were propped his and hers umbrellas, and I happened to know that Trevor and Penelope had a meeting in town tomorrow and it was forecast to rain. I started with the first umbrella unravelling the little ribbon that kept it closed, and pulled it open a little bit. Next I opened the lid on the last box, and poured around half the box of (about two-hundred) Meal worms down into the umbrella. I then closed it back up tight and wound the little ribbon back around it tightly holding it closed.

I quickly repeated this on the other umbrella with the remaining half of the box. There, when they opened them tomorrow they'd be wishing they'd got wet instead!

Inwardly laughing, I crept back into the living room to wait for Louise. I didn't have to wait long. I'd barely sat down when she came in.

I shot up to give her a hug, god I'd missed her. She returned my embrace with a very stiff hug and an expression I would have expected off Penelope.

"I've missed you Lou. How are you?" I said stroking her hair.

"Have you?" She asked sharply. She was a prickly little thing.

"Course I have, you're all I think about. Have you missed me?"

"Not particularly." She really did look completely indifferent to me.

"Are your grandma and grandad looking after you okay?"

"Fine. I prefer it here. I've got a TV and video in my room, and next week I'm getting a computer."

"Oh, that's great sweetheart, I'm glad you're happy. You do know that just because we don't live together now doesn't mean I love you any less don't you?" I was desperate for her to know this.

"Of course, but things are much better this way, grandma says now I won't learn your common ways." She said this so matter of factly I was cut to the quick.

"Come on." I said taking her hand. "Let's get your coat on and get to the cinema before we miss all the good bits."

At least in the darkened cinema as she was absorbed in the Lion King she couldn't see me crying.

However, it wasn't all tears that night. The gods had decided to throw me a bone.

As I was saying goodbye to Louise as we stood in the Pemberton's hall, the doorbell rang. I couldn't believe my eyes, it was the Lady Mayoress.

Penelope was delighted at her unexpected visitor. "Come in, come in, how nice to see you!"

She didn't seem to notice the Mayoress's obvious discomfort, or the large box under her arm. "I'm sorry to turn up un-announced like this, but this seemed like a..." She paused. "A delicate matter."

"Oh yes? Is something the matter?" Penelope wanted to know.

"Well, yes. You see, a parcel was delivered to my house today by mistake. I do believe it should have been sent to you, as it has... erm...your particulars on it, name and address and such." She was blushing terribly.

"Oh yes?" Penelope was looking pleased. "An unexpected gift how wonderful."

"Well, here you go." she handed the box to Penelope. "Now I really must be on my way. Goodbye." She practically ran out of the door.

"Goodbye!" Penelope called after her. "Do call again."

She put the box down on the hall table and went to fetch her spectacles.

All the time this exchange had been taking place I had been routed to the spot barely able to breath with anticipation.

Penelope returned with a self-satisfied smile and a pair of glasses on. She looked down at the box before her and froze. The smile on her face morphed into a grimace as she realised what the label said. All colour drained from her cheeks.

Louise noted her grandmother's strange reaction and wandered over to investigate. She peered at the label her grandmother seemed unable to look away from and asked, "Grandma, what's a butt plug?"

God bless her I nearly peed my pants.

It seemed to waken Penelope from her reverie though. "Bed time Louise. Now! Off you go."

Louise said a sulky goodnight to me and went up to bed.

Penelope finally seemed to register my presence. "It's time for you to go." She said, in a very harsh tone.

I glanced pointedly at the parcel as I went passed. "And to think you got custody of my daughter?..........Pervert!"

Then I left before I could ruin the moment by laughing.

The Door

I got back to find Darren and May both in the sitting room next to the kitchen, in front of a blazing fire. Neil's former dog Butch was curled up looking very cosy in front of the hearth. This room used to be the servants break room where they could have a comfortable seat between shifts, a quite small room by the standards of the rest of the place, but we all preferred it as it was cosier. Especially when the fire in the hearth was lit. There was an autumn nip I the air that night, so I was grateful for the warmth.

Once I had sat down, kicked off my boots and given my dog a cuddle, I told them all about who I had seen while at the Pemberton's.

"My goodness!" May said, wiping at her eyes with a handkerchief. "I bet the look on her face was priceless."

Darren joined in. "I wish I could have seen it. After the embarrassment of taking that box to the post office I can bet how she felt. But at least when I took it, it didn't have my name and address printed all over it."

"And repeat customer stamped on it!" I snorted. When I finally composed myself I continued. "I haven't told you the best bit yet; Louise wandered over to the box, and looked up at Penelope and said 'Grandma, what's a butt plug?' I nearly wet myself." We all laughed again.

Next I told them about the new little wind up with the crickets and meal worms. We all agreed the noise from the five-hundred crickets I had released into the house would be deafening when they all started chirping. It would drive them insane, and there would be no way they'd ever catch them all.

"I don't know where you get your ideas from love, but you've certainly kept me entertained." May stood up yawning. "But it's no good, I'm going to have to get myself off to bed."

"Okay aunt May, goodnight."

"Night love, night Darren."

"Goodnight May, don't let them bed crickets bite."

She left with a tired smile, she was really starting to look worn out lately, probably all those afternoon sessions were wearing her out.

Once she was out of earshot, I turned to Darren. "I can't stop thinking about that door. I'm dying of curiosity."

"Me too."

"Let's get a torch and go have another look." My eyes were shining.

He laughed. "God you're as bad as May for dragging me into things. Let me get my boots on while you find a torch."

I did one better; I found a torch and an oil lamp. "Come on Darren, we haven't got all night."

"I'm coming."

We made our way out of the back door and went the long way around, through the kitchen gardens and past the hen houses, we didn't want to go the front way around as May might hear the front door creak.

"God it's so dark out here." Darren complained.

"You don't realise how much light there is at night in a town compared to out here in the country do you?" I agreed fighting my way out of some privet that had leaped out and grabbed me.

Darren got snagged on the same privet just as I got free. "Oh bloody hell, I'm stuck!"

"Hang on I'll help." I shone my torch up to where he was struggling, and spotted the snagged privet branch stuck to his sleeve. I pulled it free from his coat and we continued.

"It's over this way I think." He said leading the way with the lantern. "Shit. Whoa!"

I shone my torch after him finding him laid across a stray rhododendron root. "Darren this isn't the time for laying down on the job!"

"Ha ha very funny."

"Come on." I offered my hand and helped heave him back up.

We were pretty much parallel with the door now. I shone my torch while Darren lifted his lantern. It was just as it had seemed earlier, a large oak, arched door. It had very old and worn looking hardware on it, black iron by the look of it. I would have sworn that door never used to be there.

Darren reached out and grabbed the handle, but he was right, it was locked.

"Bugger." I said. "Should have known it wouldn't be that easy."

Darren put his oil lamp down in front of the door and stood back looking thoughtful.

"What?" I asked, standing back with him and shining my torch on the door.

"Can I borrow your torch a minute?"

"Here you go." I offered it.

He took it and shone it at the masonry around the door. "Have you noticed how much the door is recessed into the wall? The walls around it are proud by a good ten-inch or so."

He was right. I hadn't really noticed before. I looked closer. According to what May told me, after the east wall had been repaired from the bomb damage, it had been coated with a thick rendered layer of cement to hide the scars. Now though, that render was falling off in big chunks all over the wall. Was it possible that originally the door had been rendered over? But now with the render crumbling the once hidden door was now visible?

I shared my theory with Darren.

"Looks like it doesn't it? But why cover it up, why not just render round it?"

"If we hadn't seen May going in and out of it I would just have thought it was the old blanked off door from the old wing of the house." I volunteered.

"No, it definitely is a working door that goes somewhere." He rubbed his chin looking perplexed.

"Come on then, let's go have a brew and a think. It's bloody freezing out here." I said as I picked up the oil lamp from below the door.

"Sounds like a plan."

We got back to the house without any mishaps this time, and after getting settled in the little sitting room with a cup of coffee, we continued pondering the mystery of the door.

"I don't know why aunt May would lie about the existence of the cellar. She doesn't even have the excuse of not knowing it was there, she was the one who had the east wall repaired and rendered." I was getting a headache trying to wrap my head around it.

Darren also came out with a good point. "If May was working here in the Hotel before the bomb dropped, as a servant she'd have to go down to the cellar, wouldn't she? Didn't they used to use cellars as refrigerators or something in those days?"

"Yes, and for coal storage, so yes you're right Darren, with the sort of jobs she used to do here that would have been part of her job, fetching things up from the cellar."

After a while we finally voiced the troubling thought that was on our minds. 'What was she hiding down there?' We were stumped.

"So why have it all boarded up and deny its existence for decades, and then suddenly un-board the door and start using it as a love nest?" He questioned.

238

We sat in silence pondering the situation.

"Do you think she's started using it again because she's worried that we'll catch her with the doctor? You know with him being married?" Darren questioned.

"Maybe. Perhaps it's something as simple as the render crumbled away from the door because of all the damp on that side of the house, and it's presented an opportunity as a little love nest." I was getting excited now. "Perhaps what she was hiding down there isn't there anymore; maybe whatever it was has been moved!"

"Makes sense. She hid something down there that she didn't want people to know about, got rid of the door. Then years later when the door became visible again, she's moved whatever it was out of there and started using it to play doctors and nurses."

"Ugh don't Darren." I cringed.

"I wonder if they used to play hide the sausage in the house before we moved in? Maybe it's the worry of us catching them that's forced them into the cellar?"

"Probably. She's always been very private about her love life. I once asked why she'd never been married, and she got very cagey about it. Something along the line of 'men are all bastards as soon as they've got a ring on your finger.' She did say she'd been in love once though, years ago. When I asked who with she just tapped her nose and winked."

"Do you think it's been the doctor all along?"

"Could be. They went to school together, so they have known each other all their lives." I pondered it. "I think his name's Peter."

"That's it. I knew I'd heard her call him by name the night she got arrested. Peter, yes that was it."

We speculated about it all for another hour before we got too tired to continue. Before we parted for the night we made an agreement. To find the key.

Where's the Bloody Key

The following morning was a Friday; at least Darren and I didn't have to worry about May and the doctor's bedroom antics today, and as it was May's day to go play bingo down at the community centre, she would be out of the way for a while.

The morning dragged for me and Darren, waiting for May to hurry up and leave. Minutes ticked by like hours. We both tried keeping busy, Darren out in the kitchen garden and me armed with a can of polish and a duster. But one bit of good news came with the ringing of the telephone; Matthew had the afternoon off and was coming up to join us. Brilliant. Matthew would love this little mystery, and it was one more person to search for the key.

Eventually May left for bingo - disappointed that Darren wouldn't go with her. He had too many jobs to catch up on before work later, he told her. I point blank refused to go, I've never seen the attraction in bingo, as well May knew. She'd dragged me there when I was little many-a-time. She eventually stopped taking me after I embarrassed her by sitting down cross-legged in the bingo hall and crying. That was the first time I learnt the art of passive aggressiveness. I never had to go play bingo again.

As soon as May was safely out of the way, Darren and I began the search. We went through the kitchen drawers first looking for the odd keys that were usually scattered about in there. None that we found looked big enough; these mostly looked like cupboard or drawer keys.

We were just searching though the bureaux drawers in the sitting room when Matthew arrived.

"Hey Sarah, give us a hug!" He said grabbing me and swinging me around before I had chance to say no.

I laughed as he put me down. "Nice to see you too Matt." He was a good cuddler I'd give him that. He did look funny in a suit though, I'd never get used to him looking so sensible. I preferred him scruffy.

"Darren!" He exclaimed, walking towards him.

"Don't go thinking you're picking me up like that Matt, I'll belt you one." He said trying to side step out the way.

"Come here Darren; come give your favourite brother a hug." He was chasing him now.

"Get off!" Darren was laughing as Matt caught him and bear hugged him till his feet were a foot off the ground. "You soppy sod!"

"Just glad to be home. There's nowhere like it is there?" He asked grinning. "What are you two up to anyway, why are you ransacking the place?" He was looking about him at the opened cupboards and drawers.

Darren and I looked at each other. "Long story."

After filling Matthew in on all that had happened, he wanted to see the door.

"You might want to take your suit off though; it's filthy out there in those bushes." I said.

"I've told you before." he said winking. "If you want me to take my clothes off its fifty-quid an hour. More if you're dragging me off into the bushes."

"God Matt, give over you'll have me blushing." I elbowed him.

"Yeah I saw you blush last time." He was staring at me smiling.

Maybe May was right, perhaps he did like me?

"I was blushing with good bloody reason! It's not every day you come face to face with someone's nipples." I countered.

"I don't remember it being my nipples you were staring at!"

Darren was getting impatient. "If you two have finished flirting can we get going?"

"Sorry *Darren*." Matt said mockingly before adding, "Just remember Sarah, in fairness, it was *very* cold that day."

I laughed and looked away embarrassed before changing the subject. "Why don't you two go and look at the door, and I'll have a quick look in May's room, see if she's left the key on her dressing table or something?"

"Okay, but hurry up and get changed Matt." Darren said impatiently.

"Fine, I'll be two minutes."

I left the two of them bickering and headed to May's room.

I didn't feel right snooping in her room, I felt like I was invading her privacy, but as the devil on my shoulder kept whispering, May had said that one day this place would be mine, she'd had it written into her will years ago. It wouldn't be fair to inherit somewhere like this that had some deep dark secret hiding in the cellar. Forewarned was forearmed.

I opened the door into her small but neat and tidy room. She's never had any other bedroom in the place except this one. Odd, when she could have taken her pick from any of the other lovely rooms. But that was May, she liked what she liked.

I refused to go looking through drawers or anything like that, I couldn't be that intrusive, but if the key happened to be on show, it wouldn't hurt to borrow it for a little while would it?

I was in luck; there on her dressing table was the large bunch of house keys that she often kept with her in her pinafore pocket. Hopefully one of those would be the cellar key.

I took the bunch of keys and legged it back outside to join Matt and Darren. I was out of breath by the time I got there. "Think, I've, got, it." I panted.

They gathered around me to look at the keys, many of them were far too small to be what we were looking for, but three of them seemed like good contenders.

"Give 'em here then." Matthew said, as he was closest to the lock on the door.

I handed them over and held my breath as he tried the first one.

No. Wouldn't even fit in the lock properly. Key number two, slotted into the lock but wouldn't turn. He discounted it. With a sigh and a raise of his eyebrows as he looked at me and Darren, he slotted in key number three. I took a deep breath as he slid the key into the lock. With an audible click, we were in.

As none of us had thought to bring a torch, Matt and I waited outside while Darren ran back for the torch and the oil lamp we had used the night before. While we were waiting, I filled him in on all the awful things I'd been doing to the Pemberton's. We had a good laugh over it all while we were stood dying of impatience for Darren to return.

Finally, he was back armed with lights. Time to go in.

Matthew went first, pushing the door open wider as he disappeared into the blackness with me and Darren following close behind. It was a huge stone staircase that we were descending. How this cavernous set of stairs had been here all this time without my knowing seemed impossible. We descended to a depth of around fifteen feet I estimated before it opened up before us. The cellar was enormous! It seemed as though it ran underneath the whole house. We travelled down a central passageway that had several large rooms veering off from it.

Dotted here and there on the white-washed walls were oil lamps and candle holders. This part of the house had obviously never been upgraded to electricity.

The first room that we came to looked like the love nest of May and Peter. It even had an old brass double bed. The rest of the room was empty apart from a small paraffin heater, and hundreds of candles covering the floor and walls. I broke the awkward silence. "Let's not look too closely in here, there's things that I really don't want to know about!"

"Agreed!" Matt and Darren said in unison.

The next room we came to was a coal store, still full to bursting as though a delivery had been made just before it was sealed off. Matthew shone his torch up to the roof. "Look, there's a trap door up there. Probably where they used to throw the coal down."

I looked at where his torch beam was pointing. He was right. "There's no sign of that trap door upstairs though." I said. "That must have been covered up too."

"Very odd." - Was Darren's contribution.

We continued on. The next few rooms were filled with furniture; hundreds of bedframes were stacked up to the rafters in one, dressing tables and wardrobes galore in the next.

"Why hasn't aunt May sold all of this? Some of this stuff must be worth a fortune. It's all antiques isn't it?" I really didn't get it.

"No sign of the big secret yet either though is there?" Darren added.

The next few rooms had nothing but old milk churns in them, probably from when the cellar was used as a chiller, as Darren had suggested.

The last-but-one room was completely empty; we'd been disappointed to find no clues at all. Just a ten-foot square, empty cobwebbed room. The last room to try was at the very end, but it was locked.

Help from a Busty Blonde

We were all very disappointed. Darren went back the way we came to retrieve the bunch of keys from the cellar door. Hopefully there should be the key to this door on that bunch.

"What do you think could be in there?" Matthew asked me while we were waiting for Darren.

"I wish I knew. I just hope to god it isn't a body." I rubbed my arms; it was getting cold down here.

"Cold?" Matthew asked.

"Freezing, aren't you?"

"I'm a man."

"So that's a yes then is it?" I sniggered.

"Okay yes, I'm goddam frozen actually. If Darren doesn't hurry up you're gonna have to keep me warm."

I tentatively cuddled up a little against his side, feeling his arm slide around my back.

"I'm here. I've been as quick as I could." Darren was panting from running.

"Oh now he's here!" Matthew tutted, letting go of me reluctantly.

He held up the bunch of keys to the light, looking for one a similar size to the lock. After discounting most of them he was left with the remaining two.

"I'll give it a try then eh?" Darren said, inserting the first key. Nothing. It wouldn't turn at all. "Last one then, hope to god this one fits, I can't stand the suspense!" He tried to fit it into the keyhole but, no, that wasn't the right one either.

"Bloody hell!" I exclaimed kicking the door. We had come so close! "We'd better turn back." I said with disappointment, after holding my watch up to the lamp light I could see that it wouldn't be long before May would be back. "We don't want to get caught down here do we?"

And so, feeling dejected, we left the cellar with its strange locked door for another time.

Once back in the house I slipped up to May's room and put the bunch of keys back where I had found them. It was fortunate that we had returned when we did, for when I came back into the kitchen May was already there telling Matthew and Darren about her day at bingo. She had come back an hour early with a headache. While she was chatting to the boys I made us all a cup of tea, and sought out some paracetamol for May.

"Thanks love." She gratefully swallowed them. "Hang on a minute, these aren't diuretics are they?" She teased.

"Nope, just laxatives." I joked.

"Oh good, I was feeling a bit bunged up." She teased back.

"So, what have I missed then while I've been out?" She looked at us from one to the other. We'd all frozen trying to think of something to say.

Finally, I stammered out. "Plotting again aunt May."

"Ah good! I hoped you were. I could do with a laugh, what you up to next?"

"I don't want to spoil the surprise." I genuinely did have a plan, but I wanted to show her my 'project' once it was finished.

"Oh well, something to look forward to then eh love?" She smiled at me.

"Trust me aunt May you'll love it. In fact, once I've finished it tomorrow night I'm taking you on a road trip to see it!" I raised my eyebrows at her and gave her my best mischievous grin.

She laughed, "Can't wait."

The following day was Saturday, one of the day's I was allowed to spend time with Louise and another opportunity to gain access to the Pemberton's house.

After spending the morning playing hide and seek with Matthew and Darren - much to May's annoyance, I set off to buy the new prop that I needed with which to wind up the Pemberton's. It took a few trips round different shops before I found what I was looking for, but it was well worth the trailing about for. I had to take my largest handbag with me in order to hide the large folded up and rolled up scroll that I now had tucked away in my hand bag.

As usual I was left to wait in the living room by Trevor while Louise was getting ready; I noticed Penelope was avoiding me since I called her a pervert. I presumed that Trevor and Penelope must be hiding in the kitchen until I left. Perfect. But I had to work fast.

I walked across to their large front window, and taking hold of the cord, pulled the roller blind down into the closed position. Next, I pulled out the rolled-up poster that I had purchased earlier from my handbag and unrolled and unfolded it. I then took out a couple of safety pins from my pocket, and pinned the poster to the inside of the roller blind before very carefully rolling it back up. Ha! From inside the room when they pulled the blind down it would look perfectly ordinary, however, anyone outside that happened to be passing by would see exactly what was on the outside of the roller blind!

I couldn't wait to drive past with May later. If the poster I had hung in their front window didn't make her laugh, I didn't know what would!

I sat back down on the sofa to wait for Lou. I couldn't help but grin to myself at the crickets making such a racket! It must have been driving them insane!

I sat listening to the chirruping noise smiling for another five minutes before Louise came sulkily in. She wasn't happy to see me.

"What's the matter love?" I said getting up to greet her.

"It's not fair!" She scowled back at me.

"What do you mean? Living with your grandparents?" I was concerned, perhaps she was finally realising that this was a permanent arrangement. Maybe the shock was wearing off?

"No! I mean having to go with you. Felicity was having a party today but I'm not allowed to go because I have to spend the day with YOU!"

Good god. This was a chore for her was it? Spending time with me?

After speaking to Trevor about Felicity's party that Lou wanted to go to instead, I ended up leaving without her.

They only slight silver lining was when I observed the two missing umbrellas from the hall.

I went home and sulked.

Matthew came out to the garden to find me. I was hiding in Darren's shed while he was at work at the pub. I ignored the first two knocks on the door. I hoped if I was quiet enough he'd get the message and go away. But no, he stopped knocking and charged the door until the little bolt snapped. "Ow!" He yelled holding his shoulder as he came in.

I looked the other way but said under my breath. "Big girls blouse!"

"Hey, I've just been all gallant breaking the door down to make sure you're alright. I've got a bloody war wound now!" He said petulantly.

I looked up and smiled it was a minute scratch.

He sat down on the compost next to me, and shuffled up close. "Made you smile!" He teased.

"No you didn't!" I hid my smile behind my hand.

"Yes I did!" He said tickling me under my ribs.

"Get off me you big girl's blouse." I was laughing now and slapping at his hands.

Once we stopped giggling, we sat in silence for a while.

"I hope you didn't hurt your shoulder."

"Give over." He laughed. "Told you, I'm a man!" He looked closer at my tear stained face. "It's really got to you today hasn't it?"

I nodded, I still didn't trust my voice.

"Come here you silly sod." He put his arm around me and hugged me tight.

"Sorry." I said. "I'm not usually such a girl." I wiped my eyes with the back of my hand.

"I know!" He laughed. "No one could ever accuse *you* of being a big girl's blouse, could they?"

I smiled despite myself. "No, probably not. Especially if they saw what I've just done to Penelope's and Trevor's house!"

"Can I come with you and May later for the grand reveal?"

"Course. I was going to take a photo for you if not."

"Great I can't wait." He smiled. "Do you feel like coming back in the house now? Me and May were gonna play strip bridge if you want to come and watch?"

"How can I say no to that?" I laughed.

He pulled me up from my compost bale. "Come on then comrade; let's go cheer that old bugger up."

The rest of the afternoon was spent laughing at May and Matthew who were desperately trying to outdo each other. They had each put on about fifteen jumpers and who knew how many pairs of socks, sweating away playing strip bridge in the kitchen for hours. By the time May finally won, they both still had enough clothes on to clothe an army!

As soon as it got dark, I packed them both into my little Nova and took them on a little trip to the Pemberton's house. We pulled up opposite their driveway and admired the view. Their colonial-style home with its graceful columns and archways looked magnificent in the moonlight, but not as magnificent as the large pair of breasts that were hanging in their living room window. It was a shame they hadn't rolled the blind down quite far enough, they'd cut off Samantha Fox's head!

I commented. "I thought this was appropriate, I always thought they were a pair of tits!"

We all laughed and snorted at the sight of those 36DD's hanging there in the lovely leaded bay window. Wonder what their neighbours would think?

We also wondered how long it would take the Pemberton's to notice?

What's life without a little mischief?

Over the next few days, I upped my game with the Pemberton's. Matthew had gone back to work for the week, Darren was doing extra shifts at the pub while someone was on holiday and May was out at various things, bingo, tea dances at the community centre, and of course her afternoon loving with Dr Peter.

I had been to the job centre and applied for a few different things, but to no avail. There were too many people and too few jobs. I kept popping back in and checking for new jobs every few days, but didn't have any luck.

Well as I've said before, it's not a good idea to leave me with too much time on my hands; I tend to find all sorts of mischief. My project for that week was to terrorise the Pemberton's. I'd been informed the night before that they would be sending Louise off to boarding school at the start of the next term. They didn't ask me, they told me! Louise was all for it, she thought it was wonderful, but I was NOT amused! Now I'd only get to see her when she was on holidays. I was devastated and livid. I was also determined to get even!

On the Monday morning, the sun was shining for the first time in days, a perfect day for catching up with some gardening I thought. It wouldn't be long now before autumn would turn to winter, and so there were very few opportunities left for pottering in the garden. Unfortunately for the Pemberton's, it was their garden that I decided to potter about in.

After sloping around the side of their house to see if their cars were there, I quickly deduced that no one was home. Good. The lawn was Trevor's pride and joy, he had spent a fortune on it over the years with various tonics and feeds, he regularly scarified it and raked it; throwing his hands up in despair if he caught sight of a daisy trespassing. Although he employed a gardener to trim the hedgerows and shrubbery, the lawn was strictly off limits to ANYONE but him. Once a week he would ride around on his sit-on-mower, painstakingly striping the lawn. I decided to make his trip around the lawn a little more interesting.

After walking round and round the shed trying to find the best entry point, I finally decided on trying to squeeze through the little window at the top that had been left ajar on its latch. "My god it's a good job I'm not fat." I whispered to myself as I heaved and squeezed myself through that tiny window. I landed in the shed with a bump. "Ow." Never mind I was in.

I'd been quizzing Matt and Darren about all things mechanical for a while now; it was something that I should know about. Just because I was a girl didn't mean I couldn't get my hands dirty did it? So I approached my task with a little more confidence than I would normally have with such things.

Peeling the dust cover off Trevor's pride and joy, I set to work, armed with araldite and cable ties, and proceeded to tighten his throttle cable. Now when he started his lawnmower up it'd set off like it was in a drag race! With a bit of luck he might take out a bit of the shrubbery too! Just to make sure I did maximum damage, or rather Trevor did maximum damage, I cut through the brake cable.

Next, just to *really* be a pain in the arse, I set about his spare ordinary push-lawnmower. I figured that after he'd gotten over the shock of the demon sit-on-mower, he'd probably feel much safer with his old faithful petrol push-mower. I looked about me for a spanner the right size. At least Trevor was very organised, he made my job much easier. Once I'd found the right size for my task, I unbolted the blade from the mower, turned it over, and bolted back on upside down. Now instead of cutting the grass, the upside-down blade would simply burn the grass and chew it up. Lovely.

Next I mixed a bagful of weed killer into the bag of miracle grow that I found on a shelf, a little counterproductive I knew, but, hey ho, that the way things go!

Once I was satisfied that my job here for the day was done, I squeezed back out of the little window that I had arrived through and went home.

The following day when I found myself at a loose end again - and bored, I put an advert in the personal ads in the local newspaper: -

'Personal Discreet Massage,
Other Services offered at a special rate. Customer satisfaction guaranteed! Special introductory offer, tell a friend and get a 'session' for free! Call Penelope on the number below for more details'

I would love to be there when the Pemberton's phone started ringing.

While I had been composing my advert, I had seen some other personal ads in the paper that caught my eye. Particularly one that said: -

'Attractive couple in their fifties looking for other open minded couples for fun times.'

Oo swingers eh? Well, The Pemberton's did always enjoy socialising. I called the number listed and pretended to be Penelope.

I spoke to a lovely 'friendly' woman who was desperate for a little 'get together' with me and my husband Trevor. I explained that unfortunately they would have to come to us if they wouldn't mind; Trevor and I were new to this and would feel much more comfortable in our own home. No problem at all - was the reply. And so, I gave her The Pemberton's address and arranged for a 'get together' the following Friday. (Louise was at a sleepover that night.)

Next, I called Penelope and informed her that I had just bumped into a lovely couple in the newsagents who were thinking of buying the house next door to her. They were viewing the property at half-past-seven on Friday night, and they wondered if it would be convenient for them to call in and speak to her and Trevor about what kind of neighbourhood it was before they put an offer in?

"Yes, yes, of course it is" - was the reply. I knew she'd take the bait; she was too nosey to pass up an opportunity to grill her new neighbours.

I was dying to know how *that* little get together would pan out. I could just picture it. Penelope welcoming them in, not giving them an opportunity to speak while she gave them the grand tour of their house. They would assume the Pemberton's were just nervous, too shy to get straight down to business. They'd probably even humour them a little, complimenting them on a beautiful home to set them at ease. I wonder what the Pemberton's would think during the tour when the swingers asked for a moment in private in the bedroom? They'd probably be polite and say 'of course'. Perhaps giving them five minutes before returning to see what was keeping their new guests? It would be just like the ski lodge over again, some people naked, and a lot of people screaming.

As soon as May returned from her afternoon with Dr Peter, I told her everything that I had been up to that day. She coughed and spluttered trying to drink her tea and laugh at the same time. When I read the advert out that I had placed in the classified section she finally lost it. Control of her bladder that is.

"Oo you bugger, you know not to make me laugh like that at my age!" She was still laughing though. "Now I'll have to go and change my underwear again."

"Thank goodness for tena lady!" I called after her as she departed wiping the tears of laughter from her face. I was still laughing too. I couldn't wait for time to pass so that I could call Matt when he got home from work and tell him what I'd done.

When it finally got to an appropriate time to call him he beat me to it. "I was just picking the phone up to ring you." I laughed.

"I told you I'm psychic. That how I know you love me so much."

"It's a cross I have to bear!" I sighed.

"Well you sound cheerful today what have you been up to for the last few days?" I could tell he was already amused.

"Just a spot of breaking and entering; with a dash of criminal damage, but the highlight of my day was definitely impersonating a swinger!" I said mysteriously.

"I don't know what to ask about first!"

"The swingers were my personal favourite."

"Go on then, tell me all about it."

And so for the next hour I filled him in on the last few days' worth of activities.

"God, you never fail to surprise me. Just when I think you must have run out of ideas you knock my socks off with another round." He did sound amazed I thought smugly.

"Which was your favourite?"

"The swingers!"

"Yeah me too."

He paused for a while. "When're you going to stop torturing them? When you run out of ideas?"

"I'll never run out of ideas." I thought for a minute. "I suppose I'll stop when I find a new purpose. They stole my daughter. I want them to share in my pain, it's like being stuck in limbo-land at the minute, and I don't have a clue what I'm supposed to do with the rest of my life." I paused. "Yes, that's it exactly, when I find a new purpose. *Then* I'll stop."

He sounded like he was thinking. "Let me take you out on Friday night? That'll give you something new to think about won't it?"

"What like a date?"

"Why not? It'll be fun. Just don't wear them bloody drag queen shoes, I can't carry you home if you get too drunk to walk."

"As if I would, you're the lightweight according to May!" I pointed out.

"Only because she bloody cheated! So, are you coming or not?"

"Well it is my birthday on Friday...Yes, go on then. But no funny business Matthew, don't go getting any funny ideas about taking advantage of me when I'm drunk, I'm not that sort of girl!" I added sternly.

"Bloody hell, do you really think I'd risk pissing you off and having you as an enemy?" He laughed. "I've got to go; I'll pick you up at seven."

"Okay, I'll see you Friday then, bye."

"Bye."

Good god I must be out of my mind!

When I Get Nervous I Get Creative

The next day was a Wednesday thank goodness, this meant that May and Darren were both home. I didn't like being alone so much at that time, whenever left alone to my own thoughts they would trail back to Louise, then I'd get depressed and start plotting revenge again. That day - just to make a change we were sitting in the kitchen drinking tea. (I know, but it was the warmest room in the house, and we were all tea addicts.)

"So, you and Matthew then eh?" May was digging me in the ribs and wiggling her eyebrows up at me. "Off on a date I hear?

"It's not like that!" I lied. "He's just taking me out for my birthday to cheer me up."

"I wasn't born yesterday love, I see the way you two look at each other. Even if neither of you'll admit it." She turned to Darren. "Help me out Darren."

He shook himself out of a stoned daze, (he'd only just come in from his shed.) He turned to May. "Yes it *is* a date. Matt phoned me all excited about it." He smirked at my betrayed face.

May sat back in her seat eyebrows raised and smirking. "Well, I best be getting a hat ready for your wedding then hadn't I?"

GOD!

By the time the two of them had finished ripping the piss out of me I quite wished they'd both gone out after all! Once they'd finally exhausted themselves laughing at mine and Matthew's expense, the subject came back round to the Pemberton's.

"Have you got anything else planned for them?" Asked Darren.

"As a matter of fact, I've got an absolute belter planned for tomorrow."

May looked up innocently. "So, you won't be around tomorrow then love?"

Darren and I exchanged a knowing glance. "No, I'll be heading out about quarter-to-twelve aunt May."

"Oh good." She tried to fake nonchalance but she wasn't very convincing. Too busy planning her dirty date with the Doctor. "How about you Darren? Are you busy tomorrow?"

"I thought I might pop into town or something around dinnertime May. Do you want anything getting?"

"No that's quite alright Darren, I'll be fine, you know me, and don't worry about me getting lonely or anything I'll find something to occupy myself with."

My god she was as subtle as a brick!

Darren rolled his eyes and looked over at me. "What have you got planned for tomorrow then?"

I grinned and explained my plan. But first I needed to know if Darren knew anyone who could lend me a mobile phone.

The following day, I set off for the Pemberton's, armed with a towel and a borrowed mobile phone.

I parked my car up around the corner from the Pemberton's and got out. Sneaking my way in and out of the shrubbery I made my up towards the house, I needed to check to see if they were in. I had read in the paper that there was a party on at the town hall, and assuming that the Lady Mayoress hadn't black listed them, the Pemberton's would probably be there.

I went around the back of the house and took in the devastation that was before me. The once immaculate lawn looked as though it had been used as a rally track. The lawn was chewed up in some places, large burnt looking bald spots in other areas, and a very large sit-on-lawnmower sized hole in the side of the carport. Whoops.

The more I looked, the more devastation I saw. Several of the garden statues were missing heads or arms, with some of them were laid out on the ground in hundreds of pieces. It was WONDERFUL!

I grinned to myself. That'd teach em, did they really think they could steal my daughter and get away with it?

After checking to see it their car had gone, I also decided to be on the safe side and ring the doorbell. After all I couldn't take the risk that anyone could be home. I rang the bell at the back door and held my breath. After waiting for a full five minutes, I felt confident enough that there was no one home. Right then. Time to get this show on the road.

I went back down the driveway and made my way back to my car. I turned it around and drove right up the Pemberton's driveway till I was level with the house. I took out the mobile phone that Darren had borrowed from a customer in the pub, and called the phone number that I had written down on a piece of paper in front of me.

"Hello this is Brown's locksmith's service how may I help you?"

"Hi, I'm really sorry to bother you, but I've locked myself out of the house, do you think you could get me back inside?"

"Of course Madam, but we will need to see identification to prove that you are in fact the homeowner, not a burglar!" He laughed at the absurdity.

"That might be a problem sir." I offered meekly. "I was getting ready for a bath when I heard the dog barking at the back door. Well, I shot down to let him in and somehow the door banged closed on me and now I'm stuck outside in just a towel!"

"Oh dear Miss, I'm very sorry. I'll send someone out straight away, I'll make sure the notes I send out state that ID isn't necessary." He sounded quite embarrassed.

"That's wonderful thank you. How long will they be? It's just it's very cold out here."

"What's the address?"

I gave the Pemberton's address.

"I'll have someone there in ten minutes."

"That's great thank you."

"No problem Miss, thank you for you custom."

It had worked! Now the awkward part, trying to wriggle out of my clothes inside a car, and into a towel without displaying my bottom to the whole world!

The locksmith turned up ten minutes later to find a poor girl shivering in a towel hiding behind a hedge.

"Thank you for coming out on such short notice." I bellowed from behind my rose bush.

"No problem Miss, I'll have you back inside in a jiffy."

He did. Two minutes later I was wearing Penelope's dressing gown and hunting through her bureaux for her cheque book. I made out the cheque to the locksmith, adding on a hefty tip, and faking Penelope's signature on the bottom.

Once he left, I retrieved my clothes from the car and got down to business. No more Mrs nice girl! I wanted to hit them where it hurt, as I've previously stated all they cared about was their precious reputation. They wouldn't have one left to care about by the time I finished!

I went through the many drawers in the bureaux, briefly shitting myself as a cricket leaped up at me. Ah ha, now I had the right drawer. I pulled out the file that had their bank and credit card statements. I sat down on the little telephone table and called the first credit card company, putting on my best posh voice, I called up Barclay card and reported my card as stolen, could they please cancel it with immediate effect.

I worked my way through every other card too, until I was just left with their hefty bank account, which had made my eyes water when I saw how much they had in there.

I had noticed when I arrived, the charity leaflet sat on the welcome mat. I picked it up and had a closer look; it was for a donkey sanctuary. I'd always liked donkeys. I called the number on the leaflet, and using the bank statement in my hand to refer to for the details; I donated five thousand pounds to the donkeys.

I looked at my watch; I still had a bit of time before the party at the town hall finished. I fished the keys for Trevor's Jaguar of the key hook, and headed for the garage.

Going in through the side door of the garage, I admired the sight. It was a midnight black Jaguar XJS, my favourite car of all time. It was Trevor's baby, only ever getting driven once or twice a month for special occasions. It seemed like sacrilege what I was about to do to it, but sometimes in life you have to make sacrifices right?

I unlocked the driver door and got in. It was beautiful this car, all leather and elm wood. The beige carpets were about an inch-thick underfoot, I could feel my feet sinking into it. Unfortunately for the car, it was this that I had come to sabotage.

I knew Trevor loved his lawn, which was sadly now ruined so I thought I'd make it up to him. I pulled from my coat pocket ten packets of cress seed that I had bought earlier just for this purpose. Tearing the packets open, I sprinkled it over every inch of the car's carpets, followed by six watering cans full of water. After reading the back of the seed packet I was pleased to see it guaranteed germination within a few days. Good. It would create a lovely new lawn in the car much quicker than grass seed would. His face would be a picture when he finally got around to driving it, to find that the plush carpets were now more of a meadow!

The last thing I did before I locked up and left, was to hide all the evidence of my presence. The cress seed packets went back home with me. I put all the statements away amongst a few stray crickets in the bureaux, along with the cheque book. I even thought to tear out the cheque stub that I had used to pay for the lock smith. I swept up the tiny bit of debris that the locksmith had left, got back into my car and left.

I was now starting to feel better. I thought that I may actually now have finished my reign of terror. Maybe Matt had been right, maybe it was time to move on and find another purpose. After all, looking around me at the devastation I had left in my wake, I think I'd helped them share my pain. Plus, they hadn't met the swingers they were dating yet!

A Memorable Date

'Oh my god it's my birthday again already!' - was my first waking thought that morning. My second thought was, 'bloody hell I've got a date tonight with Matthew!'

I sat up in bed, admiring the low autumn sun pouring in through the stained-glass windows of my bedroom, and yawned. I wanted to get up and get dressed, but it was just so cold in there. It was too easy to cuddle back down below the blankets and stay warm a bit longer. No such luck, May brought me a cup of tea in bed along with my dog who leaped on the bed jumping all over me trying to wash me.

"Oh bloody hell Butch, get off." I laughed as he stood on my knees.

"Happy birthday love." Aunt May said, as she put my cup down. "Sorry about Butch, he shot past me to get up here and I couldn't catch him."

"It's okay." I said cuddling him.

"When you're ready to come down, me and Darren have got a little something for you in the kitchen."

"Aw thanks aunt May you didn't have to bother."

"It's not much love, just a little token."

"I'll drink my tea and then I'll get dressed and be down."

"Okay love. Come on Butch." She stood hands on hips looking at my dog laid out on my bed on his back with his legs in the air, blatantly ignoring her.

"It's okay he can stay, I'll bring him back down with me." I said as I rubbed his belly. He was much happier in his new home with no more Neil and his unpredictable behaviour.

Ten minutes later, I had drunk my tea, got my lazy arse out of bed, and got dressed.

I walked into the kitchen to find a big bouquet of flowers on the table, and a huge box of chocolates. Bless them.

"Thank you both of you they're beautiful." I exclaimed picking up the flowers and smelling them. Lilies, my favourites. I leaned over to give Darren a kiss on the cheek. "Thanks Darren."

He blushed fuchsia all the way to his roots. "It's alright, happy birthday."

"Thanks aunt May." I got up and gave her a hug as she was walking past.

She returned my hug. "Happy birthday my beautiful girl." Once she'd released me she said - "What's the plan for today then? Dare I ask?" Chuckling.

I reached over for piece of toast off the plate in the middle of the table. "I haven't given it much thought to be honest. I think I'm just gonna potter about here till it's time to get ready to go out later. I might see if I can find something to do to make myself useful."

"I know what you can do love. You can come and play bingo with me and Darren!"

Shit.

It was hours later that May finally let me and Darren leave. We'd both completely had enough, and got to the point where we both sat down on the floor cross legged and were quite prepared to cry, if she didn't hurry up and let us leave.

Once we finally managed to pry May away from the bingo hall and got home, I only had an hour to get ready for my date, and poor Darren had to depart to the pub straight away to start his shift.

May had a blast though; she lived for bloody bingo, and had wound all the other old biddies up while she was there telling them Darren was her new boy-toy. After that, all the old ladies kept going out of their way to try and touch-up Darren. I don't know how he put it with it all to be honest, I would have been terrified. In the end, he took a leaf out of Matthew's book and started telling them it was a fiver to feel his bum. He did alright out it, he made enough to take the girl from the chemist out for a meal the following week. (After going in and buying several items before plucking up the courage to ask her.)

Once I was finally home I got a quick shower, and wriggled into my new little black dress. As Matt disapproved of my drag queen shoes, I made sure that I was wearing them. A quick bit of make-up, bit of mousse through my hair that was nicely growing back now, and I was ready.

I made my way down the stairs to the kitchen to wait for Matt, or at least I would have done if I could walk in those bastard shoes. I stood at the top of the stairs, looking down and thinking 'please don't let me fall down these.' I remembered the tumble I took down the stairs the day of the party, so in the end I did the right thing, I slid down the bannister.

"Weeeeeeeeeeeeeeeeeeeeeeeeeeeeeeeeeeeeeeeceeeeee!!!!!" I cried all the way down laughing, until I landed with a bump at the bottom.....on Matthew.

"Well that's one way to make an entrance!" He laughed. "It's lucky I caught you." He was still holding on to me, smiling down at me.

"Put me down then!" I tried to look mad but I don't think it worked.

"What if I don't want to?"

"You wouldn't like me when I'm angry." I grinned up at him.

"Fair point." He put me down gently, observing "Nice shoes."

"Aren't they!"

"Well don't you two make a lovely couple." May said as she walked into the hall. "Look after my girl Matthew, she's a real one off you know." She looked at him sternly through lowered glasses.

"She's not actually, she's a carbon copy of you May, if I was fifty years older it'd be you I'd be chasing." He pretended to grab her bottom to her delight.

"Get away with you, you little sod." She smacked him with a duster "Go on the pair of you, bugger off and give me a bit of peace." She smacked us both with her duster, chasing us out the door laughing.

I got into the passenger side of Matt's car thankfully without showing my bottom, 'getting classy in my old age' I thought smugly.

As Matt sank into the driver's seat he said "Did you get the impression she was trying to get rid of us?"

"I did actually. Plus, did you notice she had lipstick on?"

"Oh god she's got a date with Dr Love again hasn't she? Ugh I hope we aren't still doing 'it' at that age."

"Hey don't get presumptuous Matthew; it might take you till I'm that age to get me in to bed." I giggled.

"Well on your head be it. If my back's gone by then, and I miss out I won't be a happy man."

"Stop it, you'll make me blush again."

"I'd like to."

"God, drag your brain out the gutter will you." I laughed. "Where are we going anyway?"

He looked at me mysteriously. "Birthday treat."

Oo I was intrigued.

Fifteen minutes later we were sat outside the Pemberton's house.

"What are we doing here?" I was curious.

"I thought I'd bring you here for a little bit of entertainment before we go get something to eat."

"Oh god. The swingers! They're due any minute aren't they?" I looked at the illuminated clock on the dash. "I turned to Matthew smiling with delight "You really know how to spoil a girl don't you." I leant over and kissed him on the cheek.

He looked pleased and tried to pull me closer, before changing his mind with a start. "Quick, they're here, duck down."

We ducked as the blue Mercedes pulled into the Pemberton's driveway. I peeped out of the passenger window at the scantily clad couple that emerged from the Mercedes. She was around sixty I would have guessed, with bleached blonde hair trimmed into a sort of Rod Stewart hairdo. She had a pink mini skirt on that did nothing for her fat white wobbly calves. She had a sort of Spanish looking black shawl around her shoulders over the top of what looked like a belly top. I could see a fat gut hanging out of it anyway. Nice.

Mr Swinger looked about sixty-five, and had the same blonde Rod Stewart hairdo as his wife! Good god, his and hers hairdos!

He had on black baggy shorts, (Didn't he realise it was November?) and a silver shirt open at the collar displaying grey chest hair (Ugh) and a gold medallion. They looked like they'd both just stepped off the plane from Benidorm. But more than anything, they did not look like the 'fifty something's' they had advertised themselves as.

I sniggered and whispered to Matthew "This is way better than I expected. I wish I could see Penelope's face when she sees those two."

"I know, this is brilliant. Just remind me in future never to get on your bad side will you?"

"I don't give fair warning Matthew."

"True. Oo look they're going in."

I turned back to view Trevor ushering their guests in through the front door. This was magic. We watched the living room lights come on, followed closely by the dining room lights.

"They've fallen for it." I exclaimed. "Look they're giving them the grand tour!"

As we watched, all the lights came on in turn, ending in the master bedroom.

"I can't stand the suspense." I turned back to look at Matthew instead, who was ignoring the scene in front of us and staring at me.

"I think you're amazing!" He smiled. "Why don't we leave these idiots to their sad little lives and go get on with our date now."

"You're right." I sighed, disappointed. "I think my work here is probably done."

Matthew was just starting the car as the shouting started. "Wait a minute! They're kicking off!" I exclaimed with delight.

The front door flew open on its hinges as naked man came hurtling out backwards.

"WHOA!" He screamed as he landed on his back on top of a rose bush. He pulled himself back up yelping, presumably at all the thorns sticking out of his bottom, and ran back into the house.

The next person to come flying out backwards was Trevor, closely followed by Penelope who happened to be in a tight head-lock by Mrs Swinger. Mrs Swinger at least still had her skirt on, although sadly her fat saggy titties were on view for the whole world to see. One of which was currently bashing Penelope around the head.

Matthew and I were screaming with laughing in the car watching it all unfold against the backdrop of Samantha Fox's breasts that were visible in the window behind.

Penelope seized an opportunity to get the upper hand on her opponent and titty twisted Mrs Swinger until she let go of Penelope's hair. Meanwhile, Trevor had managed to overpower Mr Swinger and currently had the naked pensioner bent over the ornamental water butt in the front flower bed.

I said to Matthew "That poor waiter missed out didn't he? Look how masterful Trevor is!"

"God I wish we'd brought a camera." Matthew was wiping his eyes from laughing. I turned back again to see Penelope getting nipple twisted as Mrs Swinger retaliated. She had also managed to wrestle Penelope's cardigan off. It became apparent as Mrs Swinger tried once again to grab a nipple, that Penelope's bra contained nothing but chicken fillets. Mrs Swinger grabbed one and flung it across the garden and into the pond as though it was a Frisbee.

Now the one tittied Penelope was mad! How dare this strange naked woman disparage her small breasts! She launched into attack mode! She grabbed a handful of the blubber that Mrs Swinger passed off as breasts and proceeded to swing her round and round by them, while growling. When she eventually let go, Mrs Swinger flew across the lawn and went down with a belly-flop straight into the pond!

Penelope wiped her hands, straightened her lop-sided bra, and tried to walk with as much dignity as she could, back into the house on one broken stiletto.

Trevor meanwhile was having problems restraining the slippery naked man who kept wriggling out of his grasp. One minute he had him bent over the water butt with his hands behind his back, the next minute he was the one who was bent over the butt with his hands behind his back. Penelope came to his rescue though; she had run through the house and out into the back garden where she had found the hose pipe. She dragged the hose down the side of the house, with a steely look of determination on her face. Unfortunately, Penelope seemed to have had some sort of mental breakdown due to the warfare she had just endured. She was no longer playing!

She approached the naked man who had her husband bent over the water butt, and before he had time to react, she stuck the jet wash nozzle up his bum and opened fire.

I think it's fair to say he was surprised judging by the way his eyebrows shot up.

Matthew and I were both crying with laughter and holding onto each other for dear life.

As Mr Swinger released his grip on Trevor, Trevor seized the opportunity to grab his wife by the hand and make a run for the house. They slammed the door just in time, knocking the now soaking wet Mrs Swinger (who was running at the door full pelt) out cold.

It was over. Mr Swinger admitted defeat and pulled his hefty bulk of a wife back into their Mercedes and after climbing into the driver seat beside her (still naked) left.

I turned to Matthew, still laughing. "Thank you, this is without a doubt the best date I have ever been on!"

"I aimed to please." He grinned smugly. "Come on then, let's go get something to eat."

The Night Aint Over Yet

The rest of our date was quite sensible after the eventful beginning. We went out for a nice meal in a lovely little restaurant in the town, followed by a few drinks in the pub were Darren was working. It was the easiest date I had ever been on. There were no uncomfortable silences, no wondering what to say, we were perfectly happy in each other's company. I knew it was early days but even though, I was starting to wonder if May had been right. Maybe we did make a good couple?

We decided to walk home from the pub in the end, as it wasn't that far to go. At least that was what Matthew thought. He didn't have bloody drag queen shoes on did he?

To me it seemed to take forever, every step seemed like a step-up Everest. Eventually to my drunken delight, he took pity on me and hoisted me up and carried me home.

"Careful. My knickers feel like they're showing!" I gasped as I was bounced about as he strode up the drive way.

"Good! That's what you get for wearing stupid shoes." He smacked my bottom for effect. "It's a fitting punishment." He was laughing.

"This is nowhere near as romantic as I thought it would be." I gasped.

"You can carry me if you prefer!"

"You're too fat."

"Hey, don't get personal, I might get upset and drop you." He half dropped me, before pulling me back up again laughing at my screams.

"Not funny!"

"Depends where you're standing!"

I laughed and stopped fighting him. I looked up at the house that was looming up in front of me still grinning; the smile froze on my lips as I saw something was wrong.

"Matt look at that!"

"What?"

"That up there look. May's bedroom window."

He looked up to see the same thing that I had seen - the flashing light in the window. It was flashing on and off, on, and off, as though somebody was trying to get our attention.

Matthew put me gently down, and set off at a run.

I wriggled out of the stupid shoes and set off after him. Catching up with him as he bounced the front door open, we both charged up the stairs in a panic not knowing what to expect when we got up there. The sight we saw as Matthew kicked the bedroom door open was something neither of us were prepared for, and never forgot.

May had company. From our view from the doorway, we could see that we had caught May *in flagrante* with Dr Peter. Before my eyes burnt from their sockets with embarrassment, I had seen the Dr sprawled out on the bed, pinned beneath a half-naked May - May who was slumped and not moving.

Matthew who was braver than me went around the bed to the doctor who had his only free hand on the switch of the bedside lamp.

"Thank goodness!" The doctor said. "Could you please help me? I have been trying to alert someone for hours!"

Matthew and I were both looking in shock at May's unmoving form.

At last I found my voice. "Is she dead?"

The doctor peered over May's shoulder. "I'm very sorry Sarah, she's gone!" He was tearing up. I sank down onto the side of the bed in shock. She was gone! How could she be gone?

Matthew came over and pulled me up. Before I realised what was happening I found myself in my bedroom where he had carried me before going back to help the doctor.

I was completely numb. Surly this must be a dream? This can't be real?

But it was.

It seemed like hours later when Matthew came to fetch me.

"Come on Sarah, it's okay, you can come back in now." He gently led me by the elbow back to May's room. Everything seemed much more normal now. The doctor was dressed for one thing. For another, May was now lying in her bed wearing her best nightgown looking as though she had just fallen asleep.

She looked as though she was having a very dirty dream though looking at that wicked smile that was now permanently etched upon her lovely face. That made me smile.

Doctor Peter was much more composed now, though his devastation still showed on his grief-stricken face.

After that it was all a blur of undertakers.

Once he was satisfied that I would be okay for a little while, Matthew had gone to get Darren to break the news to him. He was devastated of course. May had become his honorary grandmother.

Later that night when May had been taken away, still with that wicked grin on her face, Mathew, Darren, and I, had sat in her kitchen and bawled our eyes out. She was our family and she was our friend. We were all her little lost children that she had taken in, fussing over us, stuffing us with food and endless cups of tea. She would be sorely missed.

After we had run out of tears to cry, we found ourselves laughing about some of the things she had gotten up to in her life. It was during this evening that Matthew and I learnt about her taking Darren shoplifting. We had smiled at the story; it was so typical of May.

Matthew told me and Darren how during his first week living with May, she had played several practical jokes on him trying to gauge how far she could push him. Silly things that gave her great delight, like sewing up the legs of all his jeans so that he couldn't put his feet through them.

Darren snorted at that. "She did that to me too! Except she did it with all my socks as well."

She'd also done juvenile things like cling filming the toilet seat, and filling their pillows with shaving cream.

"I can't believe I didn't know any of this!" I smiled at the thought of her up to mischief. "She was a bugger, wasn't she?" I would have teared up again if I hadn't already cried myself out.

Matthew held up his glass of whisky. "To May!"

"To May." - Joined in Darren clinking Matt's glass.

"To aunt May!" I clinked both of their glasses. "She went as she would have wanted, with a Bang!"

A Few Answers

After the funeral, May's wake was held at the local pub, where she had spent so much of her time antagonising the many Landlords that had come and gone over the years.

Matthew and I, along with Darren had all spoken at the funeral, fully intending to be sombre and sincere in our eulogies, but when the music started up (which May had requested years ago apparently) it became impossible. Taking her sense of humour 'a step too far', according to the vicar, though bound by the promise she had extracted from him before she had actually told him what the song was that she wanted.

The gasps in the church were deafening as the music started up. As the first few bars of music played out, we saw some of the mourners prick their ears up in surprise, as though thinking, 'No, it can't be *that* song. It wouldn't be, it's an old lady's funeral! It must just sound like that song.'

But no, it *was* that song.

In a final act of devilment, May had extracted a promise from the vicar to play 'something to lighten the mood.' The vicar hung his head in despair as his parishioners were forced to endure....'I'm A Wanker!' By Ivor Biggun.

Well we all cracked up. It was the sight of all those disapproving faces that did it. May had been right it certainly did lighten the mood.

After that, Me, Matthew and Darren got up on that pulpit and brought the church down with laughter. All our earlier prepared speeches about loss and grief were scrapped. We did what May would have been proud of and made everybody laugh.

We all went back to the pub for the wake, but after an hour we'd had enough. People were having too good of a time, discarding May and drifting into conversation of their own lives and stories. After a while the bulk of the people seemed to have forgotten why we were there.

We'd decided enough was enough and it was time to go home, when Dr Peter stopped us on the way out.

He grasped my hand gently. "I'm very sorry for your loss Sarah. May was a wonderful woman, and if I'm honest," He lowered his voice, "she was the love of my life." He dabbed a tear from his eyes and looked from me, to Darren and Matthew. "I'm sure it must have been a shock for you, finding us as you did, as well as the shock of May's death. May never wanted any of you to know about us you see. With my being married, things have been difficult." He paused before resuming. "Do you think I could call at the house tomorrow? There are some things that you need to know."

I felt very sorry for him. "Of course it's okay to call, but could you make it late in the day? May's solicitor wants to spend the day going over the will and the deeds or something. She said it could take a while."

"I shall call in around six o'clock then if that would be suitable with you all?"

We all agreed that would be fine, and so finally we were free to go home and mourn in peace.

The following morning I introduced May's solicitor Linda Porter to Matthew and Darren, and asked her to take a seat at the kitchen table. Anything she had to say to me I told her could be said in front of Matthew and Darren.

"Let me start by saying how very sorry I am for your loss. May was a wonderful person, with a huge personality."

"Thank you. We're all still in shock I think." Darren and Matt both nodded their agreement.

"I can well imagine. I'll get straight down to business then and get out of your hair as soon as possible. Now as you know Sarah, May left her entire estate to you. It's a reasonably straight forward probate that should be all sorted out within the next month or so. There won't be a hefty inheritance tax to pay, as fortunately May had the foresight to put the property into your name around ten years ago. As May only had to survive this by seven years, the inheritance tax is no longer applicable to this case."

"I had no idea that she'd put the property into my name." I was baffled.

"I believe from a conversation that I had with her last year that she had not wanted you to feel under any pressure. The maintenance bills for an estate of this size have been a huge financial burden these past few years, she thought that if you knew that it actually legally belonged to you, that you would feel it your duty to contribute financially. She was adamant that any financial liabilities were hers and hers alone."

"Of course I would have contributed, I've been worried sick for years about the state the place was in, but she just used to say that the place had character. She wouldn't hear of any financial help."

"I have the original deeds to the house here for you to peruse at your pleasure, although I would advise you to keep them in a safe place, preferably lodge them with a solicitor, me or otherwise." She slid the very grand looking deeds across the table to me. "May also had a life insurance policy payable to you Sarah in the event of her death. Once I have finished dealing with the insurance company you should receive a sum of sixty-five thousand pounds." She shuffled the paper in her hands.

"I had no idea." I sighed and put my head in my hands. "She's looked after me to the end, hasn't she?"

Matthew leant over from his place behind me and squeezed my shoulder for support. I put my hand up to his and squeezed it back.

"Now if I could just go through some other forms with you, and get a few signatures I shouldn't take up too much more of your time."

We spent perhaps another hour with Linda before she excused herself and left.

Darren put the kettle on while Matthew and I sat back down at the table.

Matthew spoke up first. "At least that's all done with now."

"Yes, I suppose. She'd really thought hard about what was best for me hadn't she? All that getting round the inheritance tax thing. It's lucky that she did, I'd probably have had to sell up just to pay the tax bill."

"She thought the world of you did our May." Chipped in Darren as he prepared the teapot.

"She thought the world of you two too." I paused for a while, deep in thought. "One thing I did think of though while she was talking, Neil can't claim half of it when I finally get him to agree to a divorce can he? 'Cause of the pre-nup. It was worded something about how we must both leave the marriage without claiming anything that the other one already owned before our marriage. He thought he was protecting his own arse with that, he didn't know I owned a mansion in the country!" That made me laugh. He'd be furious. I couldn't wait to write to him and tell him.

Matthew smiled and held my hand under the table. "Well that one bit him in the arse didn't it. Serves him right for being such a self-serving greedy bastard."

I couldn't agree more.

Darren asked. "Do you mind if I have a look at these deeds? I've never seen anything like them before, really grand looking aren't they?"

"Help yourself." I slid them over the table so he could better reach them.

Matthew turned to me. "Are you going to eat something today then? You're going to have to keep your strength up you know."

"I know, I'm just not hungry. I will try and have a bit of toast or something in a little while."

Darren looked up puzzled. "I don't get it!"

Matthew asked "Get what?"

Darren was peering down at the deeds looking confused. "It says here, that the Davenport Manor Hotel was left to Mr and Mrs Robert Fairhurst. May was married!"

"Let me see that it must be a mistake!" I stood up and peered over the deeds that Darren had slid back over. He was right. The hotel had been left to May and her husband Robert!

"I don't understand. Who the hell is Robert? May's told me a thousand times that she would never ever marry. She always said as soon as a man had a ring on your finger he turned into a bastard."

Matthew sighed and put a comforting hand on my back. "Maybe she was speaking from experience Sarah."

"I can't believe it! Why would she keep this from me? I don't understand."

Darren spoke up. "I once found a wedding ring in the garden when I was cutting the grass. A man's wedding ring. I took it to May, and when I put it in her hand she acted as though I'd just handed her a dog turd or something. She acted really strange and said it must have belonged to one of the Staines family. Looking back though, I think judging by her reaction to it she was lying. I think it was her husband's wedding ring."

"I can't believe she's never told me!" I was disappointed; I thought we'd always told each other everything. "What did she do with the ring?"

"She practically threw it back at me and told me to put it back where I found it."

"Where did you find it?"

"The east wing foundations."

"Everything comes back to that east wing doesn't it?" Matthew had voiced what I was thinking exactly. "You don't think do you…" He trailed off looking worried.

"You think she killed her husband, don't you?"

He looked to Darren. "What are your thoughts Darren?"

"I can't help but wonder, is that locked door in the cellar her husband's grave?"

Oh Jesus I hoped it wasn't that.

We spent the remainder of the day puzzling over this new mystery. I couldn't picture May killing her husband. She was all bark was May… wasn't she?

We were interrupted from our thoughts by Dr Peter knocking on the kitchen window. Hopefully he might have some of the answers we desperately needed.

The Doctor's Tale

"Thank you for seeing me." He said as he sat down at the kitchen table. He was dressed as the proper little country doctor, all tweeds and corduroy. He took his hat off and ran a hand threw his thick head of silver hair. I briefly wondered if Neil's hair had grown back?

"Thank you for coming Doctor." I replied taking a seat.

"Call me Peter." He was fidgeting nervously.

"Okay Peter."

Matthew asked if Peter would like a cup of tea or coffee.

"No thank you. Actually, would it be an imposition to ask if you have anything a little stronger perhaps?"

Darren offered. "I think we've got a bottle of Glayva in the cupboard. Would that be okay?"

"That would be splendid thank you."

I could sense Peter's discomfort and so decided to level the playing field a little.

"I just want to let you know Peter, that finding you and May like that wasn't such a shock for us. We've known for some time about your erm….relationship."

Darren poured the whisky for Peter and continued. "We discovered by accident about you and May disappearing off down the cellar on an afternoon."

"So, you know about the cellar then too." He looked a little taken aback. "Goodness." He took a big sip from his glass.

I didn't want him to feel uncomfortable. "It's okay; we're not judging you Peter. You obviously brought a lot of joy to May's life. She's been happier this last year than I've ever seen her." I paused while he finished his drink and his eyes met mine. "We didn't let on that we knew because we thought that you deserved your privacy. It was none of our business."

He cleared his throat and began. "Well that does make things somewhat easier. At least it won't be too many shocks in one day for you all. Oh dear, I'm afraid I've been dreading this conversation for a long time." He looked at the three of us in turn before continuing. "May asked me to tell you something Sarah, if anything should happen to her and she didn't get a chance to tell you herself, I'm sure that would now include both of you Matthew and Darren. She thought of you two as her adopted family. Before I tell you May's secret do you think I could have another shot of Dutch courage please? I think I'm in need of a little courage tonight."

"Of course." Matthew poured a large glass for Peter, and after taking note of the grave look on his face, he poured the rest of us one too.

"Right then, I'll begin." He took a deep breath and started his tale. "May and I knew each other all of our lives. We went to infant school together, and remained close throughout our adolescence. We always were fond of one another, but both a little too shy to do anything about it. I finally asked her to go courting just before the war broke out, and to my great delight she said yes. We had a few glorious weeks together and I was starting to think that as soon as I came of age, I'd ask her to marry me. I was completely besotted with her. But sadly life doesn't always work out the way one would hope.

I was conscripted into the army in Nineteen-forty, against my wishes I might add. I had no desire to go to war, I wasn't the adventurous type. I just wanted to go to university, train as a doctor and then get married and have children. That was it. May was obviously upset at my leaving, but none of us had a choice in the matter. Anyway, while I was gone, Robert Fairhurst had set his cap at May; he had remained behind during the war as he failed the medical. May told me later that he was charm personified while he was pursuing her, every day she left work he would be waiting to walk her home with some little gift or other. Flowers one day, fruit the next. After six months or so, I was starting to fade from her memory and the handsome man in front of her was starting to look quite appealing. Especially as all the other girls in the village were trying their hardest to pursue, him to no avail. He only had eyes for May. Once she started courting him, she quickly forgot all about me, and fell head over heels for him. Within a year they were married, but May's parents didn't approve of Robert one bit. After they were married, they got jobs working here at Davenport. The proprietors Mr and Mrs Staines grew very fond of the happy young couple that came to work for them, and treated them like family. They had never had children of their own, and after many squabbles within their own family they had pretty much lost every one but each other. It is easy to see how May and Robert invigorated them with their youthful presence. May said the first two years were bliss, she was wonderfully happy. Living in a beautiful hotel with her handsome husband, wonderful employers who doted on her. But gradually the cracks started to show. Over the next few years, the handsome charming man she had married grew cold and indifferent to her. Suddenly she couldn't do anything right for him. If she cooked his dinner it would be too hot, or too cold. Too spicy or too bland. She said she starting calling him 'goldilocks' in her head. Next, he stopped her seeing her friends anymore, and cut her off from her family. By the time I came home in forty-three, injured and unable to return to the war, she was barely recognisable as the girl I had left behind. Everything that had made her so vibrant was gone; she had this defeated look in her eyes. It broke my heart to see her like that." Peter paused and took a long sip from his glass before continuing. "I also started to notice the bruises on her arms and legs. She tried to pass it off as clumsiness but I wasn't fooled; I knew it was Robert doing it. The night before the bomb hit I had it out with him; I collared him as he came out of the pub. He tried to barge past me, telling me I didn't know what I was talking about, but I was having none of it. My dander was up so to speak. He had a good six inches of height on me, and at least two or three stone, but he was no match for me that night. I've never been an aggressive man and I can quite honestly say, other than during the war, that was the only fist fight I ever had. But by god I put that man down on the pavement with a bang. I warned him that if he didn't start treating her with the respect I'd kill him. He seemed to get the message and sloped off. I got a round of applause from the rest of the customers who had come out to see Robert get his comeuppance, it turned out I wasn't the only one that had noticed the change in May with concern. I went back to my parent's house which is the house I still live in today next door, hoping that May's life would get easier now. Sadly, I had made a grave error. He'd gone home and took his fury and anger out on May. He beat her black and blue for setting her 'boyfriend' on him. I only learnt this afterwards of course. The following night I was asleep in my bed when the explosion shook the house. Straight away I knew it was a bomb, and it had landed close.

I shot out of bed and looked out of the window across towards the hotel, and saw the devastation. The east wing roof had gone and the second story bedroom was just a mass of masonry and to my horror, fire. I dragged my clothes on and shot across to the hotel as fast as my legs would carry me. I pounded on the door but knowing it was unlikely that anyone could come; I broke the front parlour window with my elbow and climbed in. I made my way out to the hall staircase in the pitch black trying to grope my way up the stairs where I knew May and Robert would be sleeping, I had no hope of saving the Staines, nobody could have survived that bomb dropping into their quarters. As I groped my way up the stairs I found May huddled on the landing. I was so relieved to find her alive I can't tell you." He took out his handkerchief and mopped his forehead. "I was worried that she'd gone deaf from the bomb at first, as one of her ears was pouring with blood. But she was okay after a few days it was just the one ear, the other one that had been buried in her pillow when the bomb hit was fine. I could see better now that I had found May, her bedroom door was open and an oil lamp was lit in there which cast a little light out onto the landing. 'Where's Robert?' I asked her.

She was just staring at me stunned.

'May, where is Robert?' I shook her a little.

Eventually she looked up at me and shook her head. She didn't know where he was. She'd woken up alone. I could see a gaping hole in the wall on the above landing; fortunately, the staircase hadn't been affected. May and I made our way up there and looked through the gaping hole straight into a scene from hell. The room was burning on the far side, the rest of the room was just charred wood and glass, the entire roof had come down into what was once the luxurious master suite. One thing was evident though, amidst the wood and tiles and rubble was the vast amount of blood covering what was left of the floor. We didn't dare venture any further than the hole we were peering through, we'd seen enough of the strewn body parts to know there was no one left alive in there." He paused again and asked if Matthew would mind pouring him another drink.

It must be said, telling us his tale was taking its toll on the poor old gent. We were hanging off his every word. May had never spoken in detail about the night of the bomb. When he'd had another sip of his whisky and composed himself, he carried on.

"We could see by the light of the fire in there a man's foot sticking out from under the crumpled brass bed, just a foot. It wasn't attached to anything. I almost vomited at the sight. As my eyes took it all in I also saw what looked like a woman's arm across the other side of the room. I'd seen enough, I took May by the arm and turned her around to take her to safety and came face to face with George Staines. He had been standing behind us the whole time taking in the same sights as we had. Including the male foot sticking out from under his bed. His expression looked ghastly from the scene before him. Taking his wedding ring off he threw it into the carnage before turning away, white as a sheet and disappeared down the stairs. May and I were stunned. If it wasn't George in the bombed-out bed chamber who was it? I pulled May back down the stairs with me; I wanted her out of that place as quick as I could.

As I led her out of the front door she said what we'd both been thinking. 'It was Robert, wasn't it?'

I nodded.

'He was sleeping with Edith, wasn't he?' She wasn't asking me as much telling herself.

We suddenly heard the coal hatch being opened, and turned to see what was happening. George was crying and clambering down the pile of coal and into the cellar. I called after him to come back, it wasn't safe, but he carried on as if he hadn't heard me. I told May to stay where she was, sitting on the side of the fountain in the turning circle, and then I set off down the coal chute to try and get George out before he got his fool-self killed in there. He was charging down the corridor like the devil was after him, he ran straight to the end room and slammed the door on me before I could dart in after him, but not before I had seen what the room contained. It was the gun room.

The handle was unbelievably stiff, and before I managed to heave the door back open I heard the boom in there, I was too late. I heaved the door open to find that he had taken a shot gun and blown his head off with it."

Matthew, Darren and I gasped. All I could think was thank god we never managed to get into that room! Peter took a moment before carrying on.

"I leaped out of my skin as May put her arms around me, she had followed me you see. Never one to watch life from the side lines she'd come to help me get George out. She saw what I saw. She dragged me out of the way of the door as I had crumbled into a mess; it was just too horrible to take in. She slammed the door shut and taking her keys from her dressing gown pocket she extracted the gun store key and locked it up.

'What are you doing?' I wanted to know.

'Saving you Peter.' She said. 'Come on we have to get out now, people will be coming.'

I followed her back out in a trance not sure of what was really going on anymore, I think something in my brain had snapped by then with the shock of it all.

Once we were out, May slammed the coal store trap door behind us and pulled me over to sit with her on the fountain. She was more animated that I had seen her for a long time, in complete control of the situation, she was always marvellous in a crisis, and she'd have made a much better soldier than I ever did.

She sat me down and put it to me in no uncertain terms, that no one would believe that was Robert upstairs, or what was left of him, in bed with Edith. Edith was a respected pillar of society. No. What people would think is that Mr and Mrs Staines had died in their bed when the bomb dropped. The now headless corpse in the cellar would be believed to be Robert, who I had beaten up the night before in front of a pub full of witnesses and threatened to kill.

I was stunned. I couldn't believe what she was saying. But in the heat of the moment it made sense, after all, Robert and George were the same height weight and build. Although George was older, from a pampered life of luxury his body could be mistaken for that of the younger man - who'd had a harder life of manual work, and looked older than he was.

I sank my head into my hands and wept. She comforted me and told me everything would be alright. All we had to do was pretend that the bodies upstairs were Mr and Mrs Staines. No one would go looking through locked rooms in the cellar, would they?

But what about Robert I wanted to know. People would notice his absence. May thought about it for a while and said, 'I'll tell people he's run off after being humiliated by you in the pub.'

It seemed plausible; Robert was known for being a bit of a coward.

So, we made a pact, to tell the world that the poor Mr and Mrs Staines had been sadly killed by the bomb. May was in the part of the house that was unscathed, and Robert had fortunately left the morning before. When the villagers arrived to help put the fire out, that was the story we told them. Later on that night it became apparent from the blanket and whisky tumbler that we found in the library, that George had fallen asleep in there in a drunken stupor, which had given Robert and Edith the chance they had been waiting for.

For fifty years that's the story we stuck to. It was fortunate that May had been bequeathed the hotel in the will, as it meant that she could prevent anyone from going down the cellar. The smell down there was quite terrible, but neither of us could find the nerve to open up that door again, and so as soon as she could, she closed all access to it and did her best to erase its existence from everyone's minds. We could never erase it from our minds though. We both had nightmares about it for years. In the end, I had to leave; I couldn't stand it anymore and so left to go to university. I tried to put everything to the back of my mind and even met and married my wife in an effort to put May and what we had done from my mind. I never truly could though. When my parents passed away many years later, I inherited the house that I grew up in next door to the hotel, and moved my wife and I into it. A lot of time had passed by then, and I could see things better now, I was more able to cope.

May had changed for the better too. As soon as she got access to the funds that she had inherited, she had the east wing pulled down, the house repaired and more importantly the cellar door closed off forever. It seemed to make things better for her after that, she could breathe again.

Our secret was safe.

Eventually people forgot about May's husband as time passed, but whenever the subject was raised she'd simply state that he managed to pass the army medical and joined up in forty-four, sadly dying in action.

May and I remained firm friends throughout the years never mentioning anything that had happened that night in Forty-four though; that is until the render started falling off the east side wall around ten years ago. We both were terrified when the cellar door once again became visible. Well this time I wasn't going to hide behind May's skirts like a lost puppy like I did the last time, this time I would take charge. I was much older now and seen many squeamish things during my many years as a doctor. I decided to go back down the cellar and open up the door. It was time to right the wrong that we'd done all those years ago.

I must say though for all my bravado to May, my hands were shaking when I prised that cellar door open. Fortunately the awful smell that I remembered from all those years ago had gone. It only smelt a little damp. Well, that I could cope with.

Everything was just as I remembered down there, I'd relived it often enough in my nightmares to know it like the back of my hand. I made my way down to the room at the end and took a deep breath and unlocked the door. It wasn't as bad as I was dreading, in the end. There was no gore now, no horrors, just a pile of bones amidst a shot gun. I had brought a small wooden box that used to contain my portable writing desk down to the cellar with me. I thought it appropriate that it should be something pretty for a casket. I gently picked up all the bones and fragments from the floor and laid them all carefully in the box. After taking the box upstairs for safe keeping, I set about cleaning up the gun room. A good sweep and scrub down and the room looked good as new. I polished the shotgun that I had picked up from the floor and put it back onto the rack with the others after checking that both its chambers were empty.

Later that evening, as soon as it got dark, May and I snuck into the church yard and buried the box in the grave that was marked George Staines.

We both felt so much better after that, it was like a curse had been lifted from us. We fell in love again. The atmosphere in the house lifted and for the first time in years we felt free.

We continued seeing each other discreetly over the years, I never had the heart to leave my wife as she would have been devastated, the physical aspects of our marriage had been over for decades, and we were little more than companions really. But May, May was my true love. So now you know." He looked about at us, all three lost in our thoughts.

Now 2014

Over the next few years Matthew, Darren, and I got into many adventures while living in the Hotel, too many to list here for time is of the essence now. However, I made sure to leave my diary along with May's (that I found many years later) buried in a box, in the locked room at the end of the cellar. When I have finished this account, I'll add this to the box too before re-burying it. Someone may find it one day and have a giggle at many of the things that are contained in the diaries.

As the years passed here at Davenport, Matthew and I fell in love, although we never married. Whenever we were asked why we wouldn't tie the knot we both used to say together laughing 'As soon as a man gets a ring on a woman's finger he turns into a bastard!'

We were happy we didn't need a piece of paper to prove it.

Darren stayed in his old quarters rent free in exchange for a few jobs about the place as he had always done. He grew from an awkward, shy little hippy into a handsome young man with sensible short back and sides. Despite growing up though he kept his wicked sense of humour. Which was a good job actually.

Louise came to stay with us for a few months when she nineteen, her grandparents had gotten sick of her money grabbing ways and snide remarks and cut her off without a penny. I was glad to have her back with us, even if Matthew and Darren couldn't stand her. They said she used me. (Which she did.) But still, I was glad she was here. That is until she drugged Darren and then seduced him. Poor Darren, he could never forgive her for it.

She knew damn well that he couldn't bear her, he was pining over his girlfriend who had left him for someone else the month before. But as we all came to know, Louise got what Louise wanted, despite who might get hurt in the process.

I confronted her about it when I found out. I was angry. I said to her if he'd been the one to do that to her, he would have gone to jail for it. Why did she think it was okay to do that to him?

"Because I felt like it!" - was the reply.

Things have a strange way of working out though don't they?

Nine months later, out popped Malcolm.

This one bit Louise in the arse. She thought she was having a fling with a bit of rough while she found herself a proper husband, one who was rich, with prospects! The thought that she was now tied to Darren for the rest of her life appalled her.

Fortunately though, Motherhood didn't suit Louise in the early years, and so for the first four years Malcolm grew up with Darren, Matthew and I, which was the best thing for him; he grew his own little personality here with us. Much to Louise's despair I might add. When she decided to take him away from us when she eventually settled down with a rich property developer who couldn't have children of his own but desperately wanted a child, we were all devastated. So after four years of caring for him, she stole him away from us. But that wasn't enough for Lou, now she wants my house.

Six months ago, I caught her property developer boyfriend skulking about my land with an estate agent. He tried to argue that He and Louise were just looking after my interests, wasn't I aware that I was sitting on a gold mine here? He tried to convince me that I should knock the house down and let him build a housing estate on my land, 'we'd make millions' he tried to argue.

You know me; I'm not one to be bullied. I got my shot gun and ran them off my land double quick.

The next thing I heard was that Louise was seeking planning permission from the council to build thirty new houses where my home stood. I don't know how she did it; I presume she must have faked my signature or something. The first I knew of it was when the planning notice appeared on the first oak at the end of my driveway.

I confronted her last week about her underhand shenanigans to which she replied. "I wonder where I get that from then?"

She went onto tell me that if I didn't sign over the deeds to the house to her immediately, the following week she had an appointment to seek power of attorney over me! After which, she told me, she would put me in a mental hospital, and evict Matthew and Darren.

"I'd love to see you try." I laughed. She really didn't know who she was up against did she?

Apparently, actually, she did.

She'd done her research and had prepared a report on me; listing the 'bouts of depression' I had suffered in my early twenties. (Bollocks, I've never been depressed in my life; I was just reacting to living with a miserable bastard.)

She went on with her report that then included my criminal record for poisoning Neil. (Okay I'd give her that one.)

Her grandparents had written a statement about a 'reign of terror' I had inflicted upon them after I had poisoned their poor son. Next was what really bowled me over. She'd been around my neighbours collecting sworn affidavits that stated they had been questioning my mental health for a number of years! (I wonder how much she paid them to say that!)

She concluded in her report, that it was her belief that my two lodgers Matthew and Darren were taking advantage of my mental state, in order to take my money. She must gain power of attorney to (get this) save me from being taken advantage of!

I couldn't believe it. How could she betray me like this? She's already stolen my heart when she tore Malcolm away, now she was going to have me institutionalised unless I handed over my home?

NO!!!! I DON'T TAKE THINGS LYING DOWN!!!!

The little bitch had me stitched up like a kipper. I didn't dare say anything to Matthew and Darren, I needed time to think. But, while I was working out my plan, I began systematically taking down all my neighbours that had signed the affidavits against me. Let's just say they felt my wrath. After all, when I get nervous I get creative.

After days of weighing up my options I decided what would be best for everyone. The first thing I did was to change the beneficiaries name on my insurance policy; Louise no longer got a penny. Next I went along to my solicitor and amended my will. In the (likely) event of my death, my estate would be passed to Malcolm Barton, care of Darren Barton. My solicitor and I went to great lengths to get the wording in my will perfect, and to my great delight, I think we succeeded.

Darren would look after my estate on Malcolm's behalf, until Malcolm turned twenty-one. I also stipulated in the will, that both Matthew and Darren were to live in the hotel for as long as they desired, Louise however, was not. Under no circumstances was Louise to step foot on the property without prior permission from Darren, and if any attempt was made by Louise to contest the will, the current will would be discarded with immediate effect, and the whole lot would be donated to the Donkey sanctuary. (With the same stipulation that Matthew and Darren got to live there for as long as they wished.)

I had changed my insurance policy as previously stated, in which the majority will go to Matthew, around four hundred thousand I estimate. (That was one good thing that the Pemberton's did, they talked me into a hefty life insurance policy years ago.) The remaining money is to go to Malcolm and Darren to pay the inheritance tax that they will unfortunately get lumbered with.

As my insurance company won't pay out if I commit suicide, I have to make my death look like an accident. Plus, I don't want anyone to know. I think it will be easier on them in the long run if it just looks like a tragic accident.

The only regret I have, is that I can't really leave a proper suicide note for anyone to find. It would defy the point of making my death look like an accident. This account will have to stand as my suicide note for someone to find in the future, along with all my drafts to Louise which I will include in the box.

And so there you have it. I hope whoever you are that's reading this don't think that I'm a coward taking the easy way out. I'm not. Trust me this is NOT easy. But, if it protects the people I love, then it's good enough for me.

I'm dressed in my best work clothes, and my comfiest wellies, I've got a hammer tucked into my belt and a roof slate in my hand. After safely putting this account away in the wooden box buried beneath the locked room in the cellar, I'm going to climb up to the roof to fix the missing shingle that's been bugging me for months.

Good bye dear reader.

Draft Six

"To Louise Pemberton,
I wish to inform you that The Davenport Manor Hotel, and all its contents has been left to you by the late Sarah May Pemberton to do with as you wish, with a commencement date of...

Kiss my arse! It's going to the donkeys!"

Epilogue

Okay, I'm still here. Change of plan.

I climbed out of the bedroom window on the third floor and managed to clamber up the cast iron fall pipe to the roof. I'm not ashamed to tell you, my knees were knocking; I've never liked heights, having fallen out of too many trees over the years.

Once I'd finally clambered up the slippery slate roof to the ridge tiles, I sat there looking at the magnificent view before me. It's a glorious summer day out there; all I could see for hundreds of yards were my lovely oak trees, edged by the stunning yellow Laburnum trees in full blossom. The meadows were full of wild flowers, and the air was full of bird song. Even the Cuckoo seemed to sound nicer from up here.

The house was looking quite magnificent these days, after twenty years of hard work it was almost as beautiful as May had described it from before the war. I think she'd like what we've done with the place.

I looked over to my left at the village, and smiled at the havoc I had wreaked there over the past week. They would remember me alright.

I sat up there for an hour, looking out at my beautiful land and thinking on all the battles I had endured and won over the years. Against all odds I had taken down my enemies one by one. -Which got me thinking, what was I doing? Why am I getting ready to jump off the roof of the house I love, full of people I love? What I need to be doing is plotting my counter attack. I'm not a little victim. I'm a warrior. A force to be reckoned with! I'm a seven-foot amazon with the heart of a lion. I'm not going to be forced into a corner like this! This little cuckoo won't be flying off the roof today after all, for as we all know…I DON'T TAKE THINGS LYING DOWN!!!!!!

Not The End

Also by K. L. Smith

Humour

Flight of the Cuckoo – Part one of the Cuckoo series

Cuckoo's nest – Part two of The Cuckoo series

Just a little Cuckoo – Part three of The Cuckoo series -

Coming soon

The P**e in the Jam Tart – Coming soon

Thriller

The Little Pink Pill